HIS COUNTRY GIRL

LaRaine turned, attempting to subdue the excitement he was arousing, but Travis didn't move out of her way. Instead he smoothed a large hand over her cheek and lifted her head. The lazy smile on his firm mouth sent her heart tripping over itself.

"I'll make a country girl out of you yet," he murmured.

Her breath caught in her throat. At that moment he could have made anything out of her that he wished. LaRaine was suddenly ready to submit to his hands, willing to please as long as he would go on looking at her like that. Then his gaze strayed from her and his hands came away as he released her completely from his touch.

"Hi, Joe," he said.

LaRaine took a shaky breath and glanced over her shoulder to see the young ranch hand walking from the barn. His hazel eyes darted from one to the other and LaRaine wondered how much he had seen. Her cheeks grew warm, and the faint blush made her angry.

Why was she embarrassed? She had done love scenes much more torrid than this in front of a camera with a multitude of people watching. The difference was that this time her partner in the scene was Travis. . . .

from "A Land Called Deseret"

EVERYTHING

Janet Dailey

ZEBRA BOOKS
KENSINGTON PUBLISHING CORP.

http://www.kensingtonbooks.com

ZEBRA BOOKS are published by

Kensington Publishing Corp.
850 Third Avenue
New York, NY 10022

All Kensington titles, imprints and distributed lines are available at special quantity discounts for bulk purchases for sales promotion, premiums, fund-raising, educational or institutional use.

Special book excerpts or customized printings can also be created to fit specific needs. For details, write or phone the office of the Kensington Special Sales Manager: Kensington Publishing Corp., 850 Third Avenue, New York, NY 10022. Attn. Special Sales Department. Phone: 1-800-221-2647.

Zebra and the Z logo Reg. U.S. Pat. & TM Off.

First Printing: July 2004
10 9 8 7 6 5 4 3 2 1

Printed in the United States of America

CONTENTS

DANGEROUS
MASQUERADE

CHAPTER ONE

The afternoon sun tried desperately to pierce the hazy smog that hovered like a dirty halo over Los Angeles, the City of the Angels. There was nothing angelic about the traffic in the streets, however.

Laurie's cab driver weaved and honked his way through three lanes of bumper-to-bumper vehicles while she braced herself for the collision that never came. An irate driver shook his fist at the taxi that cut in front of him and Laurie sank a little deeper in her corner. She knew she could never drive as aggressively as the scowling man behind the wheel, although her cousin LaRaine would be more than his match.

The thought of LaRaine drew a weary sigh from Laurie. Laurie was supposed to have been back at their apartment before noon. Her fiery cousin would be furious with her.

It wouldn't make any difference that she had been helping Aunt Carrie, LaRaine's mother, prepare for her favorite charity's annual bazaar. Nor would it matter that LaRaine's mother had volunteered Laurie's computer skills without consulting her. No, her aunt had simply told her to get started, adding a snide comment that someone should get some benefit from Laurie's word processing course.

Resentment flared briefly in Laurie. Her own parents had been killed in a car crash when she was only seven. Her mother had no living relatives; and Paul, her father's brother, had been named as Laurie's guardian. She dearly loved her uncle, who was so much like her fading memories of her father.

It seemed like an ideal solution for her to go and live with Paul Evans, his wife Carrie and their own daughter, LaRaine, who was only nine months younger than Laurie. And it might have been if Uncle Paul hadn't been so wrapped up in his career and Aunt Carrie hadn't devoted every minute to her only daughter.

As a sensitive seven-year-old, Laurie had been quick to realize that their world revolved around LaRaine. Memories of her aunt's parties, where LaRaine was paraded in front of the women who gathered, came drifting back.

More often than not, Aunt Carrie would forget to even mention Laurie except to refer to her in passing as their "little orphan." The term wasn't meant to be unkind, but deprived as she was of her own parents' love, her aunt's tactlessness had hurt. Laurie had been glad to stay in the background while her self-confident cousin hogged the spotlight.

Although she had gone to the same schools as LaRaine, had an equally beautiful bedroom across the hall from her cousin's, and on the surface had been treated as a member of the family, Laurie had looked forward to her high school graduation.

Against the advice of both her aunt and uncle, she'd used the last of her father's money to take word processing courses and put off college for a while, hoping to earn her own living without being dependent on them.

There had been a few months of sweet success with money she had earned herself in her pocket every week. Then, beautiful LaRaine was out of school, intent on taking a trip to Hawaii. LaRaine considered herself an adult. She wouldn't dream of letting her parents accompany her and they wouldn't allow her to go by herself. The compromise: Laurie had gone with her. Laurie had attempted to protest, knowing her job could be taken by someone else at a moment's notice. But the look in her aunt's eyes plainly said that Laurie owed it to them to give it up—after all, they had raised her. Laurie had acquiesced reluctantly, figuring she could always get another job.

But after Hawaii, it had been something else, finally culminating in LaRaine's demand for an apartment of her own. It was a demand that was met only after Laurie agreed to live there as well. Any hint of rebellion by Laurie was met by the same reproachful looks that reminded her of the everlasting debt she owed, with an added "How lucky you are not to have to work for a living." A bitter smile flitted across her lips. She was a companion to her cousin, provided with room and board and a clothing allowance, at the mercy of LaRaine's whims and the dictates of her aunt. She was twenty-one—but without a life of her own or friends of her own.

"This is it, lady," the cab driver growled over his shoulder.

With a start Laurie realized the taxi had stopped in front of her luxurious apartment building. A quick glance at the meter sent her rummaging through her purse for her wallet. The grimace on his face when she handed him the money intimidated her into adding another dollar to the tip she'd thought was more than adequate. He waited impatiently while she struggled with the door handle. If LaRaine had been sitting here, she would have ordered the cab driver to open the door for her, Laurie knew. She finally managed it on her own, saying a breathless "thank you" over her shoulder as she crawled out of the backseat.

Once inside the high-ceilinged lobby with its many urns of dramatic foliage, Laurie was greeted warmly by the security guard. "Good afternoon, Ms. Evans."

"How are you today, Mr. Farber?" she returned in equally friendly tones.

"Just fine, thanks," he nodded.

"I'm running late today." A wry smile made her dimples appear. "My cousin expected me back before noon and it's nearly three."

"I believe your cousin is out." Noting the look of surprise on her face, he added, "She swept out of here about an hour after you did this morning and I'm pretty sure she hasn't returned."

That meant absolutely nothing had been done

since Laurie left. Since she'd returned before her cousin, she'd be stuck with doing it all, as usual. With a resigned shake of her head, she smiled her thanks to the security guard and hurried towards the elevators.

As Laurie walked down the hall to her apartment, she blamed her feelings of self-pity on the tight, sore muscles in her neck and shoulders, her reward for sitting in front of a computer for nearly six solid hours. The future wasn't so bleak, when she thought about it. LaRaine was engaged to be married and a tentative wedding date had been set. Four more months . . . then Laurie would be free to live her own life at last.

Dresses, evening gowns, pants, skirts, tops, and underwear were tossed over every piece of furniture in the living room. Laurie sighed, recognizing her cousin's helter-skelter method of choosing clothes to be packed in the empty suitcases set to the side. There was no note telling Laurie where LaRaine had gone or when she would be back. LaRaine Evans did as she pleased and answered to no one.

Her hasty engagement was pure LaRaine. It had begun almost two months ago when LaRaine attended yet another elegant Hollywood party, all part of her childhood fantasy that she would be "discovered" and become a famous movie star. Laurie never went and didn't even enjoy LaRaine's breathless accounts of who wore what and re-hashed gossip. LaRaine returned early from this particular party and Laurie was still up when her cousin swept into the apartment, her eyes glittering with suppressed excitement.

"I've just met the man I'm going to marry!" she announced grandly.

Laurie was astounded—and too familiar with her cousin's self-absorbed fantasies to take her seriously.

"Don't laugh, cuz," LaRaine smiled wryly. "This guy's one in a million and I want him."

"I just can't believe you could fall in love with a man you only met tonight," Laurie said.

"Oh, I'm not in love with him, but he has everything I want, if you know what I mean," her cousin had replied, tossing her evening wrap on the back of the couch before she curled on its cushions looking like a contented cat.

"You're not making sense."

"Oh, no?" LaRaine replied smugly. "You wait!"

Her cousin simply refused to discuss it, preferring a mysterious and melodramatic silence on the subject. The following morning a delivery boy stood at the door with a dozen red roses. An unsigned invitation to dinner that evening was enclosed. LaRaine, unusually for her, was ready the instant the doorbell rang, preventing Laurie from meeting her unknown caller. Flowers arrived daily after that, predictably, long-stemmed red roses. The bold, decisive handwriting on the accompanying cards was always the same as the first. None were ever signed. The messages were always crisp and concise, thanking LaRaine for the previous evening or making arrangements for another. Not one word about undying love.

It was almost two weeks to the day since LaRaine made her announcement before Laurie had met the mystery man.

She'd just washed her hair and wrapped it in a

towel. Green cucumber cream from the Body Shop was smeared over her face when the doorbell rang. Thinking that LaRaine had probably misplaced her key, Laurie raced to the door, wearing a baggy red caftan, a castoff of LaRaine's.

Without asking who was at the door, she flung it open to stare in open-mouthed surprise at the man who stood there. He was over six foot, dressed in an impeccably tailored gray suit, his hands thrust casually in his pants pockets. Hair as black as her own was combed back from his tanned forehead. The artificial light from the hallway reflected faint blue highlights in his thick, slightly wavy hair. Kind of like Superman, she thought irrationally, wondering what was wrong with her. But there was real strength etched in the aristocratic cheekbones and very masculine jaw. The slight smile on his lips got her attention for a brief moment before she made the mistake of looking into his hooded, nearly black eyes.

"Who . . . Who are you?" she stammered, unnerved to the point of wanting to shut the door in his face.

Dark brows lifted slightly and a glimmer of arrogant amusement shown in his eyes. "Is Ms. Evans in?" His low voice had a decidedly authoritative ring. Oviously this man was used to commanding and having other people obey.

"LaRaine?" she asked stupidly before rushing on, "No, no, she isn't here right now. May I tell her who called?"

His eyes flicked with merciless thoroughness over her dishevelment. "You're her cousin?"

At least the slowly drying cucumber cream hid

the sudden flush of embarrassed pink in her cheeks. Laurie could only swallow and nod.

"Well, tell her that I called and offer my apologies for not being able to keep our engagement this evening." His tanned hand reached inside the breast pocket of his jacket and removed a narrow, green velvet box which he handed to Laurie. His voice was tinged with cynical mockery as he explained, "A gift for Ms. Evans."

In that instant Laurie realized that this was La-Raine's mysterious suitor, at least mysterious to her because she had never met him. Her cousin had hinted that the man was filthy rich and drop-dead handsome. But now that she'd met him, Laurie couldn't think of him as handsome. Sexy, yes. Overpowering, definitely. Masculine, undoubtedly, but there was too much unrelenting strength in his features for him to be handsome. Yet his magnetism couldn't be ignored. Still, he wasn't the type of man Laurie would ever pick as a husband or lover, let alone a friend. And heaven help her if she should ever make an enemy of him, because Laurie instinctively knew that he would be a dangerous man to cross.

The expensive jeweler's box in her hand seemed to burn her fingers. Laurie wanted no part of him or anything that belonged to him. Hurriedly she tried to give it back.

"You'd better give it to her yourself, Mr.—Mr.—" Wildly Laurie realized that she still didn't know his name.

"Montgomery," he supplied smoothly, with an imperious nod of his head. "Rian Montgomery." The name was vaguely familiar, but as flustered as Laurie was, she couldn't immediately think why. A cynical smile curled one corner of his mouth as he refused to take back the gift meant for her cousin. "I don't think it'll matter much to LaRaine who actually hands her the present. I don't have time to argue the point with you. Please give her my message and"—he flicked a finger at the green velvet box clutched in Laurie's hand—"the gift."

Laurie was left standing in the doorway watching him stride to the elavator. Two hours later, LaRaine returned, furious when Laurie told her of Rian Montgomery's visit, but more or less mollified when she saw the jeweler's box. She snapped it open, exclaiming over the diamond-and-ruby bracelet nestled on the satin lining.

"What difference does it make who gives it to me?" she said, fastening it around her wrist and holding it up to the light, "as long as it came from him."

That was almost an exact echo of his words. As far as she was concerned, Laurie would have wanted to receive any gift directly from the giver, especially something as expensive as that bracelet—which, considering the cost, she would probably have refused.

"Well, what did you think of Rian?" LaRaine was studying Laurie's thoughtful expression.

Her impression was not what LaRaine would want to hear, so Laurie played it safe. "He was a little older than I expected."

"Thirty-five isn't old," her cousin replied scornfully. She toyed with the bracelet like a child, turning it around and around on her wrist. "He's rich, powerful, and very well known. There isn't a woman alive who wouldn't want to marry him."

Laurie knew one—herself. The man she'd marry

someday would be gentle and tender, not someone who had to dominate every female he met. "Who is he?" She still couldn't remember where she'd seen or heard his name before.

LaRaine laughed, a throaty, sexy laugh she'd practiced until it no longer held any genuine amusement although it was pleasing to the ear. "Laurie, you're so incredibly ignorant! Rian Montgomery owns the Driftwood hotel chain, and a lot of other stuff."

The recent article in the newspaper—that was it. She didn't usually read the business section, but LaRaine had left it lying around. Rian Montgomery was in town after opening a hotel in Mexico and negotiating the construction of another in some resort area in South America. Laurie also remembered that the article hinted at his reputation for ruthless deal making, and added a few innuendoes about the beauties often photographed at his side.

So it was Rian Montgomery her cousin was trying to steer to the altar—well, good luck. During the weeks after Laurie's meeting him, there had been more presents, each more expensive than the last, more dates with LaRaine, one more accidental encounter with Laurie where Rian Montgomery practically ignored her existence, and finally the stunning news that LaRaine was engaged to Rian Montgomery.

Her cousin could take care of herself, but Laurie still thought she was making a big mistake. The very day after her engagement LaRaine had been in a foul mood that not even a lavish sapphire-and-diamond engagement ring could cool, because Rian Montgomery nixed any and all publicity about it. And more than anything else, LaRaine wanted to be in the spotlight. Laurie could have told her that he wasn't the type who'd be swayed by stormy scenes or a woman's tears. LaRaine was forced to comply with his order.

And the day before yesterday, he had decreed that LaRaine was to visit his aunt in Mobile, Alabama while he flew to South America on business. Laurie had a sneaking suspicion that Rian Montgomery knew that without him around to stop her, LaRaine would flaunt their engagement to the press and public. In front of him, LaRaine had meekly agreed to the visit, only to storm in anger at the injustice of it after he had gone and Laurie had entered the room.

Rian had left for South America yesterday. LaRaine had her airline ticket to Mobile and would be flying out tomorrow afternoon. Laurie stared at the haphazard piles of clothes to be sorted and packed for her cousin's journey. She sighed, knowing most of them would need pressing. LaRaine couldn't even iron. She scorched nearly everything she touched.

Carefully Laurie began folding the scattered underwear and bras, stacking them into a neat pile by one of the smaller scarlet cases. Her cousin would have to pick dresses, pants, tops, and the rest. There was no choice but to leave them until LaRaine returned.

The front door to the apartment swung open and LaRaine glided into the front room, her dark eyes dancing with barely suppressed excitement and her glossy mouth in a wide, joyous smile. Laurie always felt so colorless when her cousin entered a room, so vibrantly alive and stunningly sensuous. The room could be crowded, yet all eyes would be on LaRaine.

"I have amazing news!" LaRaine bubbled, spinning around the room like a captivating gypsy, beautiful dark hair floating free while her flared skirt whirled to allow a glimpse of shapely thighs. "It's fantastic! Absolutely magnificent!"

"What is it?" Laurie asked, fascinated and annoyed by this manic dance.

After being in constant motion since entering the room, LaRaine stopped, letting the suspense build a moment before she announced, "I'm going to be in a movie!"

Laurie's mouth opened and closed several times as she stared unbelievingly at LaRaine's smug expression. "What are you talking about? What movie? How?" she breathed at last.

"Ted Lambert, the producer, cast me today." Her eyes gleamed with diamond brilliance. "I met him at a party last week with Rian and he called me today to test for a part in his new picture. And I got it!" For one fleeting moment, all sophistication was cast aside as LaRaine hugged herself with childish glee. "I'm in so many scenes. Oh, Laurie, I always dreamed about this."

"When does it happen?" Laurie was so stunned by the news she couldn't think straight. "Where will you be filming? When do you start?"

"I have costume fittings tomorrow." Her cousin calmed down a little. "I'll be a princess in Czarist Russia. They're going on location somewhere in Europe, but all of my scenes will be shot at the studio." She waved a dismissive hand. "Well, Russia isn't exactly a top tourist destination these days. So who cares?"

Laurie looked down at the dress in her hand, her words of congratulation momentarily forgotten. She glanced apprehensively at her cousin. "You're supposed to leave tomorrow to visit Rian's aunt in Mobile."

LaRaine turned away. "I know," her cousin murmured, her enthusiasm dying melodramatically. She spun around, her brown eyes dark and imploring. "Laurie, what am I going to do? It's what I've wanted since I was a child. This is the chance of a lifetime! Mr. Lambert said I was a natural for the part."

Silently Laurie agreed, seeing the regal fire of a princess in her tempestuous cousin. "Call Rian and explain what happened. Persuade him to postpone your visit to Mobile." It was beyond Laurie's power to resist LaRaine's sudden demand for her help.

"I don't know where he's staying. Even if I did . . ." She left the thought unfinished as she gazed earnestly at Laurie, seeming to beg for her understanding. "You see, Rian . . ." LaRaine couldn't find the words, which touched Laurie's heart more than any actressy eloquence. "I don't think . . . he would approve. You know how autocratic he is. I . . . I'm sure he wouldn't like it if I appeared in a film. But, Laurie, I want this so much." Diamond tears hovered on the edge of her lashes. "If . . . if only— it's sort of one last fling before I . . . I get married. You know it's always been my dream."

"I'm sure there's a way," Laurie murmured, confusion deepening her brilliant blue eyes.

"Ted . . . Mr. Lambert said they would probably shoot my scenes right away since they're filming that sequence first. He said it wouldn't take longer than three weeks, at the most," LaRaine mused aloud, sinking forlornly on the sofa. Her tight laugh had a bitter edge. "Not much longer than my visit to Rian's aunt."

"Well, call her and explain the circumstances," Laurie suggested, missing the speculative gleam in her cousin's eyes.

"And have her tell Rian? Then he really would be angry with me," LaRaine sighed, suddenly looking like a shadow of her former self. "I can't fake illness and plead a cold or the flu. Rian might find out and come flying back or something."

Her cousin's sadness touched Laurie. "Then you'll have to turn down the part and go see Rian's aunt," she concluded somberly.

"The only problem is that I've already signed a contract to appear in the film." The rustle of the chiffon dress lying beside LaRaine sounded like electricity crackling in the sudden silence of the room. "If I don't fulfill the terms, the studio can sue me. Maybe even Daddy."

"Oh, LaRaine, no!" Laurie gasped. "Why did you do it? You signed a contract without having a lawyer look it over? What were you thinking?"

"I sort of wasn't," LaRaine pleaded, leaning forward to gaze with tear-clouded eyes into Laurie's expression of displeasure. "Thinking, I mean. I was still pinching myself, not believing I'd actually been offered the part. Before I knew what I was doing, there was my signature on the dotted line. Now do you understand? I don't want to risk my engagement to Rian, or hurt my parents."

LaRaine burst into tears, looking more amazingly beautiful and feminine than before. Just as suddenly, the tears stopped, and a look of determination spread over her cousin's face.

"I can't feel sorry for myself," LaRaine declared firmly. "I got myself into this mess and it's not fair to ask you to help me out of it. But maybe the two of us can brainstorm a solution."

Laurie smiled tentatively, in sympathy with her cousin. But there seemed to be no way out of the situation. LaRaine rose and walked to the large picture window that dominated the apartment's living room, looking out at Los Angeles.

"What I need to do is split myself in half," LaRaine said jokingly. "One half could go to Mobile and the other half could do the picture."

"Perfect. Or we could clone you," Laurie laughed lightly.

LaRaine turned around suddenly to stare at her. "I think we can do it," she breathed. "I know we can!"

"What is it?" Laurie demanded as LaRaine almost jumped for joy.

"You take my place." Mischief danced in her dark eyes. "I just know it will work!"

"You mean, send me to Mobile?" Laurie swallowed, drawn into the whirl of her cousin's enthusiasm. "Instead of you?"

"It's so simple!" LaRaine exclaimed. "Why didn't we think of it before? His aunt has no idea what I look like—Rian doesn't carry photos in his wallet and he hardly ever sees her, or so he said. She won't be coming to the wedding, which is why I'm visiting her now."

"But Rian will find out about the movie role," Laurie protested half-heartedly.

"I can convince him that I did it before we were engaged. It takes months and months of post-production before it hits the theaters. By the time he finds out about it, it'll all be in the past. Over and done with," LaRaine declared. "Please,

Laurie, you have to do it—if not for me, then for Daddy.''

All well and good—but it still seemed like an odd way to demonstrate her loyalty to the people who had brought her up. Would she ever not feel obligated? The prospect of masquerading as La-Raine frightened Laurie into raising another objection, however weak it might seem.

"When his aunt calls me LaRaine, I'll look around for you."

"Oh, there isn't much difference between Laurie and LaRaine," her cousin answered sharply before tempering her irritation. "Tell her Laurie's your nickname. She'll believe you."

"I don't like it."

"Do you have a better suggestion?"

Laurie was forced to admit that she didn't. Except for the deception involved, she could find nothing wrong with the mechanics of the plan. Though she never actually said she would do it, LaRaine took her silence for a tacit yes. And LaRaine kept up a steady stream of chatter, trying to convince her what an adventure it would be. But a chilling thought occurred to Laurie more than once: there would be hell to pay if Rian Montgomery ever found out about this masquerade.

CHAPTER TWO

Right up to the minute she boarded the plane, Laurie kept hoping some other solution would present itself, but the doors had closed and she was on her way to Mobile, Alabama, to pretend to be her cousin LaRaine Evans.

The Gulf of Mexico was a shimmering deep turquoise in the late afternoon sun as the plane made its approach to land. After fastening her seat belt, Laurie put a reassuring hand to her black hair, making sure that none had escaped the shining coil around her head. She had chosen a sleek, sophisticated style to give her the poise she needed to pull off this masquerade.

There was barely a crease in her traveling clothes, but she loosened the knotted neck scarf that matched the silk blouse. Her oval face looked serene and composed except for the anxiety in her deep blue eyes. There was nothing she could do about that.

Laurie knew she would be met at the airport. As the passengers disembarked, she listened intently for her cousin's name to be announced over the PA system. She kept assuring herself that nothing could go wrong. Vera Manning, Rian's aunt, had no picture of LaRaine and, Laurie hoped, only the sketchiest details of what she looked like. With a slight stretch of the imagination, Laurie could fit her cousin's description.

She watched her fellow passengers being greeted by friends and relatives, and followed the stream of travelers to the baggage area, still listening for her cousin's name. The more time that went by without hearing it, the stronger the urge became to take the first flight back to Los Angeles. Tricking a nice old lady into believing she was Rian's fiancée seemed more and more wrong, regardless of the motives.

Minutes later, LaRaine's scarlet suitcases were piled around Laurie's feet. The sapphire ring on her finger seemed to weigh her hand down. What should she do now? She looked around anxiously. No one had come forward to meet her. Laurie had no address for Rian's aunt, only the name Vera Manning. The impromptu plan was becoming more hopeless with each heart-pounding second.

"Pardon me."

A hand touched her shoulder and she turned, startled. A tall, tanned young man with golden hair was smiling down at her. Her blue eyes were wide and frightened as she stared into his handsome face.

"Are you LaRaine Evans, by any chance?"

Paralyzing fear robbed Laurie of her speech for a moment. His searching eyes seemed to unmask her even as she nodded yes to his question.

"What a relief!" He laughed, extending his hand towards her in greeting. "I'm Colin Hartford. Vera Manning asked me to meet you, but I got caught in traffic and your flight had landed by the time I arrived." His manner was apologetic, but matter-of-factly courteous. He was a true Southerner, that was clear, accustomed to charming his way out of a situation. "I was just going to have you paged when I saw you standing here looking so . . ."—his gaze roamed admiringly over her—"so lost."

High color rose in her cheeks, her guilty conscience telling her that LaRaine never would've looked lost, only impatiently angry at being kept waiting.

A glint of amusement gleamed in Colin Hartford's eyes at the delicate blush in her cheeks. He appreciated beautiful women and LaRaine Evans was all that and more.

"Are these your suitcases?" He politely changed the subject for which Laurie was grateful.

"Yes," she answered breathlessly, wondering if he thought she'd brought too many for her short visit. Of course, LaRaine had directed the packing, supplementing Laurie's limited wardrobe with her own. "I came prepared for anything," she explained with a nervous smile.

"Well, the Gulf Coast climate is pretty mild in the middle of February. Might get a few cool, rainy days now and then, though. That's so people appreciate the sunshine." Colin smiled, motioning to a porter to take the luggage. "My car's right outside."

A gentle hand on the back of her waist guided her to the automatic doors leading out of the airport. Colin ushered her to the garage where his gold SUV was parked. Laurie watched as he supervised the loading of her suitcases in the back, idly thinking a golden man should have a golden car. Now that she was actually playing the role of her cousin, some of her tension eased. She managed a polite smile when Colin helped her into the passenger seat before he slipped behind the wheel.

"Is Mrs. Manning's home very far?" she asked.

"Just a few miles outside of the city," he answered smoothly, putting the SUV into gear and driving out of the parking area. He slid a twinkling glance her way. "You'll learn very quickly that she likes to be called Vera and not Mrs. Manning. And don't ask her age. That's a touchy subject. You either know her well enough to call her Vera or you don't know her at all."

It sounded like this aunt was as formidable as Rian Montgomery—not a comforting thought. "Have you known her long?" Laurie asked.

"My father's land adjoins hers, which is why I was deputized to meet you at the airport," he explained. "Vera hates crowds or she would've met you herself. She's quite anxious to meet you, La-Raine. May I call you LaRaine?"

Laurie appreciated his old-fashioned Southern courtesy, and his slow, drawling voice was a balm to her jangled nerves. "My friends call me Laurie." She talked fast and glibly, wishing she could get out of LaRaine's crazy scheme right here, right now.

"Laurie it is. And you can call me Colin."

"Thank you . . . Colin." A genuine smile lit up her face for the first time.

"I have to confess"—his attention returned to the road ahead of them—"the Judge—my father—and I had a bet as to what you would look like." At Laurie's wide-eyed surprise, Colin laughed. "You've been the subject of a lot of speculation since the great Rian Montgomery announced that he was engaged. Vera thought he would never marry."

Her hands were clenched tightly in her lap as she tried to seem only mildly interested in the subject, unconsciously twisting the sapphire ring on her finger. She must stay calm, she told herself, and not let Rian Montgomery's name upset her. Since her name was going to be coupled with his often for the next weeks, she had to become accustomed to it.

"How do I measure up to your expectations?" She forced a lightness to her voice that she didn't feel.

"Well, I thought you would be a beautiful, temperamental woman with a sensual allure that no man could resist." His hazel eyes glinted with amusement, while Laurie thought what an accurate description that was of LaRaine. "The Judge, on the other hand, imagined you would be the quiet, shy type, someone who let others take the lead."

"True enough," Laurie supplied softly, turning her gaze out the window and thinking about the way she always seemed to give in to her cousin's caprices. Although she didn't have to act like that just to please Rian Montgomery. A tiny smile brought her dimples into play as Laurie thought how ironic it was that she'd been so determined to have nothing to do with the overpowering Mr. Montgomery, and here she was pretending to be his fiancée.

"Oh, there's more to you than that." Colin's drawling voice drew her back. "Now that I've met you, I'd have to say that you are a little shy—but real sexy. I believe the Judge and I were both right and wrong."

The conversation disconcerted Laurie. She was too used to comparing herself with LaRaine and seeing a pale shadow of her much more glamorous cousin. She'd met most of the men that hung around LaRaine, who seemed to fall in love or in lust with her cousin the instant they were introduced. It had always hurt to know she was second-best, even now, when she was only an imitation LaRaine.

"There's nothing special about me, Colin." Her candid words were meant to change the subject.

"Now, now," he teased gently. "There's no need to be so modest. Hey, you're as beautiful as that ring on your finger. Which solves another riddle."

"What's that?" Laurie seized the opportunity to change the subject again. Any praise embarrassed her, since it was so undeserved.

"You know that Rian's parents died when he was in his teens. Between his grandfather and Vera, they raised him. When his grandfather died ten years ago, Vera became the keeper of the family heirlooms." Colin was filling in gaps in Rian's background that Laurie didn't know, and LaRaine either hadn't known or considered unimportant. "When Rian flew back to Mobile a couple of weeks ago to select an engagement ring for you, he chose the sapphire instead of the more traditional diamond solitaire surrounded with pearls. Only Vera would dare question any of Rian's decisions, but she did. She said he'd thought that his bride-to-be would prefer the sapphire-and-diamond ring. As usual, Rian was right."

"How do you mean?" Laurie asked blankly, again aware of the weight of the stone on her finger.

Colin glanced at the gleaming, richly blue stone. "No other jewel could match your big blue eyes. Oh, yes," he mused softly, "I do see how you've been able to ensnare Rian Montgomery."

An innocent game of pretend. That was what LaRaine had called it in the security of their Los Angeles apartment. But carrying it out wasn't easy at all. Laurie hadn't realized how ashamed she would feel until she saw how many nice people would be deceived by her cousin's self-serving scheme.

"How much farther is it?" Her voice was sharper than she intended it to be, but she couldn't stand any more talk about her engagement to Rian.

As she stared out the window at the suburban landscape now giving way to pine trees, she wondered how she was going to be able to go through with this misguided plan. It had seemed so simple . . . but not anymore.

"Are you changing the subject?" Colin chuckled, meeting Laurie's confused glance briefly. "Hey, I'm not seriously flirting with you. I wouldn't dare make a move on Rian's fiancée."

"Oh, I didn't mean that. I'm sorry," Laurie apologized quickly, "I'm nervous about meeting Mrs. Manning, I guess." That was only half true. She wasn't anxious. She was dreading it, knowing that

Colin's friendly questions were nothing compared to what Rian's aunt would probably put her through.

"I wouldn't worry about Vera approving of you. She's been wanting Rian to marry for years. She'll adore any woman who gets him to the altar." There was a blessed moment of silence as Colin turned off the main road onto a peaceful tree-lined drive in the countryside. "Rian has been kinda close-mouthed about you, but then he is about everything. Tell me, how did you meet?"

"At a party in Hollywood."

"That's a surprise." An eyebrow raised slightly. "Rian hates big, pretentious parties. You don't seem the type who would go for that kind of thing yourself."

"I don't," Laurie answered honestly, before plunging back to the business of pretend. "Maybe that was why Rian noticed me. We left early when he offered me a ride home. He asked me out to dinner the following night, and that was that."

"Love at first sight, huh?" The statement didn't seem to require an answer from Laurie. "Those two stone pillars on your right," Colin pointed through the car window, "mark the entrance to the Judge's home. The hot pink azaleas ahead are where Vera's lane begins."

"How beautiful!" Laurie murmured, catching sight of the brilliant shrubs.

"We've had a mild winter. They're blooming early this year," he commented casually, "which will make Mardi Gras just that more colorful."

"Mardi Gras? Are you going to New Orleans?" she asked as he made the turn into the lane.

"Traitorous words," he said sternly. "Mobile is

the American home of Mardi Gras, where it was first celebrated and still is, but we don't get the publicity that New Orleans does.''

"I didn't know that."

"Most people don't. The parades and festivities start this week, so you'll be able to see it for yourself."

Laurie studied Colin, guessing the immaculately dressed man was no older than his late twenties. He would be a great escort, though she hadn't come here to date cute guys, strictly speaking.

She looked out at the numerous magnolias and oak trees dotting the well-kept lawn. The narrow drive ended in a cul-de-sac in front of a brick mansion with four white columns. The columns, a Southern tradition, supported an upper balcony, and freshly painted white shutters flanked the windows on both stories. Flowers grew everywhere in tropical profusion: azaleas, roses, and many more that Laurie didn't recognize.

From the corner of the house, a young-looking woman walked gracefully towards the SUV and stopped in front of the steps, a basket of freshly cut flowers on her arm. Her skin was petal-smooth and her hair was an attractive shade of silver blonde. No mention had been made of a woman Laurie's age, and she wondered who this was.

"Here comes Vera," Colin smiled, getting out of the car and walking around to open the passenger door.

Laurie glanced towards the still-closed front door, looking for the elderly woman who was to be her hostess. There was no sign of anyone but the woman she saw.

"I've been waiting so long," a melodic voice

interrupted Laurie's thoughts. "I was beginning to think I should've gone to the airport with you, Colin, to make sure you didn't spirit her away."

Only now was Laurie able to see the faint lines of age on the slender throat and at the corners of her sparkling, light blue eyes. The hair wasn't silver blonde; it was silver gray, but styled in gentle waves that enhanced her delicate features. All of La-Raine's images of a doddering old lady were blown away when Vera Manning gave Laurie a wide welcoming smile after Colin had brushed his lips against the proffered cheek.

A wry smile touched Laurie's mouth as she remembered her concerns about spending two weeks with an older woman and having staid conversations about Rian Montgomery. There was nothing staid and dull about Vera Manning. Her outgoing personality had kept her young.

"If she weren't Rian's fiancée, I would've," Colin was saying. "But I brought her safely to you."

A beautifully manicured hand reached out for Laurie's. "I'm so happy you could come, LaRaine," Vera Manning declared with obvious pleasure and sincerity. "You're just as I hoped you would be."

"It was very kind of you to ask me to come, Mrs. Manning," Laurie replied, accepting the warm greeting and knowing she was going to like this woman more than was good.

"Kindness had nothing to do with it," the woman laughed. "I had to satisfy my insatiable curiosity and meet the girl who's going to marry my only nephew. And I insist that you call me Vera." After releasing Laurie's hand, the older woman put her arm around Laurie's slim shoulders and directed her towards the house, ordering Colin airily to bring in the luggage. "We must have a drink to celebrate your arrival. You'll join us, won't you, Colin?"

"Now you know I would never deny myself the company of two beautiful women, Vera," he said playfully, following them up the steps with the scarlet suitcases under his arms and dangling from his hands.

"How glad I am that Rian had to go on that South American trip," said Vera, squeezing Laurie's shoulders briefly before removing her arm and opening the large front door with its brass knocker. "This is a heaven-sent opportunity for us to get to know one another, LaRaine."

Laurie cringed. The way her conscience was pricking her, it was more hell-sent.

"Laurie," she corrected quickly, explaining, "My friends call me Laurie instead of LaRaine."

Vera nodded sagely. "Laurie, of course. LaRaine is much too la-di-dah for someone as nice as you." They had stopped in the cool hallway that served as an entrance hall, and Vera turned to Colin. "Take Laurie's suitcases upstairs to the white bedroom."

"Yes, ma'am." Colin slanted Laurie a knowing look. "That room is reserved for very important people."

"She's more than that," Vera corrected, bestowing a warm, loving look on Laurie. "Now she's family. Our best is never too good for those who belong to us."

Laurie would have preferred that Vera disliked her on sight or mercilessly cross-examined her. Anything rather than this instantaneous affection for the future wife of her nephew.

"You're embarrassing the girl, Vera," said Colin, drawing the woman's attention to Laurie's blush.

"No, not really," Laurie protested at the slightly hurt expression on the older woman's face. "I'm not embarrassed. It's . . . it's only that you don't know me yet. And what if you don't like me when you do?" she asked with a nervous laugh.

"If Rian has chosen to marry you," Vera said reassuringly, "then that's all the endorsement I need."

"Ah, Rian," Colin mocked. "He's a lucky man. I've always admired his taste in women and his uncanny ability to keep them all happy."

"Those days are over. Now Rian has Laurie and he won't need all those other women," Vera sighed before glancing sideways at Colin. "And I thought I told you to take the luggage upstairs." With a mockingly deferential bow, Colin complied with her request. "Excuse me, Laurie," the woman turned back to her, "while I put these flowers in water and make us some iced tea. Would you like to freshen up or anything first?"

"No, thank you." Laurie didn't want an opportunity to relax, needing the nervous tension to get her through the charade.

"Why don't you wait in the living room, then?" Vera suggested, ushering Laurie into a brilliant gold and green room. "Colin will be down in a minute and it shouldn't take me much longer than that."

Cream white walls softened the richly hued carpeting and the vivid green satin curtains and pale sheers. The golden oak furniture warmed the room, and Chinese porcelain planters held lacy ferns and climbing philodendrons. Ornately scrolled high ceilings were dominated by a magnificent crystal chandelier. It was a bold room, much like its elegant owner, bursting with vitality.

But the prospect of staying here and pretending to be LaRaine Evans, taking advantage of Vera Manning's trusting and loving nature seemed more distasteful by the minute. A long, weary sigh came from the depths of her soul. Why, Laurie wondered, had she ever allowed herself to be talked into this? Helping LaRaine fulfill her childhood dream of becoming an actress and still remain engaged to Rian and, lest Laurie forget, protecting her dear Uncle Paul from a possible lawsuit wasn't good enough reasons to lie to Vera Manning.

"Do you feel a little more at ease?" Colin spoke from the doorway. "Now that you've passed inspection?"

"Actually"—Laurie walked to a green brocade sofa and sat down, unwilling to meet his gentle, inquiring gaze until she could slip back into the role of Rian's fiancée—"I'm kind of overwhelmed."

"Why?" he asked casually, taking a seat in a nearby chair.

"I didn't know what to expect," she smiled weakly. "Rian didn't tell me much about Mrs. Manning . . . Vera. I wasn't expecting her to be so young."

"Don't tell Vera that," Colin laughed. "I think she's found the fountain of youth."

"I like to think so." Vera appeared in the doorway, a tray of drinks in her hands, smiling. "Age is purely relative. It grates on my nerves when people ask how old you are. The French put it much more tactfully. 'How many years have you?' That emphasizes experience instead of deterioration.''

"No one could accuse you of that, Vera," Colin stated.

"It's one of my eccentricities," she replied, directing another smile at Laurie. "You'll find I have many."

"I don't quite believe that," Laurie smiled, accepting the iced tea.

"I'm disgustingly old-fashioned, too," Vera declared. "I still won't fly in a plane no matter what. I truly believe that old saying that if people were supposed to fly, they'd have wings. And I hate cars and ride in them only when there's no other method of transportation. No, the only two means of travel that I enjoy are horseback riding and walking."

Which was why, Laurie realized, Vera wouldn't be attending Rian and LaRaine's wedding.

"Do you ride, Laurie?" Vera inquired.

"I have," she admitted, since riding had been one of the activities at the exclusive girls' school she and LaRaine had attended. "But I'm no expert."

"Vera has a small stable behind the house," Colin explained. "She rides every day."

"The Judge, Colin's father, joins me quite often, and Colin is always welcome, too." A knowing glance was darted towards the golden-haired man studying Laurie with open admiration. "When Rian's here—which isn't very often—he rides out with us."

Laurie changed the subject from Rian to the horses Vera owned and into a discussion centered on horses in general. A half hour later, Colin rose to leave, despite a mild protest from Vera that it was still early.

"I know the Judge is anxiously awaiting news about our guest," Colin smiled, extending his hand in good-bye to each in turn . . . and holding Laurie's a little longer.

"The two of you must come over for dinner tomorrow night," Vera said.

"We will. And thank you for the invitation," he nodded, sending a glittering glance towards Laurie. "I'll look forward to seeing you tomorrow."

"Yes," Laurie said. "And thanks again for meeting me at the airport."

"My pleasure." His hazel eyes glowed when he looked at her.

"He's a wonderful young man," Vera declared after Colin had left. "So charming and kind, like the Judge. He's attracted to you, too." She darted a teasing glance at the veiled expression in Laurie's eyes.

That was a complication she didn't need and hadn't expected. The borrowed ring on Laurie's finger was a reminder not to become too fond of Colin Hartford. Unconsciously she touched the cold sapphire of her ring, drawing Vera's attention to it.

"As much as I adore Colin," Vera continued, her reassuring hand touching Laurie's arm, "I'm glad you met Rian first."

"So am I." Her tremulous smile didn't add much credence to her lie.

"You look tired." The older woman smiled sympathetically. "Let me show you to your room. You'll want to unpack and shower before dinner. Try to rest a bit first. I'm afraid I don't get out much and

I was so excited at finally meeting you that I forgot how tiring traveling can be.''

Laurie's fatigue undoubtedly showed in her face, but it wasn't from traveling. Pretending to be Rian's fiancée was exhausting. Meekly she followed the silver-haired woman down a wide hallway to a curved staircase leading to the second floor. Gold flocked paper decorated the walls of both hallways, and vases of fresh flowers added bright color to the sunny interior.

"I do hope you'll like your room," Vera said, opening a highly varnished oak door to the right of the landing.

The white room—she had referred to it when Vera had directed Colin to bring her suitcases there. Thick white carpet covered the floor and the walls were also white. A richly quilted satin bedspread adorned the oak bed, with matching draperies at the windows. Brass lamps flanked the bed with linen-white shades on top. It was elegant without being ostentatious or cold.

"It's beautiful!" Laurie breathed in admiration, walking slowly towards the oak dressing table where fresh yellow roses turned their dewy petals towards her.

Then a gilt-framed picture on the bureau caught her eyes. She grew pale and her knees threatened to buckle. Cold black eyes stared out from an aristocratic male face. Laurie experienced the same unnerving feeling she'd felt the first time she saw Rian Montgomery so long ago in L.A. It was as if he were in the room, the uncompromising set of his mouth condemning her as a fraud, a liar. Her heart stopped beating. A terrible fear swept over her again . . . Would he discover this foolish masquerade and send the world crashing down around her?

"I thought you might like to have Rian's picture in your room." Vera's voice came softly from behind Laurie's shoulder. "It's the only one I have, or I'd give it to you."

"It's a really good photo of him," Laurie said weakly, unable to take her gaze away from the masculine face.

"Do you think so?" the older woman asked, a mild disagreement in her tone. "He looks so hard and cynical in that photograph, but sometimes," she shrugged ruefully, "that's how he is. I always hoped that Rian would find someone who loved him for himself and not for his money and power. I do believe, honey, that he has found that woman in you."

"Vera—" Laurie began, but the lump in her throat stopped her. Tears brought an added brilliance to her blue eyes and made her black lashes even blacker.

She couldn't go on with the masquerade. It had to end here and now. But her voice wouldn't cooperate.

The older woman mistook the tears in Laurie's eyes for tears of gratitude at being accepted as a member of the family.

"You don't have to say anything. I understand." Vera hugged Laurie's unresisting shoulders and hurried from the room, her own pale blue eyes filling with happy tears.

The moment of truth had come—and gone.

CHAPTER THREE

During the next three days Laurie discovered how Vera Manning stayed in shape. They went horseback riding every morning through the quiet country back roads with Laurie astride a gentle, well-mannered bay gelding named Briar, while Vera rode a spirited chestnut. The weather remained unseasonably warm, so their afternoons were spent in or beside the swimming pool in back of the house. Laurie enjoyed the hours she spent at the beautifully designed pool, admiring the natural stone used in its landscaping and the potted ferns and trees that made the area look like a small paradise.

They had even taken a rare trip by car, with Vera's gardener acting as chauffeur. It was a sightseeing tour of Mobile, stopping to explore antebellum homes, two of the museums and galleries, a stroll along the Azalea Trail, and a visit to the

U.S.S. Alabama, a battleship permanently docked in Mobile Bay. Despite Laurie's protests that she didn't need to be entertained, another outing was planned for next week to Dauphin Island, with Judge Hartford and Colin accompanying them for a picnic on the Gulf Shore beaches and a walk through old Fort Gaines.

The dinner the night after her arrival had been undemanding fun. Judge Hartford was a tall, distinguished man with iron-gray hair that was a dignified white at the temples. It was obvious that he adored Vera Manning and it was equally obvious that his affection was returned. Only during the introduction did Rian's name come up. Colin had been politely attentive to Laurie, but never overstepped the bounds of friendship.

The days after the dinner, Colin had found reasons to come over, once to go riding with them in the mornings and twice to swim. His lighthearted banter helped ease Laurie's tension. She was constantly on her guard.

Not that Vera was at all suspicious that Laurie was putting on an act. The whirlwind of physical activity that Vera Manning enjoyed left little time for chitchat. The introduction of Rian's name in any conversation was always casual, about his preference for some food or something equally unimportant. No, Laurie's concern was that she would accidentally refer to LaRaine's parents as aunt and uncle, or mention that her own were dead. And Vera was the kind of woman she could have confided in, which only made it more difficult.

Laurie couldn't help returning the affection that Vera bestowed upon her so generously. Her own giving nature longed to reciprocate tenfold, but she had to hold it in check. Realistically Laurie knew that LaRaine wouldn't get along all that well with Vera. Once this visit was over, Vera would probably never see LaRaine, because if she did, she would discover the deception immediately. That had to be avoided at all costs. So Laurie had to conceal her growing regard for Rian's aunt. Vera would be hurt if LaRaine didn't immediately like her before or after her marriage to Rian, whether or not they ever met. Laurie cared too much for Vera to have that happen.

For the first time in her life, Laurie wasn't being compared to her cousin. The total acceptance and admiration, not only from Vera but also from Colin and his father, gave her a wonderful sense of confidence. The experience was ego-building, even though she felt so bad about the deception.

This is the end of the fourth day, Laurie told herself as she lay between the white satin sheets of her bed. In another ten days she would be returning to Los Angeles. She reminded herself that she would never see these people again. Ten more days of pretending and it would all be over. Her tired muscles silently thanked Vera for being so physically active. Tonight was the first night she hadn't fallen asleep the instant her head touched the pillow. Laurie turned her head to the side, her black hair spreading over the white pillow like an ebony fan. She closed her eyes in anticipation of the sleep that would soothe and restore her raw nerves.

There was a light rap on the door. Because of the nearly all-white interior of the room, it never seemed completely dark. Laurie sat up to switch on the brass lamp beside the bed as the door swung open and Vera walked in, her eyes shining with excitement.

"Were you sleeping?" she asked.

"No," Laurie shook her head. "Is something wrong?"

"There's a phone call for you." A beaming smile spread across the older woman's face. "It's Rian. You can take it on the extension by your bed."

"Rian?" Her voice broke as she said his name.

"Yes, he's calling from South America. I've already spoken to him, so I'll leave you to talk to him in private."

Vera waited long enough to see Laurie's trembling hand pick up the white receiver. Her heart was racing at top speed as she moistened her lips several times before finally saying a stammering "hello" into the phone.

"Is that you, LaRaine?" The crisp male voice sounded like it was coming from the next room.

Her hands were clammy. She was afraid to answer him for fear he would detect the difference between her voice and LaRaine's. She had no choice, she told herself firmly. She had to bluff all the way through.

"Yes," Laurie answered, trying to achieve the purring sound that came so naturally to LaRaine, "I didn't expect to hear from you, Rian."

"I was curious as to how you were getting along with Vera and vice versa."

"She's an absolute sweetheart." Laurie used one of LaRaine's gushy terms, waiting for the axe to fall on her head.

"Hm. Vera said almost exactly the same thing about you." Something resembling disbelief came across the line, mixed with cynicism.

"You sound surprised."

"I can't quite imagine you riding horses and swimming all day," Rian returned.

Laurie remembered too late LaRaine's aversion to swimming. Her own love of water had led her into an unforgivable mistake. "I can put up with anything if it's only going to be for two weeks," she said quickly. "Lazing around the pool has done wonders for my tan. I'll be a golden goddess when you see me again." Laurie knew she was talking too much, but what else could she do?

"Vera said you were in bed when I called. Did I wake you?" His swift change of subject surprised her.

"Yes, yes, you did. I must've just dropped off. I still feel a little groggy. I keep thinking this is a dream and I'll wake up and find out you didn't call at all."

"I guessed you'd been sleeping. Your voice sounds a bit different, like soft velvet." That was a compliment, but it was delivered with marked indifference. "I'll be turning in shortly myself."

"How's the trip going?" Laurie asked, trying to fill the gap left after his last remark.

"Just fine," he replied dryly. "I suppose I should hang up now so you can get your beauty sleep."

"You must be tired yourself," she said nervously.

"You sound concerned." There was arrogant amusement now in the vital, masculine voice.

"Of course I am."

"I almost believe you mean that. Since we both seem to be tired, I'll say good night."

"Okay. Good night, Rian." Relief tinged her voice with a throaty sound.

"Is that all? Just good night?" he mocked.

Her mind raced, trying to think what LaRaine would say. "There's more I'd like to say, but I'd rather do it in person."

"Such as?" he prompted with infuriating calm.

"Such as," she forced a lightness to her voice that she didn't feel at all, "I love you and I miss you."

There was a long silence. Laurie felt sure he could hear the pulsating beat of her frightened heart over the telephone.

"Those words won't give a man a peaceful night's sleep when he's half a world away from you."

"They aren't meant to," Laurie replied, inwardly sighing with relief at the answering chuckle on the other end.

"Good night, LaRaine."

"Good night, Rian." She let out a sigh of relief when the receiver clicked on the other end only seconds later.

A wave of exultation rippled over her as Laurie silently congratulated herself on fooling Rian Montgomery. She sounded a lot like her cousin on the phone—after all, they'd grown up together—the excuse of sleep, and the long distance satellite connection combined had made it possible. She hugged the knowledge to herself as she sank back against the pillow. Oddly, deceiving Rian Montgomery brought none of the guilt she usually felt as LaRaine. Now that the fear of discovery had passed, it had almost been fun.

Her sapphire-blue eyes looked at the photograph on the bureau. Not even the brooding look on his face could quell the excitement she felt, but it did remind Laurie of the fine line she had just walked. She didn't want to think of the consequences if

he ever did find out. Before the thought could
diminish her sense of triumph, Laurie switched off
the light, snuggling into the covers with an elated
smile still dimpling her cheeks.

The following morning Judge Hartford and
Colin joined Vera and Laurie for a ride over the
back roads. Colin was astride his own roan hunter,
while the Judge expertly controlled the gray Arabian that was Rian's mount when he visited. After
the phone call last night, Laurie was confident she
could handle anything. Her new poise added a
freshness to her appearance, already enhanced by
the slim-fitting black riding pants and the black-
and-white-striped blouse. A folded, white silk scarf
held her black hair away from her face to cascade
down her back and shimmer in the sun.

The gentle wind tousled Colin's golden hair as
he turned his head to silently admire the woman
riding beside him. Laurie gave him a warm smile,
not really seeing the answering warmth that leaped
into his gaze. She wished they could ride on forever—that this contentment would remain.

"What a glorious morning!" Laurie declared,
gazing out over the dew-kissed meadows, vibrantly
green backgrounds for the rich browns of the tree
trunks. "I wish every day could begin like this."

"So do I," Colin agreed soberly, his eyes drinking
in her fresh beauty. She flashed him another smile,
noticing how handsome he looked in his riding
pants and matching jacket. His shirt opened at the
top to reveal his tanned throat, she noticed.

"I don't believe I've told you how beautiful you
look, Laurie," said Judge Hartford, looking back
over his shoulder from his position at the front

beside Vera. "You make me wish I were Colin's age again."

His teasing comment drew a friendly laugh from Laurie. "As handsome as you are, Judge," she replied, "you would turn any woman's head regardless of her age."

"That may be," the Judge smiled, "but I wish I knew the secret of your radiance this morning."

Laurie was about to credit it to the company she was with when Vera spoke up. "It might have something to do with a certain phone call last night. Am I right, Laurie?"

The expectant look on the older woman's face forced her to agree. "It had something to do with it," Laurie admitted, not wanting to explain much more.

"Ah, Rian called." The Judge nodded sagely while Colin maintained a quiet silence. "That's why. There's nothing more beautiful than a woman in love, except one who's on the brink."

"Did Rian mention when he would be back?" Colin asked sharply.

"No, he only said his trip was going just fine," Laurie replied.

"That means he's making money hand over fist," Colin murmured with a wry smile.

"I did ask if he would be back in time for Mardi Gras," Vera commented, bestowing an apologetic smile on Laurie. "But he said he didn't think so."

"Mardi Gras starts this week, doesn't it?" She pounced on the subject like a lifeline.

"Yes," Colin replied. The relief on his face almost matched Laurie's. "Now plan on attending some of the parades and at least one of the balls, Laurie."

"I'd like that," Laurie agreed eagerly. "What do you think, Vera?"

"Never fear," the Judge declared with a twinkling smile. "Leave it to me, Laurie. I'll convince her it would be a major crime for you to miss our most festive season."

Vera laughed, sounding as if she was going to enjoy being coaxed by the Judge, for whatever the reason.

"Would Rian object?" Colin asked in a lowered voice, slowing his roan so the two older riders could pull ahead.

"Of course not," Laurie declared with an airy toss of her head. She didn't want her fiancé spoiling her day when he wasn't even here. "I'm sure he knows that Vera will show me around."

"I was thinking," Colin hesitated, "that he might object to me. You are his fiancée."

"And you're a friend of the family." Softening her voice, she added, "And my friend, too. I won't allow him to object. Please, let's not discuss Rian."

If Colin thought her request was strange, he didn't comment in so many words. Gradually the subject shifted to the man and woman riding several yards ahead of them.

"Your visit has been good for Vera," Colin stated. "The Judge just might persuade her to attend a ball, because of you."

"Why do you say that?"

"These past years she's become somewhat of a recluse. I know she told you that she hates cars, planes, and crowds. She doesn't get out much, and only her closest friends have stayed in touch," he explained.

"That's hard to believe. Vera is so warm and

outgoing." Laurie murmured. "She's always so active, constantly doing things."

"But never involved in anything except Rian's life." A corner of his mouth quirked.

Laurie let that pass. "Vera never discusses her husband. Is he the reason?"

"Yes," Colin nodded.

"Well, go on. Tell me what happened. Does it have something to do with his death? Vera did say he died some years ago," Laurie prompted.

"From what the Judge has told me, the problems started long before that," Colin said, slowing his mount so there would be more distance between the riders in front of them. "Charles Manning was from a good family who, like a lot of others, lost their money during the Depression. But Charles was a charming opportunist. As lovely as Vera is now, she was that much more beautiful as a young woman. The Judge was in love with her even then. If Charles hadn't come along, I'm sure he would have married her."

"But she married Charles Manning," Laurie sighed, remembering how she had guessed the first time she had seen the Judge with Vera that he was in love with her. Her heart went out to the gray-haired man riding so energetically in front of her, happy to be by Vera's side.

"She eloped with Charles Manning," Colin corrected her. "Vera's father thought Manning was a fortune hunter and refused to let Vera see him. The Judge used to wonder whether Vera would have seen through Charles if the old man hadn't been so dictatorial."

"What happened after they eloped? Did her father disinherit her?"

"No, and he wouldn't hear of a divorce. In his old-fashioned way of thinking, his daughter didn't have enough sense to realize what a mistake she'd made. Once they were married, he tried to put Charles to work in the family business. From what I understand, Charles made an effort to be the family man and business executive he was expected to be. But my father says he was a born philanderer. Before anybody realized what was happening he was having an affair with his secretary. Vera always took the blame for his straying because she couldn't have children. She pretended not to notice every new mistress and the rest of the family had to do the same."

"Poor Vera!" The lump in her throat was hard to swallow. Such a life would have broken the spirit of a lesser woman.

"Everyone turned a blind eye except Rian," Colin continued. "Now did I tell you that after his parents were killed, he went to live with Vera and Charles? They were staying here, in her father's house. Rian was fourteen or fifteen at the time. Yet he never hid his contempt for Charles Manning. And he never understood Vera's saying that she loved Charles despite his faults. He must have been a thorn in Charles's side, always ragging him about his fooling around, never caring who was there, even Vera."

"Sounds like the man I know," Laurie said. According to LaRaine, Rian was famous for speaking his mind, especially as a teenager.

"If Vera's father hadn't died, it's hard to say how long Charles would have gotten away with it. Rian was twenty-five at the time, a young age to become CEO of a sprawling conglomerate. Charles got reckless. He began appearing in public with his women and forgot all about Vera. In fact, he was rarely home, and usually only when Rian was expected." Colin paused, staring off into the quiet countryside before looking back at Laurie. "Then one day Vera met Rian for lunch. They went to one of the more exclusive restaurants in town—and there was Charles with a blonde. Vera wanted to walk on by, but Rian grabbed Charles by the collar and damned near beat him to death before they were able to drag him away."

Laurie's gasp of surprise brought a sympathetic glance from Colin.

"So the Judge intervened. Charles didn't press charges, and the power of the Montgomery name kept it out of the papers, but everyone knew about it soon enough. Vera filed for separation, although her religious principles wouldn't allow her to divorce Charles. She rarely ventured out of the house for two years. Then, when she was beginning to enjoy some social activities again, Charles was killed in a car crash—he was with a married woman, who died too. And the whole scandal was revived again."

"No wonder she never discussed any of this with me." Laurie sighed. "Vera is too loving to have to carry that burden the rest of her life."

"My father agrees with you," Colin smiled. "And he's a patient man."

"You really would like to see them get married, wouldn't you?"

"I don't remember my own mother. She died when I was two. Vera's been like a mom to me." He glanced at the woman riding beside his father. "Besides, I'm a sucker for a happy ending. And the Judge has been in love with her for too many years for me not to want to see that love fulfilled.''

"Maybe Vera's afraid to fall in love again," Laurie commented.

"I think she was more afraid that Rian wouldn't marry." A frown creased Colin's forehead. "The Judge believes that once you and Rian are safely wed, Vera might be more susceptible to his persuasions."

"Do you think so?" A whimsical smile played over her face as, for the first time, Laurie hoped that Rian and LaRaine would marry soon.

"To tell the truth, when I first heard Rian was engaged, I thought he might be doing it to just please Vera and to have children to carry on the family name. Remember," Colin said with a half-smile, "I hadn't met you yet and I couldn't picture Rian marrying for love. Now I can't see how anyone could help falling in love with you."

The need to dim the glow in his eyes brought an instant protest from Laurie. "Colin, please, I—"

"Don't say it," he interrupted swiftly, a resigned look in his eyes. "I know you're in love with Rian and that you'll marry him. I've got a crush on you already, but friends it will be."

Even if she wanted their relationship to be more, like Colin, she would have to be satisfied with a brief friendship.

"Let's catch up with Vera and your father," she suggested.

Colin nodded, nudging his roan into a canter, and Laurie followed.

CHAPTER FOUR

The salty tang of the Gulf breeze mingled with a faint whiff of chlorine from the swimming pool. The fiery yellow glow in the afternoon sky warmed the flagstones into burning rocks, as Laurie climbed out of the pool. Her long black hair glistened wet, like highly polished ebony.

She turned to watch Colin on the diving board. He looked more than ever like a golden god with his blond hair and the even tan of his body contrasting with the white of his swimming trunks. Expertly he jackknifed off the board, slicing into the water with barely a sound. Swimming the length of the pool underwater, Colin surfaced beside the ladder.

"Coming back in?" he asked, his hazel eyes flicking admiringly over her daisy-print bikini.

"I think I'll rest awhile," Laurie replied, a little out of breath from her exertions in the water. She ignored the big beach towel lying on the redwood table, choosing to let the sun evaporate the water and warm her skin. "Vera will be out in a minute anyway, and I want to make sure the Judge will be over for dinner tonight," she added as she stretched out on the cushioned redwood lounge chair.

"You're a real matchmaker," Colin laughed, clambering up the pool's ladder to join her in the cooling shade of the trees. "These last couple of days you've wangled an amazing number of invitations for my father."

"Vera planned them all," Laurie grinned. "Maybe the sound of wedding bells is contagious."

"I have to admit I never thought anyone would be able to persuade her to attend that parade yesterday afternoon. But the Judge found a secluded balcony to view it from, so she wouldn't be bothered by the crowds."

"She sure seemed to enjoy it."

"So did you," Colin commented, toweling off briskly before stretching out in a chair beside her.

"The evening parade tomorrow night might be more difficult. I was thinking," Laurie said with a conspiratorial twinkle in her eyes, "that we could all go out to dinner and then when it was time to go to the parade, you and I could suggest that they stay behind . . . alone together."

"That's a stroke of genius!" Colin chuckled as he rose to his feet. "Which calls for a celebration soda." Laurie laughed as he took her hand, made a mockingly gallant bow over it before bringing it to his lips. "You're a remarkable woman."

"Thank you, noble sir," Laurie teased.

Colin sent a jaunty salute in her direction before

ambling towards the house. Laurie leaned back against the bright cushions, a contented smile on her face. The days had passed much more swiftly since Colin had explained so much about Vera's unhappy marriage. Laurie had become so involved with finding ways of bringing Vera and the Judge together that her nervousness about masquerading as Rian's fiancée had lessened. It seemed so important that something good should come out of her visit that she devoted nearly all of her attention to that end. Even Colin admitted she had been successful.

The slight breeze had increased. Now that she was out of the direct sunlight, a shiver danced over her skin. As much as she hated to move from the relaxing comfort of the lounge chair, Laurie rose to her feet, walking over to the redwood table to retrieve the flowered sarong that matched her swimsuit.

As Laurie was securing the ties, a pair of masculine arms circled her waist, then moved up to cup her breasts. Instinctively she stiffened, gasping with surprise as she was drawn back against a hard, muscular chest. Warm breath fanned her neck while a man's lips kissed it just in back of her ear, sending a fiery trail of tingling awareness through her entire body.

"So that's what you've been doing while I've been away—twisting poor Colin around your finger," a deep voice said huskily.

A cold shaft of fear pierced Laurie as she recognized Rian Montgomery's voice. It wasn't possible, she told herself. He couldn't be here. He was supposed to be in South America for another week or more. But even as her heart cried that it couldn't be true, her mind acknowledged the inescapable reality.

With a sob of panic she turned in his arms, trying to use her body as a wedge to halt his searching caress. He allowed the turn, his head raising slightly to claim her lips possessively. Her hands pushed ineffectively against his chest, fighting the whirling sensation in her head as he forced her unyielding body to the hard contours of his thighs and chest. The sensual mastery of his kiss was gradually melting her until her fingers almost had to hold onto the lapel of his jacket for support.

When he pulled away from her, her flaming embarrassment was all too clear in her face. Her rounded blue eyes stared into the cold fury building in his dark gaze. He grabbed her left hand, twisting her wrist to confirm the presence of the sapphire ring on her finger before his accusing eyes mercilessly raked her face.

"Who are you?" Rian rasped out, not relinquishing his iron grip on her wrist and keeping her pressed against the muscular outline of his body.

"Laurie," she whispered, trembling at the anger in his face and the havoc he had made of her senses.

"Oh, the good little cousin," he said softly, as a flash of recognition lit his black eyes. "What are you doing here? Where's LaRaine?" he demanded.

"Please!" Her deep blue eyes held only fear. "I can explain."

A muscle twitched near his mouth as he stared down at her. She had no doubt that whatever she said wouldn't matter.

"Isn't this a wonderful surprise, Laurie?" Vera's

voice cut the heavy silence that had descended between Rian and Laurie. Rian's wide shoulders effectively prevented his aunt from seeing Laurie's frightened expression.

"You'll never know how much of a surprise it was to her," Rian replied calmly.

He looked scornfully at her pleading eyes and trembling lips, but he released his hold on her wrist, letting his hand move to her shoulders. His dark head bent down to her neck in what probably looked like an affectionate caress from Vera's vantage point, but it was only a ruse. Rian made sure his command was for Laurie's ears only.

"I'll handle this. Say nothing," he murmured harshly.

He studied her face, noting her silently obedient expression before his arm circled her shoulders and he turned to face his aunt.

"Dear Laurie," Rian put a sardonic emphasis on her correct name, "is overwhelmed to find me here."

"I'm not surprised," Vera smiled widely, mistaking the shimmering sparkle of tears in Laurie's blue eyes for tears of happiness. "You were so sure you wouldn't return in time for Mardi Gras when we talked to you on the phone."

The numb shock was beginning to subside. Her limbs were still trembling and the firm grip of his arm around her bare shoulders burned her skin. Yet Laurie couldn't understand why Rian hadn't denounced her as a fraud. He surely wouldn't go along with the masquerade and not say anything. He wasn't the kind of man who held back, she knew that much, thanks to her talkative cousin. Her lips retained the sensation of his scorching kiss. It was not something she was likely to forget very soon.

"Deal's done, contracts signed. So I got on a plane," Rian was saying, turning his head to look down on Laurie's raven hair. "But the thought of my beloved waiting so impatiently for my return probably had something to do with it, too."

The jeer in his voice made her blush. He must have found her humiliation amusing, as he added with a biting chuckle, "See, Vera? My desire to be at her side embarrasses her."

"Rian—" Laurie began her protest with his first name, so accustomed to referring to him that way that she momentarily forgot she had no right to be so familiar. But as she met his gaze, her own faltered and she just couldn't ask him right then and there to reveal her true identity.

Vera seemed to sense Laurie's unease. "You know, I think Laurie would like to freshen up a bit. You caught her completely unaware, without makeup and in a wet swimsuit," she laughed. "It puts a woman at a disadvantage."

"That's the way I like her," Rian replied, unwillingly removing his arm from around her shoulders. She took a quick step away, freed at last from the power of his touch. He nodded arrogantly at her as he gave her permission to leave. "Okay, go get changed and paint your face. Just make sure you don't look so different I don't recognize you."

Laurie could only smile weakly at Vera as she retreated towards the house. The hot tears that had been burning her eyes flowed with abandon as she swung open the back door and entered the cool hallway. Her blurred vision didn't see Colin approaching with a tray of drinks until he called out to her.

"Laurie, you're crying!" he exclaimed with genuine concern. "What's wrong? What happened?"

"Rian's here," she sobbed, then choked back the rest. Rian had ordered her to say nothing. Undoubtedly he wanted to do the unmasking. Besides, Laurie couldn't bear to witness Colin's reaction when he learned she was an impostor.

"I know," he smiled with relief, guessing as Vera had that she was crying from happiness. "I'm bringing out drinks to celebrate. Where are you going?"

She wiped the tears from one cheek. "I need to freshen up," she said, using the lie that Vera had offered.

"Lucky Rian!" Colin grimaced playfully as Laurie slipped hurriedly past him to the staircase.

There was really nothing she could say in her defense, she realized as she reached the safety of her room. Nothing that would be a good reason for deceiving Vera, Colin and the Judge for these past days. They believed she was LaRaine, offered her their affection and their hospitality, and she'd taken it, to her everlasting shame. How could they not look at her with disgust when they eventually heard the whole story?

Only five more days, Laurie told herself bitterly, as she entered her bathroom and turned on the cold tap. Five more days and she would've been back in Los Angeles with no one the wiser except herself and LaRaine. She soaked a washcloth, wrung it out and pressed it against her eyes to cool the redness. No, the worst of it wasn't being caught, Laurie thought, it was agreeing to the masquerade in the first place. She knew it was wrong, but she'd allowed herself to be talked into it. She was just as much to blame as LaRaine.

Removing the clasp that held her hair in place, Laurie shook it free from the braid. She turned the shower on, stepping under the spray to shampoo the chlorine from her hair and skin, hoping the pelting water would ease her tension. In truth, Laurie was attempting to postpone a confrontation with Rian Montgomery until the last possible moment.

As Laurie toweled herself dry a few minutes later, she wondered again why Rian didn't reveal that she wasn't LaRaine the instant he saw her. After rubbing her long hair nearly dry, she took heart. Maybe Rian wanted to hear an explanation before he condemned her completely—otherwise he would've denounced her on the spot. Slowly and methodically, she combed her silken hair as she considered that possibility, finally deciding it was the only thing that made sense.

Stroking on a deep blue eyeshadow with a tiny brush, Laurie said a silent ''thank you'' to Vera for giving her time to collect her wits. Rian's sudden appearance had knocked her for a loop.

Yes, the outcome was still in question, she realized as she applied mascara to her sooty, thick lashes, but now there seemed to be a chance to retreat from Mobile with a little self-respect. All of it depended, of course, on how Rian took her explanation of why she was here instead of LaRaine and what his reason was for not revealing that she was an impostor.

By the time she had put on panties and a bra, Laurie felt more in control of herself, though still nervous about the coming evening. She flipped through the clothes hung up in her closet, searching for the right dress to wear. Laurie was going to need all the confidence she could get.

A knock on the door took her by surprise. "Who is it?" she called out sharply, turning towards the door as it opened and Rian Montgomery walked in unannounced. As Laurie grabbed for the robe hanging on the closet door, she blushed at his insolent appraisal of her. "Sorry to keep you waiting!" she snapped, hating him for catching her unaware again.

"Your bikini's a lot more revealing than what you have on now." He smiled unpleasantly as he crossed the room to her side. "You gave Colin quite an eyeful."

Laurie wanted to say that Colin didn't treat her as though she were just waiting to be pawed, but the situation was tense enough as it was.

"Next time," she spoke with forced calm, "ask to enter my bedroom." She slipped on the robe and tied the knot tightly.

"Do I need permission to enter my fiancée's bedroom?"

She met his mocking gaze, pride making her ignore the pain that his stinging words evoked. "We both know I'm not your fiancée."

"Everyone here thinks you are. Their glowing words of praise for you are still ringing in my ears." The sarcasm in his low voice lashed out at her like a whip, drawing an involuntary flinch.

"I'm sorry about that, Mr. Montgomery. I—" Laurie began humbly.

"Oh, please call me Rian," he sneered.

She clutched the ivory satin robe tighter around

her throat, faltering for only a moment. There was a flash of anger in the depths of her blue eyes.

"I'm sorry," Laurie repeated more forcefully.

One side of his mouth quirked. "I'm sure you are. My arrival was inopportune . . . for you."

"That's not what I meant and you know it." There was a desperate ring to her voice, but Rian only found amusement in her discomfort.

"You don't honestly expect me to believe you're sorry for ingratiating yourself with my aunt." Contempt was sharply etched in his expression, his tallness making Laurie feel all the smaller.

"You're making this sound like a cheap trick," she protested weakly, her chin beginning to quiver from the turmoil of her emotions. "But I never intended to hurt anyone."

"Would you like to explain that to Vera?" Rian demanded harshly.

Tears of shame filled her eyes, fixed on the white carpet beneath her bare feet. It was a silent admission of defeat. What had started out as an innocent deception had reached a critical point. When Vera discovered who Laurie really was, there would be bewilderment and pain.

"I would like to explain," Laurie murmured.

"I'm sure I'll be fascinated by your tale, but not now." He cut her off sharply, his disdain clear in his voice. "My romantically inclined aunt thinks that since we've been separated for so many days, we should be alone this evening."

"You haven't told her yet?" Laurie's eyes widened with disbelief.

"I'll meet you downstairs in half an hour," Rian said, deliberately ignoring her question. "That should give you enough time to make up a believable explanation." He took a step towards her and Laurie involuntarily backed away. But all he did was reach behind her and take out a blue jersey dress from the closet. "Wear this," he ordered. "It matches your deceptively innocent eyes."

With the backhanded compliment ringing in her ears, Rian thrust the dress into her unwilling hands, then left the room. His departure left her gulping for air, only then realizing how his presence had overwhelmed her. On wavering legs, Laurie stumbled to the velvet-cushioned bench in front of her dressing table.

So she was expected to spend an entire evening with him, listening to him tear her story apart! Remembering how the scheme had been hatched made Laurie realize how unbelievable it sounded, how totally selfish the motives were.

A hysterical laugh rose in her throat. From the outset she'd had a feeling that Rian Montgomery would make a dangerous enemy. Why hadn't she listened to her own instincts? There would be hell to pay if Rian ever found out, she'd even told herself once. Staring at the blue dress in her hands, Laurie knew Rian was going to make sure to get even, and there was nothing she could do to prevent it.

Exactly a half hour later, Laurie walked out the door of her bedroom, unnecessarily smoothing the clinging fabric of the dress over her hips. The design of the simple but stunning dress effectively accented her shapely figure. The low neckline set off the graceful column of her throat and revealed a tasteful glimpse of the rounding swell of her breasts. Skillfully tailored darts nipped in the waist, then widened over her slim hips and allowed the silken skirt to flow.

Her raven hair was pulled primly back into a chignon at the nape of her neck. Laurie gripped the polished oak banister for support. She wanted to command her legs to carry her away from this house and Rian Montgomery, but she was afraid that if she did, they would refuse to move. She was caught in a waking nightmare.

A door opened near the base of the stairs and Rian walked out, looking darkly compelling in a black dress suit and tie. Yet it made him look no more civilized than a black panther wearing a jewel-studded collar. Laurie froze in the shadow of the stairs, her heart beating a rapid tattoo as she waited for Rian to see her. There was another man with him, several inches shorter, with close-cropped brown hair and dark-rimmed glasses; and it was he who caught the flash of her blue dress on the stairs.

His brown head immediately turned in her direction, a wide smile softening the thin face. "You're looking more beautiful than ever, LaRaine," he called out.

As Rian's dark eyes coldly inspected her appearance, Laurie forced her trembling legs to carry her down the stairs into the light. With quailing heart, she watched the other man's expression change to one of astonishment.

"You aren't LaRaine," he murmured, darting a curious look at Rian's unfathomable expression.

"You're kidding, right? You haven't forgotten what my fiancée looks like," Rian drawled blandly, moving to the base of the stairs to meet Laurie. The scorching touch of his fingers was on her elbow, firmly leading her to the other man. "You remember my right-hand man, E. J. Denton, don't you, Laurie?''

Meeting the short man's incredulous gaze was impossible. But he held his hand out to her, mumbling a greeting which Laurie returned with equal embarrassment. The man's puzzled glance returned again to Rian, seeking an answer to his unspoken question. None was forthcoming.

"Get hold of David tonight," Rian ordered crisply. "Tell him I want that report on the Rexler company tomorrow. He can fax it if he has to, or bring it himself."

The obvious dismissal sent E. J. Denton scurrying back into the study. His departure left a fragile silence behind. Laurie was vividly conscious of the man standing beside her, his strong hand still gripping her arm as if he expected her to flee. He didn't have to know that she was incapable of moving. Her gaze was wary as it rose to meet the enigmatic expression in his eyes.

Once again Laurie was struck by the strength in his face, so compellingly handsome and cold and so relentless at the same time. His aristocratic features were stamped with arrogance and he had the eagle-sharp perception of a man accustomed to command. If she weren't so frightened, she might have thought how crazy it had been for her and LaRaine to think they could fool him and get away with it.

"Have you found it yet?" Rian said softly, breaking the silence.

Laurie almost jumped. "Found what?"

"I imagine you were looking for my Achilles' heel."

"If you have one, I'm sure it's well guarded," she declared with surprising vehemence.

"I'm glad you realize that," he said grimly, holding her arm even more tightly. Then he turned her towards the front hallway. "My car is outside."

Laurie jerked her arm free, tilting her head defiantly as she walked to the front door. She wanted to get the inquisition over with quickly while she still maintained a precarious hold on her composure. Her sensitive radar told her Rian was only a step behind her. The back of her neck tingled where his dark gaze had to be looking at her. As she reached the oak entrance door, a masculine arm reached in front of her to open it.

"You two aren't leaving already, are you?" Vera's voice sounded from the living room door.

Rian's hand touched Laurie's waist, the electric contact stopping her when she would have bolted through the open door. She looked out, knowing that there was too much of her agitation in her face for her to allow the other woman to see her.

" 'Fraid so," said Rian, successfully keeping his tall figure between the two women. "We have early reservations."

"I was hoping you could have a drink with us before you left," Vera sighed before her voice brightened. "When you come back, we can get together."

"Sounds like a plan." There was dry amusement in his voice before he removed his hand from Laurie's waist and she was free to walk out the door.

A white Mercedes was parked in the drive next to Colin's gold SUV. Laurie briefly thought how much more enjoyable an evening it would be if she were climbing into that car instead of Rian's. But the door was being opened and Laurie slipped gracefully in, the white leather seat wrapping her in luxury. Clasping her hands in her lap, she stared straight ahead as Rian climbed in behind the wheel. She swallowed nervously, waiting for the sound of the motor starting, only to hear continued silence. A sideways look at Rian found him staring coldly at her, his eyes raking her stiffly controlled appearance.

"Take your hair down," he ordered suddenly.

"No." Her angry refusal was accompanied by a protective hand moving to the smooth chignon of raven hair coiled against her neck.

Before she could prevent it, rough fingers pulled the pins out of her hair, raking through it to send it into a billowing black cloud around her shoulders.

"You don't have the sophistication to carry off that style," Rian decreed, a dark brow arching cynically at the rebellious expression on her face.

"How would you know?" she demanded, regretting the response at the answering flash of anger in his eyes. As quickly as the fire in his gaze burst into flame, it was banked.

His hand reached up and flicked down the visor in front of Laurie. He pointed towards the mirror. "Tell me whether you see a poised young woman or an inexperienced girl."

A vulnerable, almost childlike face looked back at her, shimmering blue eyes sparkling. Rian's smile seemed to mock her reflection as the soft curve of her lips drooped with defeat. Her sharp retort had been as effective as the pathetic hiss of a kitten trying to hold a snarling jungle cat at bay.

CHAPTER FIVE

The restaurant Rian took her to was one of the more exclusive places in Mobile. It was still early in the evening and most of the tables were empty. But Rian asked the maître d' for a secluded corner table nonetheless. A potted palm provided even more privacy from the nearest table. A black-suited waiter appeared instantly.

"Drinks before dinner, sir?" he queried.

Rian shot a quick glance at Laurie who was nervously clutching the gold-tasselled menu. "I—" she began, preparing to say no to any alcoholic beverage. She had never liked the taste of liquor.

"A Cosmopolitan for the lady and I'll have Jack Daniels on the rocks," he said with a dismissive nod of his dark head.

"I don't drink," Laurie protested as the waiter withdrew from their table.

"You're too tense," Rian mocked, noting the

pallor of her face. "A cocktail will relax you so you can enjoy your dinner."

The condemned ate a hearty meal, Laurie thought bitterly, knowing she had little choice. Under his watchful eye, she took an experimental sip of the drink when it arrived. The cranberry juice and grenadine pretty much covered up the taste of the vodka. At least it didn't make her gag.

"Like it?" Rian inquired.

"Yes, thank you," Laurie nodded, setting the martini-style glass back on the table. She glanced hesitantly at him, envying the languid ease with which he reclined in his chair.

Trivial conversation was impossible and the silence between them became an invisible barrier. Laurie had expected the interrogation to begin when they had left the house, but Rian seemed preoccupied during the drive to the restaurant. Although his hooded gaze strayed to her often, there were none of the endless questions she'd anticipated. To fill the awkward stillness, her hand kept reaching for the drink until finally the glass was empty. His own drink was barely touched.

The waiter reappeared at Rian's side. "May I order for you?" Rian asked with condescending politeness.

Food was the last thing she wanted and Laurie willingly left the choice up to him. With the air of a man who always knew exactly what he wanted, Rian gave the waiter their order without consulting the menu. Laurie planned to pick at whatever arrived at their table. The before-dinner cocktail plus two glasses of white wine with her meal did wonders for her appetite. She had polished off a platter of delicious fried shrimp. The dinner plates were removed, a cup of steaming black coffee was set in front of her. Laurie was leaning comfortably back in her chair, no longer on the edge of her seat as she had been.

Rian looked at her approvingly—and then asked his first question.

"Explain to me how you came to be at my aunt's," his crisp voice commanded decisively.

The brief truce was over. Laurie fought to meet his watchful gaze without flinching.

"I don't know where to begin," she murmured helplessly.

His mouth quirked cynically. "The beginning will be fine. I already know the end."

Laurie's gaze fell to the china cup in front of her. "LaRaine really was going to come to Mobile. She was already packing for the trip when she received a telephone call from Ted Lambert," she began hesitantly.

"And who is Mr. Lambert?"

"A Hollywood film producer." She glanced up as his gaze hardened with uncompromising severity. "She met him at a party you'd taken her to the week before. He offered her a small part in a movie he was doing." Laurie swallowed nervously, unconsciously edging forward in her chair, seeking to convey the importance of the opportunity to La-Raine. "You see, LaRaine dreamed of becoming a movie star since she was a child. So when the offer came, it was like that dream came true. If she had turned it down, the chance of her ever being considered again would be just about nil."

"Oh, yes, the opportunity of seeing her beautiful face on a ten-foot-high movie screen is not an offer to be lightly refused," Rian drawled sarcastically.

Laurie blanched, feeling like he was criticizing her, and not LaRaine. "LaRaine was thrilled. Totally, one hundred percent thrilled. When Mr. Lambert offered her a contract on the spot, she accepted it."

"And afterwards she suddenly remembered—she was supposed to visit my aunt."

"Something like that, yes." The icy disdain in his eyes sent cold shivers down Laurie's back. "She didn't know how to get in touch with you to explain what had happened and postpone the visit to Mobile. LaRaine couldn't very well call Vera and explain what had happened. The contract was already signed, committing her to appear in the movie."

"Is that when the bright idea of sending you in her place popped up?"

A tentative smile curved her lips. "Actually, that started out as a joke. LaRaine just wished she could be two people—one to go to Mobile and the other to do the film."

"I can take it from there," Rian said dryly. "But what made you agree to it? Do you want to become an actress, too? Pretending to be LaRaine would give you experience."

"No," Laurie said quickly and a bit breathlessly. "Nothing like that. LaRaine was legally committed to appearing in the film and morally obliged to come to Mobile. If she didn't live up to the first commitment there was a chance—a remote chance, I admit—that she or her parents could be sued. Uncle Paul runs a successful business. A lawsuit is the last thing he needs," she explained earnestly. "At the time, it seemed pretty innocent—pretend to be LaRaine, come here, be super nice to everybody, and leave with no one the wiser.''

"I see. It was a case of what Rian doesn't know won't hurt him," he jeered, smiling derisively as he saw the shame in Laurie's expressive face. "That's what I thought," he ground out.

"LaRaine didn't want you to think less of her, and she was afraid you would," Laurie murmured.

"Oh? Guess she planned to keep her scheme a secret until after we were married, I suppose." His jaw clenched.

"I don't know," Laurie mumbled truthfully.

"What a farce."

Laurie nodded numbly, feeling shame wash over her afresh. "You have every right to be angry. But please," she turned a pleading look on him, "don't blame LaRaine entirely for this. That movie role was sort of one last fling for her before you two headed down the aisle. She never meant to hurt you or anyone else." The arrogant, austere expression on Rian's face frightened Laurie. Somehow she had to salvage LaRaine's engagement. By the look on his face, Laurie guessed it was about to be broken. "After all, it was my idea to come here in her place," she lied. "I don't think it would've ever occurred to her to deceive you this way. I convinced her I could do it."

Her false admission was met by stony silence as Rian signaled for their check. *Now what?* Laurie wondered, following Rian's lead as he rose from the table. He wasn't going to leave it at that. She had told him how and why she'd pretended to be his fiancée. Didn't he intend to tell her what he was going to do?

The tables were nearly filled now with elegantly

dressed men and women. Laurie noticed the way heads turned as she and Rian walked by, but his presence always seemed to dominate any room. She wasn't aware of the way his masculine dark looks complemented her own shy, sultry beauty or that her inner agitation had put a glowing color in her cheeks. Next to Rian Montgomery, Laurie felt utterly inconsequential.

When they reached his car, he still maintained the silence between them until Laurie thought she would scream. He was doing it deliberately, exactly the same way he had prolonged her explanation. He probably enjoyed seeing her squirm, she thought angrily, casting a mutinous glance at his sharply defined profile.

The city was quickly left behind them. Yet Laurie sensed that this wasn't the way to Vera's home. But she refused to ask about their destination. It wouldn't do for Rian to know that she preferred the safety of numbers when she had to be in his company. Laurie thought nervously he had probably guessed that already. Did he know how his hardened reserve intimidated her? Her mind was racing so swiftly, trying to second-guess his motives, that she didn't notice the speed of the luxury car decrease until the sound of tires slowly turning over sandy gravel penetrated the silence.

Laurie surveyed her surroundings. They were parked on the shoulder of a country road with the shadowy pine woods behind them and no sign of any buildings. A few feet in front of the car were the shimmering waters of Mobile Bay, reflecting the silver moon. Across the bay the fairy lights of the city blended into the starry sky.

She swallowed nervously, wanting to know what

they were doing here but refusing to ask. Rian turned on the dome light to illuminate the dim interior. Pushing dark curls behind her ear, she turned to meet his relentless gaze.

"Now that you've got yourself into this situation, how do you plan to get yourself out?" Rian asked sarcastically.

Her finely arched brows lifted momentarily. So she was to name her own punishment. Laurie understood instinctively that a man like Rian Montgomery didn't forgive and forget. But her conscience wouldn't want that anyway.

"There are really only two alternatives," she replied, determinedly keeping a tremor out her voice. "I can pack my suitcases tonight and leave in the morning as LaRaine Evans. Or I can go to your aunt, explain who I really am, and how came to be here."

"And shatter all her precious illusions if you do," he added grimly.

Laurie bowed her head in acknowledgement. "I know," she murmured. The last thing she wanted to do was to hurt the woman who had welcomed her so openly and so completely into her life. "The most logical thing would be for me to leave tomorrow morning."

"It would be the easiest," he agreed sardonically. "But what's going to happen when Vera eventually meets the real LaRaine?"

"She won't . . . I mean, LaRaine said . . ." Laurie stammered, "She said you hardly ever see Vera. The chance of you bringing LaRaine here was practically nonexistent."

"I wonder why she thought that?" he remarked

indifferently, leaning back against the luxurious leather seat with indolent disregard.

"That's true, isn't it?" Laurie whispered. "Vera told me herself that she hardly ever sees you."

"In Vera's terms, three or four times a year is hardly ever seeing someone." His gaze narrowed on her stricken face. "So what do you propose now? That I lie to my aunt to protect you?"

Laurie sighed heavily, "No, you can't do that. I'll . . . I'll just have to tell her the truth and hope she doesn't hold this against LaRaine. It was mostly my fault."

"And everyone concerned is just supposed to forgive and forget that any of this ever happened, is that it?" Freezing contempt glittered in his dark eyes.

"Do you have any other suggestions?" Laurie demanded sharply, tired of the cat-and-mouse game he was playing with her, wishing that if he was going to pounce on her, he would do it and stop toying with her.

A twisted smile lifted one corner of his mouth. "Yes, I have one. You can stay here as my fiancée and we'll forget there ever was a LaRaine."

"You can't be serious!" Laurie gasped in disbelief. "You aren't going to let this break up your engagement to LaRaine! You can't!"

"As far as I'm concerned," Rian stated coldly, "our engagement was broken the day she took off my ring and put it on your finger."

The sapphire ring fitted snugly, defying Laurie's attempts to pull the burning circle of metal from her finger. Before she could succeed, her right wrist was seized in a powerful grip.

"No, no!" Laurie protested vehemently, struggling to free herself from his hold. "I can't let you blame LaRaine. She loves you! All she talks about is getting married to you and how much it means to her. All of this was my idea," she repeated, willing to shoulder all responsibility rather than see her cousin's engagement broken. "She wouldn't have agreed to it if I hadn't convinced her. She even said she didn't want to be in the movie if it meant risking her engagement to you! You two love each other. You are going to be married. I can't let you hurt LaRaine because of my stupid plan."

"Touching how you defend your cousin," Rian commented cynically, not releasing the hold on her wrist that brought his lean, hard face so close to her. "But you don't know her any better than you know me."

"What's that supposed to mean?" Laurie breathed. She couldn't read the enigmatic expression on his face.

"LaRaine didn't love me any more than I loved her." His eyes glittered with mocking amusement. "It was a case of satisfying a mutual need. I wanted a trophy wife. Well-dressed. Beautiful. Someone who wouldn't demand too much of my attention. LaRaine wanted a rich husband who would buy her jewels, clothes, and bankroll her social climbing."

"How can you say that!" Laurie exclaimed in a horrified whisper. "You don't know how LaRaine really felt about you. Not if you believe what you just told me."

"I'm sure she wanted you to believe that she loved me." His cynical reply struck a cold shaft of doubt in Laurie. "But LaRaine loves herself most of all." Laurie did know LaRaine well enough to know that Rian might be telling the truth. Her cousin could be calculating and unfeeling, even selfish when she went after what she wanted.

"It doesn't change anything," Laurie murmured, lowering her gaze to the lean brown fingers holding her wrist. "If you don't really care for her, then it doesn't make any difference whether or not your aunt likes her."

"Vera is incredibly romantic." His low voice softened. "She wouldn't understand why LaRaine would allow you to come here pretending to be my fiancée."

"So do you want to keep on lying then?" Laurie asked caustically, suddenly hating him for being so cold and inhuman. Marriage was a sacred bond to her, not something to be undertaken to satisfy material or physical needs. At the same time, her loathing didn't seem to apply to her cousin, who was guilty of the same sin, according to Rian.

"I don't want to hurt my aunt unnecessarily," Rian corrected with cold anger.

But Laurie's slow to rise temper didn't pay heed to the warning. "And you think you'll prevent that by passing me off as your fiancée? How will Vera feel when our engagement ends?"

"Why should it?" He mercilessly raked her face, noting the blue eyes sparkling with anger, adding a volatile beauty to her face. "You're an orphan, right?" His words cut her to the quick with the harsh reminder of her lonely childhood. "Don't you want a rich husband?"

"Money isn't the most important thing in the world to me," Laurie declared proudly. "When I marry, it will be to someone I love, someone who loves me. He'll be tender and warm and kind."

There was a flash of white teeth, indicating a smile, but his expression revealed only contempt for her romantic notions. "Sounds like you have someone in mind. I can't believe the love of your life is waiting at home while you're here pretending to be my fiancée. Or is it someone you met recently? Colin, for instance?"

"Colin is all those things," Laurie said defiantly, not caring whether Rian thought she was implying that she'd fallen in love with the other man.

"Do you think you're in love with him?" he jeered.

"I haven't really known him long enough." It was a brave attempt to protect herself from his biting cynicism.

"Hey, I thought love strikes like a lightning bolt," he mocked, openly amused by her defensive attitude. The quelling look she gave him bounced off without leaving a mark. But then his manner changed, and his cold disdain vanished. He turned on a virile and disarming masculine charm, full force.

"Have you ever been in love?" His low laughter accompanied the rising color in her cheeks. "I thought not." The gleam in his eyes unnerved her. A tanned hand touched a pink cheek, tingling her senses with the feather lightness. The tips of his fingers trailed down to her lips, brushing the sensual line of her lower lip. "I wonder what you'd look like if I made love to you?"

"Stop it!" Laurie demanded hoarsely, pushing his hand away. She had already experienced his seductive strength when he had kissed her by the pool, and she had no doubt that he knew how to arouse any woman.

"You didn't fight me off this afternoon," Rian reminded her, a dancing gleam in his dark eyes.

"You took me by surprise then," Laurie replied, almost breathless.

"And now?" His mouth moved hypnotically closer.

"And now I don't want you to touch me," she answered quickly.

In the next instant her wrist was released and Rian was leaning back against his own cushioned seat, an amused chuckle shattering any impression that her weak words could have stopped him if he'd really wanted to kiss her.

"You don't have to worry," he taunted. "Seducing sweet young things in the backseat of a car is not my style. I prefer a kingsize bed and more experienced women."

Utterly humiliated, Laurie let her temper explode. "I hate you!" she cried in a voice trembling with anger. "You're a despicable, arrogant beast! LaRaine is lucky to be rid of you."

"But you aren't so lucky." His slight smile straightened into a grim, forbidding line. "You're my fiancée, and don't forget it."

"I'll never marry you!" she declared vehemently. "And you can't make me!"

"Don't be too sure about that." There was a proud fury in his eyes that she didn't want to tangle with. "For the time being, I'll settle for your agreement to the engagement."

"Why should I?" Laurie demanded, tossing back her black hair to eye him coldly.

"Have you forgotten Vera?"

At his baleful stare, she hesitated, all thought of anyone else but the man sitting next to her momentarily wiped from her mind. Laurie knew she didn't want Vera to find out about the deception. Becoming Rian's real fiancée wasn't a price she would pay to keep Vera's respect.

"Are you getting cold feet?" Rian mocked. "After all, she's already convinced, thanks to your acting skills."

"I won't marry you." Her voice was quiet, but it held grim determination.

Rian smiled without amusement. " 'Let the day's own trouble be sufficient unto the day.' We'll cross the other bridge when we come to it," he said.

"That was . . . a quotation from the Bible," she announced with surprise.

"You forgot," he said softly, "Satan was once an angel."

Had she just made a pact with a devil? Laurie studied his arrogantly handsome face, his black eyes and brows and rakishly curling jet-black hair. The interior car light switched off, plunging her into darkness. As the motor came to life, Laurie shivered and huddled deeper into her seat. She had yielded to his overpowering masculinity, succumbed to the temptation of an easy way out . . . and there was no turning back.

CHAPTER SIX

Laurie spent a restless, uncomfortable night. Her troubled conscience made sleep impossible. Morning came all too soon with the grim reminder that she *was* Rian's fiancée and Rian was here in the same house with her. She waited as long as possible in her room before finally trekking downstairs after she dressed. Rian was standing near the front door talking to Vera, an attaché case in his hand, as Laurie reached the hallway.

"I was trying to persuade Rian to wait a few more minutes," Vera called out, "and told him you were usually an early riser like me."

Ignoring Rian's speculating gaze, Laurie kept her attention fixed on the silver-haired woman. She knew his keen eyes would pick up the shadows under her vivid blue eyes and guess that he was the cause of her sleeplessness.

"You woke up in time to say good-bye to me,"

he declared sardonically as she stopped next to Vera.

"Good-bye?" Laurie repeated with a frown of disbelief, unwillingly glancing up at his aristocratic face to make sure she had heard correctly.

"Yes," Vera made a rueful face. "He barely unpacks before he has to dash off on another business trip."

"I have a flight to catch," Rian informed Laurie. "You can walk me to the car."

"Have a safe trip," Vera said before squeezing his hand in farewell and quietly retreating to leave Laurie and Rian alone.

His smile mocked her disconcerted expression as he opened the door and waited for Laurie to pass. His hand rested lightly on her waist as she walked unresistingly towards the white Mercedes.

"Curious about where I'm going?"

"No." There was a mutinous gleam in her clear blue eyes. "Only how long you'll be gone."

"Don't be sarcastic, Laurie love," he warned, scowling at her defiant expression. "I know you'd like to see the back of me, but I didn't get you into this situation. You did."

"You were quick to take advantage of it," she accused, flinching under the velvet whip of his false endearment.

"Do you blame me for protecting my family?" Rian asked. "That's what you claim you were doing."

"Not claim," she corrected sharply. "I was."

"I would advise you not to give in to any momentary impulse and tell Vera the truth, or attempt to run away. E. J. has been fully informed of the situation," Rian told her coldly, "and he has orders to take whatever action is necessary to stop you before you make any more trouble.''

Laurie couldn't honestly say that running away hadn't crossed her mind, but she was too proud to tell Rian. ''Don't you trust me to keep our bargain?'' she demanded instead.

''I don't trust any woman, least of all you.''

''I don't trust you either.''

Dark eyes glittered down at her as his mouth curved into a mocking smile. ''Strange you should say that. Only a few nights ago I heard you say that you loved me and missed me.''

Laurie couldn't stop the swift rush of color to her face. ''You know why I said that.''

''Well, you convinced me,'' he teased wickedly. ''I think you're a much better actress than La-Raine.''

Her eyes rounded as she stared up at him. ''Did you guess then that I wasn't LaRaine?''

''No.'' He gave her a hooded look. ''The phone call bothered me because I didn't expect Vera to exhibit so much affection for LaRaine. And you, as LaRaine, weren't very talkative, but it didn't occur to me that someone was impersonating her. Does that satisfy you?''

''Yes,'' Laurie replied quietly, not knowing whether it did or not.

Rian tossed the attaché case on to the passenger seat, then turned back to Laurie. ''Vera's watching from the window. Good test of your acting ability. You get to kiss me a fond farewell.''

''I will not!''

With the lightning swiftness she was beginning to associate with him, Rian seized her chin in his hand, holding it up for her mouth to receive his kiss. He claimed her lips, lingered for a wildfire moment, then moved away so he could laugh at her indignant glare. Her chin was still imprisoned by his lean fingers, but she raised a hand to wipe away the burning kiss from her mouth. Rian captured it, too, before it could accomplish its task.

"I wouldn't do that," he warned, a malicious light in his eyes as they danced over her outraged expression. "I would only have to repeat that kiss with another . . . unless that's what you want me to do."

He released her, openly challenging Laurie to try to defy him. Her hands dropped to her sides, clenched into useless fists of frustration.

Rian smiled complacently. "Now you're being smart. Stay that way until I get back."

"How long will you be gone?" The question was asked through clenched teeth.

His gaze narrowed for a moment. "A loving fiancée would want to know *when* I would be back."

"How long will you be gone?" she repeated, defiantly tilting her head.

"I'll see you tomorrow."

Her feet were rooted to the spot, incapable of carrying her away even when he got into the car and left. She stared after it, aware that she must look just like a dutiful fiancée savoring the last moments she had spent with her lover. But the fire that consumed Laurie was one of burning rage.

Her peaceful nature had undergone a dramatic change, sparked by Rian's volatile and forceful personality. She had sworn last night to remain indifferent to him, to ignore him as much as possible. The powerful feelings that raced through her when she was with him were deeply troubling. Laurie

wanted to believe that her dislike for the man was
the reason behind the unnerving sensation.

Still staring after the already vanished car, Laurie
didn't hear the horses approach until the Judge's
booming voice broke into her reverie.

"Don't look so downhearted, Laurie."

She turned sharply, taking in the saddled horses
he was leading.

He noticed the troubled frown on her face.
"Don't tell me Rian left you already."

"Yes, on a business trip," Laurie sighed as Vera
walked out of the front door wearing her tan riding
breeches and followed by Rian's bespectacled secretary, who was to be her watchdog.

"When will he be back?" the Judge asked, waving
a cheery salute to the lovely older woman coming
towards them.

"Tomorrow."

"Then there's no reason to cancel our plans for
this evening, is there, Vera?" he declared.

"No, I don't suppose there is," she agreed
absently while Laurie caught a questioning look
from E. J. Denton.

"What plans are those?" Rian's right-hand man
inquired with an unassuming smile.

"Colin was escorting Laurie to an evening Mardi
Gras parade after the four of us had dined," the
Judge explained. "When Rian arrived yesterday we
intended to cancel our plans, but there's no need
to now that he's gone away again."

The hesitant look on E. J. Denton's face prompted
Laurie to endorse the Judge's idea. "Of course
there's no need to change our plans," she declared
with false cheerfulness, glad of the opportunity to
thumb her nose at the absent Rian. "Colin told

me so much about the evening parades, and who knows when I'll be back here again during Mardi Gras? Rian couldn't possibly object." She glared at E. J., daring him to raise an objection.

"You're more than welcome to join us," Vera said warmly.

E. J. Denton glanced at Laurie, realizing that she knew he was supposed to keep an eye on her. "No, thank you," he refused politely. "I have a lot of paperwork to catch up on for Rian. You all go ahead and enjoy yourselves."

"If that's settled, are you ladies ready for a morning ride?" The Judge's twinkling gaze was directed lovingly at the smiling Vera.

"Laurie hasn't had breakfast yet," Vera hesitated.

"Fine. I had Mrs. Lawson prepare brunch. We can ride directly to my place so Laurie can eat."

"That sounds like a wonderful idea," Laurie declared with a laugh, wondering with wicked glee how poor E. J. Denton was going to keep an eye on her at that distance.

But the thought didn't trouble him as he lifted a hand in good-bye. "Have a good time." Then he retreated towards the house, probably knowing that Rian's threat had been sufficient to keep Laurie in line. Recognizing her own weakness, Laurie had to admit he was right.

The day passed swiftly, too swiftly for Laurie, who felt like a bird freed from its cage. She felt she had to savor each moment of freedom before her master returned. Some inner sense told her Rian wouldn't be pleased to discover she was spending the evening with Colin. So Laurie was doubly attentive to her good-looking escort.

The frenzied festivities of Mardi Gras only intensified her high spirits. The laughing, shouting crowd that gathered along the parade route helped Laurie lose her inhibitions as she joined in, adding her gleeful shouts to their joyful noise. Dress was unimportant. A few people were dressed in outrageous costumes while others wore casual clothes. Some, like Laurie and Colin, wore dressier attire. But the contagious hilarity made her lose all thought of the expensive silk dress of large black flowers against a background of white or the hand-crocheted shawl that covered her bare shoulders.

A self-propelled golden dragon wove through the congested street, a hidden generator system providing the power to light the myriad bulbs along its snaking back. A group of masquers, this time men in bright oriental costumes and masks, were ensconced in a howdah on the dragon's back, tossing candy, toys, and costume jewelry to the delighted shrieks of the crowd. Laurie and Colin both raised their hands in a riotous effort to persuade the masquers to throw booty in their direction.

Young and old alike scrambled for the trinkets tossed from the floats, playfully fighting over the inexpensive gifts and mementos as if they were made of gold. Equestrian units separated the floats and the marching bands. Elaborately dressed riders sat astride beautiful prancing horses, their hooves gilded in silver or gold, with ribbons in their manes and false tails arching high over their backs.

There was a lull in the procession and Laurie happily remembered Colin's earlier remark that Mobile went a little crazy on Mardi Gras. Every decadent whim was freely indulged and the party-hearty crowd ran rampant. Mardi Gras—Fat Tuesday—was followed by Ash Wednesday and the strict fast of Lent.

"Colin, this is much more fun than watching the parade from the window!" Laurie exclaimed, her face upturned so he received the full glow of her excitement.

"I haven't had this much fun at a parade since I was a kid," Colin admitted laughingly.

"I've never had this much fun," Laurie declared fervently. "I feel like letting my hair down and going a little wild."

"Your hair is already down." A huskiness came into his voice as he captured a silken black lock in his hand. "I feel like taking you into my arms and asking you where you've been all my life. Where have you been, Laurie?"

The ardent light in his hazel eyes sobered Laurie. After the possessive sensuality of Rian's kiss, she wondered what it would be like if Colin kissed her. Would he be tender and gentle, as she had always wanted a lover to be? Or would he be demanding and passionate like Rian? Colin's hand moved from her hair to her shoulder as he saw an unspoken invitation in her sparkling eyes.

The crowd surged around them, jostling forward as another float drew alongside. The moment when Laurie wanted the answer to her tantalizing question passed and she eagerly turned to the colorfully decorated float, concentrating on the parade. Colin was quick to sense the change. Although a flash of regret passed across his eyes, he immediately picked up the carefree mood of the revelers around them again.

When the float passed, the crowd eased back to

permit a Dixieland band to march by. Laurie rubbed the back of her neck, trying to rid herself of the odd prickling sensation that was tingling down her spine. A strong force compelled her to glance over her shoulder and her eyes locked with a tall man's leaning negligently against a tree. Oh, no. Rian.

With languid grace, he straightened, and, still holding her gaze, made his way through the crowd to her side. He was wearing the dark business suit from this morning, but his tie was loosened and the buttons of his white shirt were undone to reveal his tanned throat.

"Rian! We didn't expect you back tonight!" Colin exclaimed.

Laurie couldn't speak; her gaze was fixed on the enigmatic expression on Rian's carved face. "So I understand," he replied smoothly, his dark eyes not leaving Laurie's.

Colin glanced hesitantly from one to the other, feeling shut out by their concentration on each other.

"I hope you don't mind my bringing Laurie to the parade." An apologetic tone crept into his voice. "She's never been to Mardi Gras before."

"You seemed to be enjoying yourself, Laurie," Rian commented.

"I was . . . I am," she quickly corrected herself, but not before there was a cynical lift to Rian's mouth.

"Sorry if I spoiled your fun," he said softly. "I just thought my fiancée might miss me."

"Colin and I are friends," she said hastily, not wanting Rian to jump to conclusions. The catch in her throat made her voice sound soft and breath-less.

"In that case,"—for the first time, Rian turned his gaze on Colin's uncomfortable expression—"you won't object if I take Laurie home."

"Of course not." Colin nodded in agreement; fully aware, as Laurie was, that Rian expected no other answer.

Lines of fatigue were etched around Rian's dark eyes. Laurie didn't quite know what prompted her to suggest, "Would you like to leave now?"

"Would you excuse us?" Rian made a courteous nod in Colin's direction before slipping a guiding hand on Laurie's shoulders and moving her through the crowd before she had a chance to take back her suggestion. "I had to park several blocks away. Hope you don't mind walking," he said, releasing her once they were free of the milling crowds.

Laurie assured him that she didn't as they walked down a tree-lined street.

"I suppose Mr. Denton told you where we were." Her voice sounded sharper than she intended, but his presence always set her on edge.

"E. J. was under the impression it was to be a foursome. He was a bit upset when the Judge and Vera returned to the house without you and Colin," said Rian, casting a downward glance at the defensive tilt of her chin. "The poor guy thought there might have been a conspiracy to spirit you away."

"Is that why you came looking for us? Weren't you afraid you wouldn't find us in the crowd?"

"Hey, I know the best places to view the Mardi Gras parade. I had a fair idea where Colin would take you." He answered Laurie's questions with a dismissive shrug of his shoulders. "As for spotting you in a crowd, you have a face and figure no man could miss."

"Really?" Laurie retorted with chilling disbelief. "I doubt that you even knew I existed in Los Angeles."

"Can you blame me? Why would I be anxious to renew my acquaintance with LaRaine's cousin after our first meeting? You had green cucumber cream all over your face, your head swathed in a towel, and that weird red robe on," Rian mocked. "The only thing worth looking at then was your blue eyes. The next time I saw you, you were much more presentable, but you did your damnedest to fade into the wallpaper rather than attract my attention." Laurie blushed. "Why was that?"

"I didn't like you very much," she defended herself, while surprised to find out that he had noticed her.

"And you like me even less now."

"That's true," she answered, hoping to zap at least some of his complacency.

"Honesty is the best policy, Laurie, but don't overdo it." His words acted as a gentle slap on the hand. "And you're playing with fire the way you keep leading Colin on."

"I don't know what you're talking about!" A deeper flush of color betrayed her words as she wondered how long Rian had been standing there watching her and Colin.

"I've seen that look on a woman's face before. You were wondering what it would be like to be kissed by him. I advise against it," he told her firmly, an unspoken threat of some kind in his voice.

The way he was dictating to her was irritating Laurie. She reared her head back like an unbroken filly bridling at her first touch of the bit. "You don't own me!"

His fingers closed over her left wrist, holding up her hand so the dim streetlight reflected inside the deep blue sapphire. "For the moment, I do."

"You blackmailed me into wearing that ring." Her voice quivered with anger. "It doesn't mean any more to me than it did to LaRaine."

"I warned you not to push me," Rian snarled, whirling her round to face him while capturing her other wrist in his hand. "Why did you do it?" His dark gaze rested on her, satisfied that she couldn't struggle much, if at all. "Did you hope to make me angry enough to send you away? Or was it something else you wanted?"

"Let me go!" Her order sounded more like a plea.

Rian chuckled coldly, tightening his grip ever so slightly. His mouth covered hers with demanding fierceness. Laurie tried to turn her head aside, but Rian made her turn back to him. Her back was arched against the granite strength of his body and she could feel the thudding of his heart against hers. There was an irresistible sensual power in the burning kiss that melted away her resistance. But Rian demanded total submission.

His virility had Laurie reeling as his touch became less forceful and more sensually persuasive. Her light-headedness made her lose touch with reality. When his hold loosened on her wrists, she wasn't aware of it, although she knew his hands were moving across her hips and back. At his insistence, her lips parted to allow his masterful exploration of her mouth. When Rian had her clinging to him, overwhelmed by her desire for him, he released her, holding her away, his dark eyes looking triumphantly down at her face.

Instinctively Laurie swayed closer to him, the spell of his embrace still holding her captive. She could feel his black eyes dwelling on her lips, softened by his passion and parted in an unwilling urgency to know again the soul-destroying fire of his kiss. Never before had she been so stirred by a man's touch or made so aware of the difference and delights of being a female in the arms of a male.

"You're so hot," Rian murmured, his voice a caress. "I can see how you got Colin hooked with those big blue eyes. Too bad I'm not so easily fooled."

"What do you mean?" she breathed hoarsely, unwilling to believe the coldness in his soft voice.

"You can summon up any emotion that works, can't you? Sweet innocence. Anger. Passion. What will you try next to get your way? Tears?" Rian taunted. "Chick tricks won't work on me, Laurie. I can't be wrapped around your finger like Colin. And I won't let you out of our engagement since your pretense forced us into it."

She refused to let the tears scorching her eyes fall, knowing he would never believe she was crying because of his arrogant accusation. Obviously he was used to women falling at his feet. His ability to shrug off the embrace that had shattered her was chilling.

"You forced me to kiss you! I never asked for it

or invited it," she declared in a choked voice. "How dare you condemn me!"

"Guess I'm braver than you think," he mocked, her indignant outburst amusing him. "But we did settle one question. You do belong to me."

"Never!" Laurie said vehemently—before her traitorous heart could declare otherwise.

Rian ignored her reply and placed a hand on her back to guide her to his parked car. His sureness that she was his to command was a little frightening. But it was much, much worse for Laurie to know that she wasn't as indifferent to him as she had thought. The attraction was magnetic, compelling her senses to acknowledge his masculinity, forcing her to admit the desires of her flesh.

The Mercedes seemed like a luxurious prison. She trembled at Rian's nearness even as her mind railed against it. Before he started the car, he tossed a sparkling object in her lap.

"Add this to the baubles you collected tonight," he ordered.

Despite the dim light, Laurie recognized the diamond-and-ruby-studded bracelet that had been Rian's first expensive gift to LaRaine. A stunned expression flashed across her face as she glanced at the chiseled profile of the man beside her.

"Where did you get this?" she whispered.

"LaRaine had a hissy fit and threw it at me."

"LaRaine?"

"I'm sure she regrets it now. It's an expensive bracelet."

"When did you see LaRaine?" She held her breath as she waited for his answer.

"Today. She was nearly as stunned to see me as

you were, but she recovered quicker than you did."
Rian redirected his attention to the road.

"I thought you were away on a business trip."

"That was secondary. I went to L.A. mostly to
confront LaRaine."

"Was she very upset?" Laurie asked, imagining
her cousin's reaction when she learned their masquerade had been uncovered.

"At first she was contrite, until she realized there
would be no reconciliation—our relationship was
truly finished. Her new acting career seems to have
first place in her life now, although she did get
kind of worked up when she learned that I was
engaged to you."

"Why did you tell her that?" demanded Laurie.

"It's the truth. Why shouldn't I tell her?" said
Rian.

"This is make-believe for your aunt's benefit, not
a real engagement."

"That's what you keep saying. Do you feel guilty
that you've taken me away from LaRaine? As your
cousin pointed out to me today, you only get what
she doesn't want. Is a secondhand fiancé much
different from a dress?"

"As far as I'm concerned I don't have a fiancé,
secondhand or otherwise," Laurie retorted coldly.

"Don't dismiss me so easily. You belong to me
for the time being." His tone was cutting.

The hard stones of the bracelet in her hand
seemed as unyielding as Rian. "Why did you give
me this?"

"Why should you care? Doesn't every woman
equate love with how much money a man is willing
to spend on her?" he sneered cynically.

"Maybe your women do." She didn't care how

she sounded as long as she could strike back with equal sarcasm. "They probably knew expensive presents were all you could give. You're incapable of love."

"Damn you, Laurie!" Rian was furious. But the heavy traffic around them prevented him from stopping the car and really losing his temper. "Nobody talks to me that way!"

"High time somebody did, then." It was her turn to settle complacently in her seat.

But his hand seized her wrist, and he drew her closer to him, his gaze never leaving the highway. "Why do you want to get me angry?" he demanded. "Is that better than being ignored?"

"No, that's not it at all." Her soft voice shook.

Rian spared her a contemptuous glance. "You're afraid of me, aren't you? Hissing like a little kitten unable to defend herself."

"Yes," she whispered, knowing there was a lot of truth in his statement.

Her hand was released and Laurie sank back in her seat as Rian stopped talking. The silence of night enfolded them.

CHAPTER SEVEN

Rian was not at the breakfast table the following morning, much to Laurie's relief. When she'd walked by the study, she'd heard voices and the sound of shuffling papers. She had hoped that Rian was in there, but she didn't know for sure until she reached the dining room. The light meal of a grapefruit half, toast, and coffee was quickly finished so Laurie could escape to the stables without enduring Rian's unsettling presence.

The cook had already told her that Vera was there, and the horses were saddled and waiting when Laurie arrived. A bemused smile crossed her face as she saw the Judge hovering near the silver-haired woman. They looked so right together, he so tall and dignified and Vera so feminine and petite.

"Good morning, Laurie," the Judge greeted her

enthusiastically. "Did you enjoy the parade last night?"

"Yes, it was amazing. So colorful and so much fun!" She flashed him a brilliant smile as she took the reins he handed her.

"Colin's on his way over. Here he comes now," he declared as he gave Vera a boost into her saddle and turned to look at the roan cantering towards them.

The horses stamped impatiently, eager to be off, and the four riders set out towards the beckoning countryside. As usual, Colin and Laurie trailed the older couple, already engrossed in a private conversation.

"I never got a chance last night to tell you how much I enjoyed the parade," Laurie said after they had ridden some distance and the horses were less frisky.

"I'm glad you did," Colin smiled, his gaze straying to the riders in front. "Last evening must've gone well for the Judge, too. He was singing this morning at the breakfast table. I haven't seen him that happy for ages."

"They do act as if they're sharing a wonderful secret, don't they? I hope so. It would make all this worthwhile," Laurie mused wistfully.

"What do you mean—all this?" Colin immediately picked up on Laurie's slip of the tongue. "Don't tell me Rian was jealous about last night?"

There was a pause before Laurie answered as she searched for the right words. "I hadn't told Rian about our plans for the evening, so he was upset. He didn't expect me to be gone when he returned."

"That explains it," Colin nodded. "For a minute there last night I thought Rian was going to hang

No Trespassing signs on you. He can be very possessive about anything or anyone he considers his."

Laurie paled as she remembered the aggressive way Rian had said she belonged to him. She longed to deny her engagement to Rian, to prevent his brand from being stamped on her, while also remembering her own unqualified response to his embrace. She never dreamed it was possible to love and hate a man at the same time, flames of anger mixed with those of passion and desire.

"Not that I blame him," Colin added with a flirtatious twinkle in his eyes.

It was meant as a joke to lighten the moodiness clouding her eyes. In answer, Laurie kicked her mount in the side, sending it off at a rapid canter while she tossed a laughing challenge at Colin. His roan bounded out immediately after her, its superior speed drawing it even in two strides. The pair swung out ahead of Vera and the Judge, racing down the road to turn off into a meadow, then slowed their pace to a brisk trot.

"Say, what about the Mardi Gras ball? Have you told Rian that I have tickets? I can get an extra one for him." Colin raised his voice slightly to carry over the blowing snorts of their horses.

"No, I haven't mentioned it. I'm not sure what Rian's plans are." She didn't want to discuss Rian. Her feelings towards him were too complicated and there was too much beauty around them to ignore. Checking her mount down to a walk, Laurie breathed in the fragrant country air. "I'm going to miss these early morning rides. They're a perfect way to begin the day." As she shrugged regretfully, she reminded herself that her departure would mark the end of her fake engagement to Rian. If only it could be over sooner . . . before she was completely captivated by his animal attraction. "Only three more days."

Colin raised his eyebrows in surprise. "Vera said that Rian would be staying at least another week. You aren't leaving before he does, are you?"

Another week! Laurie successfully concealed her astonishment at that statement as she silently wondered whether Rian was going to force her to stay until he left. She felt her heart skip a beat because she knew he would.

"I haven't decided," she replied, knowing the decision wasn't really hers to make now that Rian had appointed himself dictator. "Don't you think we should wait here for Vera and your father to join us?" she asked brightly, hoping to change the subject.

Their ride had taken them almost full circle back to the house. The dark shingles of the Judge's roof could be seen through the treetops. Colin halted his horse and turned in the saddle.

"Hey, I thought Rian would be working this morning," he remarked casually.

Laurie whirled around, instantly picking out the dappled gray Arabian and the erect masculine figure astride it from the trio of riders approaching them. Rian separated himself from Vera and the Judge, swinging out the Arab in an extended trot that had them gliding effortlessly over the gently undulating meadow. A superb horse with a superb horseman on board, looking all the more imposing and ruggedly attractive in fawn-colored breeches and a white shirt, his jet black hair rakishly tousled by the breeze. Laurie didn't stop staring even when Rian halted his spirited horse beside them.

"Good morning." Rian's greeting was to them both, but his sardonic gaze rested on Laurie's flushed face, coloring when she realized how rudely she had been staring.

"I didn't know you were going riding with us this morning," she murmured, feeling the need to say something. "I heard you in the study working when I came downstairs."

"That must have been E. J.," he said, his hooded gaze moving from her to the tossing head of his horse. "Sitar and I were out watching the sunrise while you were still playing Sleeping Beauty. I considered going in and kissing you awake, but the temptation to join you under the bedcovers might have been too great."

"Rian!" Her embarrassed anger was clear enough. Laurie glanced at the disconcerted expression on Colin's face.

"I think this is a private conversation," Colin remarked, touching a finger to his forehead before reining his horse away to join the Judge and Vera.

"You said that deliberately so he would leave." Laurie turned an accusing glance on Rian.

"Yes." He seemed awfully pleased with himself. "Which doesn't mean that I didn't think about doing exactly what I said."

"I might have had something to say about it," she retorted.

"Maybe . . . maybe not." His dark eyes boldly took in the quick rise and fall of her breasts. A scarlet stain crept into her cheeks.

"What an ego!" she spat.

Her angry accusation drew a chuckle from Rian. "Go ahead and lash out at me," he mocked. "But you know you always end up purring when I touch you.''

The sensually intimate look in his eyes momentarily robbed Laurie of her ability to breathe. Silently she acknowledged the physical attraction that drew her to him like a moth drawn to a flame. With luck, she'd escape with no more than singed wings.

"That isn't enough," she declared angrily.

"This is the new millenium. Don't tell me I've become engaged to a prim and proper Victorian miss," Rian said with considerable amusement.

"Hardly Victorian." Laurie didn't attempt to deny the rest of his description. "You don't know me very well, do you?"

"Maybe I do," he nodded, stilling the prancing horse with the touch of his hand, "you're going to be in love with the man you marry, aren't you? What was it you said—he'll be tender and kind like Colin? Is that why the two of you separated from the Judge and Vera, so you could compare mutual likes and dislikes and discover whether you were compatible? How sweet."

"No, that isn't why Colin and I were off by ourselves," she declared, barely suppressing her rising temper. "If you must know, we were giving Vera and the Judge a chance to be alone. That's also the reason we went to the parade without them."

"A pair of innocent matchmakers," Rian drawled sarcastically.

"Twist it any way you want to." Flashing him an angry glance, she moved her mount towards the slow-walking horses and riders.

The pushing shoulder of Rian's gray forced her own horse to fall in behind the others instead of drawing level with them as Laurie had planned. She fought an urge to put a quirt to her horse's flank and race away, but she knew Rian's horse was faster than Briar and he would catch up with her in minutes.

Vera turned slightly in her saddle so she could see Rian and Laurie. "The Judge suggested we have a party this Saturday to celebrate your engagement, for our closest friends. But Colin reminded us that Laurie is leaving on Wednesday."

"Those plans were made before she knew I would be coming to Mobile," Rian replied, his bland expression unchanging when Laurie darted an angry glance at him.

"You know I have other commitments in Los Angeles." The sweet smile on her lips matched the honey-coated tone.

"So postpone them," he said arrogantly, challenging her to disagree with his edict.

Obviously, he was trying to prolong her stay— and their phony engagement. Laurie was furious.

"You say that, darling," she murmured loud enough for the others to hear as she put extra emphasis on the endearment, "because you have no idea all the things a bride has to do to prepare for the wedding."

"Such as?" One corner of his mouth twitched in amusement, laughing at the kitten trying to best the panther.

"Oh, choosing bridesmaids, the church, the dresses, the wedding gown, the place for the reception, the guest list, the invitations, bridal showers, and all that," Laurie replied brightly.

"Have you set the wedding date?" Colin asked.

"No—" Laurie began, only to have Rian interrupt her.

"Yes, in two weeks. We're going to elope." The certainty in his voice caught her off guard.

"We are not!" Laurie exclaimed, the denial that she was ever going to marry him springing instantaneously to her lips. "I told you—"

Her words were broken off by the steel fingers that gripped her arm and the hardness of his leg brushing against hers. "Watch it," he hissed for her ears alone, the glittering fire in his eyes as effective as his grip on her arm. A traitorous weakness flowed through her body, sapping her anger.

"We aren't going to elope," Laurie finished in a quieter voice.

"You can't blame her, Rian, for wanting a big wedding with all the trimmings," the Judge put in. "Every young woman pictures herself walking down the church aisle in a white satin gown."

"Is that your fantasy?" Rian baited her. "Walking down the aisle to me?"

Laurie couldn't answer. The image he put in her mind stole her voice. She could visualize it completely, even to Rian's dark eyes compelling her to walk towards him. She could almost hear his low voice making the vow of a lifetime of love. The mysterious light in his eyes closed out all thought of anyone outside the two of them.

"Cat got your tongue?" Rian whispered, releasing her arm and touching a finger to the softness of her lips.

Her heart skipped a beat as her lashes fluttered down over her blue eyes, concealing the desire that his intimate caress sparked.

"You don't play fair, Rian Montgomery," she accused in a tight voice.

"I always get what I want, though," he replied with triumph in his eyes.

"Are you two lovebirds going to join us for brunch?" the Judge broke in.

Laurie was startled to see the path leading to the Judge's rear patio. She hadn't realized they had come so far so quickly. She trembled with relief to know that in a few minutes they would all be occupied with cool drinks and sandwiches, which would eliminate the possibility of more of Rian's private asides to her.

"Laurie and I will pass this time, Judge," Rian drawled, turning his horse and so forcing Laurie's horse to turn in the direction of home as well. "We'll grab a bite at the house with E. J."

Knowing smiles were exchanged between Vera and the Judge, and Laurie knew they were putting the wrong spin on Rian's words. They were obviously thinking that the two of them wanted to be alone, though that was the absolute last thing she wanted.

"See you later," Vera waved.

Large oaks draped with Spanish moss soon separated Laurie and Rian completely from the others as they walked their horses along the worn path to Vera's stables. Her tight-lipped silence didn't go unnoticed by Rian.

"What's eating you now?" he taunted, checking his Arab as it tried to hurry its pace.

"Nothing," Laurie answered.

"Just so you know, I declined the invitation because I thought it was what you wanted."

"Why should I want to be alone with you?" Her cheeks colored as she made the angry retort.

"Perhaps I misunderstood." His calmness was infuriating. "I thought you wanted the Judge and Vera to be alone."

His answer flustered her. "I did . . . I do."

"But not if it means being alone with me, is that it?"

"I didn't say that."

"You didn't have to," he replied.

Rian dismounted at the paddock gate, reaching out to hold the bridle of Laurie's chestnut as she too slipped off her horse. She was thankful that his attention had shifted from her to the animals.

"They're still a bit warm," he said, shoving the chestnut's reins into her unwilling hands. "Let's walk them for a while."

It was difficult walking beside Rian without being aware of him. The top of her tousled hair was even with his chin. A white shirt accented rather than concealed the rippling leanness of his muscular figure. The breeches and riding boots suited his rugged looks more than elegant suits did. Rian Montgomery was a man of action—arrogant and autocratic, sure of his own power to control the lives of others.

Living with him, Laurie thought, would be like living on the side of a volcano. At times the solid foundation would be comforting, but when the rumblings began it would be terrifying.

She shouldn't think like that, she told herself firmly, aware that she was almost thinking of their relationship as a permanent thing. It was the silence dominated by the compelling man walking beside her that made her so introspective.

Three more days—just three more days—and she would be gone. All of this would seem like a dream that had never really happened. Then Laurie remembered Vera mentioning the party.

"What about the party this weekend?" she asked hesitantly. "My plane reservations, or rather La-Raine's plane reservations, are for this Wednesday."

"They can be changed," his mocking voice reminded her.

"I know, but . . . you don't really want to have Vera give an engagement party for us."

"How do you know what I want?" Now there was a knife-sharp edge to his mockery.

Laurie didn't want to delve into that subject and subsided into silence.

"What prompted your sudden interest in my aunt's love life, anyway?" Rian asked, changing the subject with lightning swiftness.

Laurie blinked up at him briefly. "The first time I met the Judge, I knew he was smitten with Vera. And Colin mentioned later that his father had been in love with her for years." She didn't want to mention that Colin had also told her about Rian's part in the breakup of Vera's previous marriage. "I thought it would be a wonderful thing if they finally got together."

"One disastrous marriage is enough for her," Rian said bitterly.

"Why would a marriage between the Judge and Vera be disastrous? He loves her very much."

"Love! Love!" he exclaimed. "You keep coming back to the same subject."

"What's wrong with love? It wouldn't be a marriage without it." Confusion darkened her blue eyes.

"Love destroys. It turns a man into a henpecked husband and a woman into a dispirited housewife," Rian bit out.

"That's not true," Laurie gasped.

"Do you know any couple who's truly in love, the way you mean it? Aren't they together just working to meet basic needs—food, shelter, clean clothes, companionship, and the physical gratification of the opposite sex?" he jeered.

Laurie knew very few people and none well enough to speak with authority on their personal lives. Her failure to answer brought more derogatory remarks from Rian.

"What about LaRaine's parents? I never met a more greedy, selfish woman than Carrie Evans. No wonder your uncle spends most of his time at work!"

"But look at the Judge," she protested, not a match for his suddenly vicious attack, "he's loved Vera for a long time."

"Yes, and that same love destroyed his marriage. Jealousy consumed Colin's mother until she didn't want to live any more. I know Colin must have told you what kind of a marriage Vera had," Rian said sarcastically. "Her husband was looking for a meal ticket, not love. He didn't even have to maintain a pretense of a happy marriage to fool Vera. She adored him no matter what he did." Laurie was mesmerized by the anger and contempt in Rian's face. "Love is just an empty word. It means nothing."

A twisting, wrenching pain tore into her heart,

making breathing almost impossible. She couldn't believe she was hearing any of this.

"What about your parents?" she asked.

"I saw my father nearly go bankrupt trying to buy my mother's love with presents. He was an important man, a powerful man, but she was never satisfied. I don't think the car crash that killed them was accidental. I think he just couldn't take it anymore." His mouth was a grim line, making him look more ruthless than Laurie thought possible. She couldn't meet his cold gaze.

"Then why on earth do you want to get married?"

"I told you once," Rian said tightly. "A woman is much more useful out of bed. I need a hostess, a housekeeper, and someone to bear my children. I'm an old-fashioned guy with old-fashioned ideas."

"What about what your wife wants?" Her voice barely squeezed through the hard knot in her throat.

"She'll have everything. You forget, I'm rich."

"I was right about you." Tears were spilling down Laurie's pale cheeks. "You don't have a heart," she gulped, fighting to get the ring off her finger.

But Rian pulled her hand away, resting it on his chest, against his thudding heart. "Yes, I do," he said harshly, sweeping an arm about her waist and drawing her to the firmness of his body. "A woman doesn't want a husband, she wants a lover."

His mouth met hers, the salty taste of her tears flavoring the kiss. His body transmitted his desires to her, sparking an answering flame that consumed all resistance to his touch. Laurie clung to him, her fingers sinking into the ebony blackness of his hair, until Rian lifted his head, breaking off the passionate embrace.

"Damn! I want you, Laurie!"

"No!" The ragged denial was torn from her heart.

With a strength she didn't know she had, Laurie twisted free. One backward step, then she turned and raced to the house while she still had the strength to resist his overpowering attraction.

CHAPTER EIGHT

A wide, tree-lined plaza marked the end of the long bridge that joined Dauphin Island to the mainland. The road was divided by lush green grasses dotted with spiky palmettos. Not a cloud marred the blue heavens and the golden sun was pleasantly warm. Laurie dutifully studied the scenery, keeping her gaze averted from the dark, compelling man behind the wheel of the luxury car.

"Rian," Vera spoke up from her place in the backseat with the Judge, "would you take Gerry and me to the harbor? He wants to check on his boat and I'm sure you'd much rather show Laurie around the island yourself."

"I didn't know you had a boat, Judge," Rian commented, ignoring his aunt's reference to Laurie.

"Oh, just a cabin cruiser, big enough for deep sea fishing in the Gulf," he replied. "But I haven't been out since late fall. I thought I'd better make sure everything is all right there. You can pick Vera and me up later to picnic down by the beach.''

"Would you feel safe in my company for a few hours, Laurie?" Lazy, half-closed black eyes seemed to laugh at her rigidly controlled expression. Since their disastrous conversation yesterday morning, Laurie had kept away from Rian. His harsh words on the subject of love still rang in her ears.

"What a silly thing to ask!" Vera exclaimed with a curious laugh. "She's your fiancée."

"Well, she doesn't seem to be saying yes or no." His statement forced Laurie to reply. She'd hoped this excursion would include the older couple and knew that Rian realized it, too.

"On the contrary," the lightness in her voice was slightly brittle, "I think it'd be very interesting to have you as my tour guide, Rian. You have a unique point of view about so many things."

The barb in her comment wasn't lost on him as he acknowledged her reply with a single nod.

After they left Vera and the Judge at one of the docks, Rian drove slowly along the marina so Laurie could see the different boats tied up there. Sailboats large and small bobbed beside cabin cruisers and fully rigged-out fishing boats.

"Every year there's a blessing of the fishing fleet," Rian told her. "The shrimp boats are all decked out in lights and flags. You see," he tossed her a mocking glance, "I take my duties as tour guide seriously." Not for anything would Laurie admit that his information interested her, though it did. "Our next stop is Fort Gaines."

"How familiar are you with the history of this

area?'' Rian asked when they walked into the inner courtyard of the fort.

"I don't know a thing about it," Laurie admitted, expecting a scornful glance, but she was met by a smile.

"Well, listen up." He tucked her hand under his arm and walked her towards the ramp leading to the top of the fort wall. "Isle Dauphine, as the French called it in 1699, was an important military base before the founding of the Louisiana Territory, which eventually stretched from the Gulf of Mexico to the Great Lakes and westward. The city of Mobile was the provincial capital of this French territory and Dauphin Island was the port of entry for two-thirds of the North American continent.''

"Did you memorize all that?" Laurie murmured.

He pointed to a historical plaque she hadn't noticed nearby. "No, I didn't. Moving right along . . . Have you heard of the 'cassette' girls of New Orleans?'' Laurie shook her head. "Before arriving in New Orleans, the French ship *Pelican* anchored at Dauphin Island. On board were twenty-four young girls who were sent by the King of France to marry the men here and eventually settle near the fort on Mobile River, which became the city of Mobile. They were later known as the '*Pelican* girls,' arriving in the colony almost a quarter of a century before their New Orleans counterparts. The cassettes were the boxes they brought with them, like hope chests.''

"Did they marry the men?"

"Of course. They came here to serve their king." There was a slight pause during which Laurie could feel his dark gaze resting on her. "What? Nothing to say about loveless marriages?" he jeered. "Or does the notion of traveling halfway across the world to marry a total stranger seem romantic?"

She shot him a cool look. "I don't believe I have to answer questions from a tour guide. I get to ask them, though."

A humorless smile was directed at her. "Sorry. Didn't know I couldn't ask a few questions now and then—"

"You never ask, Rian. You order," Laurie sighed, knowing how easily he could intimidate her.

"Okay, I'll ask," his velvet-soft voice whispered near her hair as she stopped to look out of the southeast bastion.

"Do you like this?" His hand stroked her silky long hair, slipping underneath to caress her neck.

"Rian, please!"

"I like the way you say my name," came his husky declaration. "Say it again."

"No!" She took a quick step forward to evade his unnerving touch. The Gulf shimmered blue-green, almost turquoise in color near the white sand beach. "What's that out in the water?" Laurie pointed, hoping she could distract him.

"That's the lighthouse on Sand Island, at the mouth of Mobile Bay," Rian replied, a tinge of frustration in his voice. "There's been a lighthouse there since 1838 to guide the ships to a safe anchorage. This side of the lighthouse and beyond is where the famous Battle of Mobile Bay took place during the War Between the States.

"Admiral Farragut commanded the Union ironclads while Confederate warships formed a battle line protecting the entrance. It was here that Farragut made his famous command 'Damn the torpedoes, full speed ahead!' The ironclads won and

Mobile fell to the North." His hands settled on her shoulders, pulling her back against the hardness of his chest. "I shouldn't say this as a son of the South but the damn Yankees always win. Including you."

"I'm not a Yankee. I'm from California, remember?"

For a moment, Laurie relaxed against him, glorying in the masculine nearness that swept her breath away, inhaling the scent of his maleness, totally intoxicated by his overpowering virility. In that one split second, she wanted to just give herself up to his capable hands. But the momentary weakness didn't last as she swallowed back her desire for his touch.

"Right. I remember."

She was relieved when Rian's hands dropped to his side. If it ever came to a battle, the victory would be his.

They continued along the path to the east bastion where Rian pointed out Fort Morgan guarding the other side of the Bay, then walked on to the restored northwest bastion to look at the vaulted ceilings and arches.

"The bricks used to construct the Fort were made by slaves," Rian explained. "The work was done near Dog River on the mainland almost twenty miles away. All these bastions were cannon ports, and the roofs served as catch basins for rainwater. It was then strained through shells and sand and carried to cisterns beneath the floor of the fort and the yard. Ingenious system."

Laurie nodded politely, not wanting to seem too bored with antebellum plumbing.

"Was the fort ever used during the World Wars?" Laurie inquired, sticking to the safe topic of history.

"Yes. A small garrison was stationed here in World War II, mostly to watch for saboteurs landing from enemy submarines, which were sometimes sighted off the mouth of Mobile Bay."

With their tour of the fort completed, Laurie and Rian viewed the artifacts on display at the Confederate Museum on the grounds before returning to the car. From the car windows, Laurie admired the island's country club and the lush greens of an eighteen-hole golf course, the white beaches along the Gulf, and the large oak trees in Cadillac Square, named after one of the three French governors who lived on the island. As they headed back to the marina, Rian pointed out the oak trees growing atop large mounds of oyster shells left by the Indian tribes that lived here long before the first French explorer set foot on the Isle Dauphine.

When the foursome gathered again, the talkativeness of Vera and the Judge made up for the lack of conversation between Laurie and Rian. The laughter and happy voices of the older couple made Laurie feel that she and Rian were chaperoning them. The stretch of beach that Vera chose for their picnic was empty except for the gulls that danced at the water's edge or flew screeching above the gentle waves.

It was an idyllic setting—a colorful picnic blanket on white sugar sand, the salty tang of the Gulf breeze, and the calming sound of the surf rushing in to kiss the shore. But Laurie couldn't relax. The expertly prepared seafood salad was tasteless to her. She was almost glad when everyone was finished and the leftovers packed away in the hamper.

For all the notice Rian took of her, she might as well not have been there. An hour before, he had turned on the charm, undermining her defenses and twisting her in knots. Laurie had been telling herself that she didn't want him to pay attention to her, to touch her, to cast his spell on her. Now that he was doing none of these things, she wanted him to. *Go figure,* she thought.

"How about a stroll along the beach, Laurie?" Rian was on his feet, looking down at her with a gleam in his eyes.

A second ago she had craved his attention, but faced with an actual invitation, Laurie hesitated to accept. Any time spent alone with Rian Montgomery was dangerous to her peace of mind. Then a brown hand stretched out and she found herself taking it as he helped her to her feet without a word from her.

"Looks like they want to be alone," Rian commented with a half smile after he and Laurie walked away.

"I thought you didn't approve of . . . Vera and the Judge?" Confusion clouded her eyes.

"Vera prefers to make her own mistakes. I can't interfere," he replied with a wink. "Besides, there's a lot to be said for companionship in old age. I should've listed that as one of the considerations for marriage."

"You aren't exactly old." Her cheeks were flushing for no apparent reason.

"I'm older than you. By several years."

"So's Colin." The instant Laurie said that, she wanted to take it back. She didn't mean to start another argument. "I'm sorry," she apologized quickly, not daring to meet his eyes. "I only meant that someone is bound to be older than someone else. Or something like that."

There was a moment of silence before Rian replied, "Okay. Whatever you say."

An indefinable truce had been declared. The white beach stretched out as endlessly as the sea on the horizon and Laurie felt she could walk forever. There was no need for conversation. There was only a genuine desire to savor in the magic of these moments with Rian, who shortened his long strides to match companionably with hers. They didn't touch, not even their hands, but Laurie felt closer to him than she ever had before. They were as one with the earth and sky and sea.

"We've lost sight of Vera and the Judge," Laurie murmured.

"So we have. Well, we wouldn't make very good beachcombers." Rian's steps slowed to a halt as he gave her a whimsical smile. "We can't lose touch with reality and keep going."

"Think how bored you would be with the monotony of a beachcomber's life," she remarked casually, tilting her head sideways to study him. "You enjoy the challenge of the business world, organizing companies and watching them grow."

A sudden puff of wind from the Gulf whipped her black hair across her face. Before her own hand could brush it back, Rian's was there, gently lifting it from her face and tucking it behind her ear. Then his hand cupped her cheek.

"Right now, I'm enjoying being with you." The softness of his voice melted her reserve.

"Rian." His name was a husky sound, born in her aching need for his warmth. For an instant his hand tightened, promising to close the space that separated them, then a rueful smile tilted a corner of his mouth, followed by a sigh.

"Let's go back," he said firmly, dropping his hand from her cheek and leaving her with a cold feeling that wouldn't go away even in the brilliant sun.

"Yes," Laurie breathed a reluctant agreement. It was just as well that she didn't get too close to his compelling masculinity. Too much time spent in Rian's company was dangerous.

The walk back was over quickly. So was the drive to Vera's house. Almost the instant they set foot in the door, Rian excused himself, saying he had work to do. Laurie watched him striding towards the study, a sense of loss stealing over her.

Almost an hour later Laurie saw Rian from her bedroom window as he got into the white Mercedes and left. Restlessly, she prowled her room, eventually wandering downstairs in search of Vera, only to find she had gone over to the Hartford house. The swimming pool sparkled invitingly in the late afternoon sun, but Laurie wasn't in the mood. Finally she settled in one of the living room sofas and leafed through a magazine. The telephone jingled on a nearby stand. Laurie waited, expecting E. J. to pick up the extension in the study, but it kept on ringing. Hesitantly Laurie picked up the receiver.

"Is Rian Montgomery there?" a woman's voice asked.

"Not right now," Laurie replied. "He should be back later. May I take a message?"

"Is this his aunt?"

"No, this is Laurie Evans." She was reluctant to explain her tenuous relationship to Rian.

"Are you Rian's fiancée? He mentioned that you were staying with Vera."

The woman's comment surprised Laurie. Her "yes" was hesitant. She wondered whom the melodic voice belonged to on the other end of the line and how the woman was associated with Rian.

"I'm so glad I have a chance to talk to you!" the woman exclaimed. "You're so lucky to have someone like Rian."

"Yes, thank you," Laurie stumbled, unable to think of any other reply.

"Oh, sorry. I didn't introduce myself," the woman laughed. "I'm Liz Trevors. My husband Arnold works for Rian. Or at least, he has been working for him. That's what I was calling to tell Rian—that the doctors have said he can go back to work in a month. They're releasing him from the hospital tomorrow."

"I'm glad to hear that," Laurie replied, wondering if LaRaine had known the Trevors.

"Rian probably didn't mention it to you. My husband was hospitalized after an automobile accident three months ago. Rian's been our guardian angel ever since, making sure I had transportation to and from the hospital, arranging for childcare, taking care of the medical bills.

"And he's been a tremendous boost to my husband's morale by keeping Arnold up to date with the company's transactions and assuring him that the position would be open whenever Arnold was able to come back. And Rian kept him on the payroll the whole time. Every time we try to thank him, Rian just shrugs it off. I'm so glad I can tell you how grateful we are for all your fiancé has done."

The picture Mrs. Trevor painted of Rian didn't match Laurie's image of a domineering and ruthless man whose charm was used mostly to get his own way.

She was still mulling over this discovery when she replaced the receiver and heard E. J. walk in the front door. He waved a greeting to her as he walked past the arched doorway.

"A Mrs. Trevors just called for Rian," Laurie told him, walking into the hallway to follow him.

"Arnold Trevors's wife?" E. J. asked, adjusting the black-rimmed glasses on his nose.

"Yes, she wanted to let Rian know that her husband is being released from the hospital tomorrow and should be back to work in a month."

"That's a relief." He raised his eyebrows in an expressive gesture. "Rian and I couldn't keep doing Arnold's work for much longer."

"Does Mr. Trevors have an executive position?" Laurie asked curiously.

"He was handling the South American deal until the accident, when Rian had to take over. That was about the time Rian met LaRaine." As soon as Laurie's cousin's name was out of his mouth, E. J. cast her an apologetic look.

"Yes, well—" Laurie breathed in deeply, not wanting to go into any details about all that. "Please give Rian Mrs. Trevors's message when he comes back."

"You bet."

Rian didn't return for the evening meal and Vera and Laurie ate alone while E. J. had sandwiches served for himself in the study. Not until nearly ten o'clock, when Laurie was mounting the stairs to her room, did Rian return. He glanced briefly at his watch and gave her an absent "good night" before continuing on to the study where E. J. was still working.

Laurie turned and tossed in her bed, dozing off, then awakening, unconsciously listening for the sound of Rian's footsteps in the hall. After awakening from another fitful doze, she glanced at the digital clock on the night stand. The luminous face said three o'clock. Rising from the bed, she slipped on her ivory satin robe and walked quietly into the hallway, deciding that a glass of warm milk might help her sleep eventually.

At the bottom of the stairs she saw a light shining from the study door. Rian couldn't possibly be working this late, Laurie thought idly as she tiptoed towards the door. But when she glanced in, she saw Rian sitting behind the desk, his suit jacket tossed over a chair with his tie, and his white shirt unbuttoned at the throat. He was wearily rubbing his hand across his forehead while holding the telephone receiver to his ear. Some infinitesimal sound betrayed her presence and caused him to glance up.

He cupped a hand over the receiver. "What are you doing up?"

"I couldn't sleep," Laurie answered softly, clutching the robe more tightly around her throat. "I was going to get some warm milk."

"Make it cocoa and I'll have a cup," Rian ordered, taking his hand from the receiver to speak into it while Laurie retreated quietly towards the kitchen.

Rian had hung up by the time Laurie came back carrying two steaming mugs of cocoa on a serving tray. Raking his fingers through his hair, he rose from the desk chair.

"Set it down over by the sofa," he instructed.

Obediently Laurie walked to the brown leather sofa and placed the tray on the oak coffee table in front of it. Uncertain whether to stay or go, she remained standing, picking up her mug from the tray. Rian sank down into the leathery cushions, glancing up at her in surprise that soon turned to bemusement.

"Don't stand there like that. You're making me nervous. Sit down and keep me company."

She chose a large armchair in matching brown leather, folding her fingers around the warm cup to still their trembling. Rian looked so tired, leaning forward as if he would fall asleep if he settled into the sofa.

"Do you have to work so late?" she murmured.

"Late?" One corner of his mouth tilted in a humorless smile. "It may be three o'clock here, but it's nine o'clock in the morning in London."

"Is that where you were calling?" Laurie asked, watching the lean hands as they lifted the mug to his mouth.

"Mmmm, yes," he replied, replacing the cup on the tray to press his fingers against his forehead.

"Do you have a headache?"

"Tension, more than anything," Rian shrugged.

Laurie hesitated, longing to offer to massage his neck and ease those lines of fatigue around his eyes and mouth, but afraid he would take it the wrong way. Finally she gathered the courage.

"Would you like me to rub your neck?" she asked.

He nodded. Then Rian obligingly moved towards the end of the sofa, stretching his long legs out on the cushions. Her hands trembled as she tentatively touched the taut cords of his neck. Then gently she began the massage, enjoying the sensation of unrestricted touch. As her nervousness went away, she felt Rian relax and the stiffness leave his neck.

When her hands moved to his temples, he moved slightly in surprise, then settled deeper in the cushions to rest his head against the arm of the sofa. The lids were closed over his dark eyes so he couldn't see her studying the harsh lines of his face and watching them soften.

Her fingers were beginning to ache when she noticed his even breathing and knew Rian had fallen asleep. Laurie smiled down at him, thinking how much younger and gentler he seemed. Very quietly she moved to the far end of the room where a crocheted afghan, undoubtedly made by Vera, lay folded on a table. For a moment Laurie held it against her breast, staring down on the sleeping man on the couch. A warm glow spread happily through her, filling her with a burning tenderness as she realized she had fallen in love with Rian Montgomery. Perceptively she knew she had been in love with him for a long time, but had refused to admit it.

A tiny sigh broke from her lips. It was a futile love, one that Rian didn't return, although admittedly he seemed to want her in a purely physical way. The silent acknowledgement of her love for Rian was bittersweet.

Unfolding the afghan, Laurie gently draped it over Rian's still form, wishing she could curl up in his arms and nestle her head against his chest. As she reached out to bring it over his white shirt, she saw his eyelids flutter open.

"Are you tucking me in for the night?" he asked lazily.

Laurie caught her breath, knowing how vulnerable she was at that moment and blushing at the thought. If Rian should learn of her feelings for him, it would give him unlimited power over her. She hadn't decided yet whether she wanted to marry a man who didn't love her even though she was deeply in love with him.

"Yes," she answered briskly, lowering her gaze so he couldn't read her thoughts.

His hand closed lightly over her wrist. "Are you going to kiss me good night, too?"

Laurie knew that if she didn't take the initiative, Rian was quite capable of forcing her to kiss him. Bending over, she lightly brushed his lips with hers and moved away.

Rian chuckled softly and released her wrist. "If I weren't so tired, I'd make you do better than that." A crooked smile curved his mouth as he closed his eyes. "Good night, Laurie."

She doubted whether Rian heard her wish him good night before he was asleep again.

CHAPTER NINE

The click of heels on the sun deck made Laurie open her eyes. Behind her sunglasses she saw Vera approaching, looking like a spring day in a dress of mint green.

"Rian said he thought you were here by the pool," the older woman said. "There was a phone call for you, but I couldn't find you."

"Who was it?"

"Colin. He said he'd call back later."

Guiltily Laurie remembered that she had forgotten to ask Rian about the Mardi Gras ball that evening. Too many things had happened since Colin had mentioned it, although it had crossed her mind. But, since the tour yesterday of Dauphin Island and the moments spent with Rian last night, the ball had been the last thing on her mind.

"Is Rian busy?" Laurie asked.

"He was on the phone," Vera nodded. "I'm

going into town to do some shopping. Would you like to go along? I'll be back by four o'clock and I doubt Colin will call before then.''

''No, I don't think so,'' Laurie refused politely. ''I'd rather laze in the sun.'' *And think,* she added to herself.

''I don't blame you. It's a beautiful afternoon,'' Vera laughed, lifting her hand in good-bye. ''I'll see you later.''

As soon as Vera was gone, Laurie settled deeper in the wide chaise, adjusting her wide-brimmed white hat to keep the sun from her face. It was blissfully warm and peaceful with the gentle rays playing over her skin, bare except for her yellow and blue bikini. The silence was only broken by the melodic call of the birds flitting through the trees.

When Laurie had gone up to her room after leaving Rian, she'd thought she would lie awake, mulling over the complications falling in love with Rian would bring into her life, but she'd fallen asleep almost the instant her head touched the pillow.

Deciding whether she wanted to take a chance on a loveless marriage in the hope that someday Rian would grow to care for her wasn't easy. He'd made it plain several times that he wanted a wife, implying that he would compel her to marry him. And more than anything else, Laurie wanted to become his wife, in the true sense of the word. But she couldn't ignore the bitter, sinking feeling that she would become one of his possessions if she married him, something he remembered when it suited him.

Yet he wasn't completely without heart, she knew.

He had helped the Trevors family, though logic could reason that away.

Mr. Trevors was an integral part of his company, and Rian could afford to do double work and pay the additional costs as long as he was sure that Arnold Trevors would recover and be back on the job in a matter of months. Gratitude made Mrs. Trevors sing Rian's praises the way she had, and Laurie well understood how effective Rian's charm could be.

No, her feelings for him would probably only amuse him or arouse his contempt for her weakness. Any declaration of how much she cared for him would be a mistake. Rian couldn't find out that she was as attracted to him as he said he was to her.

But if—and that was a big if—they were married, would she be able to keep her love a secret? Somehow Laurie doubted it. She was never one to hide her feelings, especially something as deep and emotionally profound as love.

The sound of a diver slicing into the water of the pool drew her sharply out of her reverie. Her heart skipped a beat as Laurie recognized the black-haired swimmer surfacing in the middle of the pool. She watched the sinewy muscles of his darkly tanned arms cleaving the water with the expertise of an accomplished swimmer. After completing several laps, Rian halted at the side nearest Laurie, his teeth flashing in a wide, mocking smile as he hauled himself up on the natural stone edge.

The sun glinted off his wet skin, making him look like a polished bronze statue. "Aha. Lorelei sits on the rock, luring men to their destruction," he intoned as he reached for the large towel on the table to wipe himself dry. "Is that what you are, Laurie? One of the sirens?"

"That description fits LaRaine, not me," Laurie replied calmly despite her nervousness.

"You underestimate your power to attract," Rian remarked, walking over to tower above her. The sight of his mostly bare body, clad only in swimming trunks, disturbed her more than she cared to admit. She certainly didn't underestimate his power, fighting the overwhelming desire to run her fingers through the black hair on his chest.

"Perhaps," Laurie shrugged, closing her eyes to shut out the intoxicating sight of Rian.

Before she realized what was happening, Rian reached down and removed her smoke-colored sunglasses. "I don't like looking at my own reflection when I'm talking to someone," he declared with infuriating complacency.

The sun's glare momentarily blinded her as she attempted to block its rays with her hand. "The sun's in my eyes," Laurie protested.

He placed her glasses out of reach on the chair that held his towel. Then Rian sat down on the edge of Laurie's lounge chair, a hand on each side of the back where her head rested, his lean body effectively blocking out the glare of the sun after he had sent her hat sailing across the sun deck.

"Is that better?" he taunted.

"Give me back my glasses," Laurie gulped as Rian came dangerously close. An unwelcome yearning for his touch throbbed through her body.

"No. Your eyes are too beautiful. Sometimes I feel like I could drown in them," Rian murmured, ignoring her request.

"S-stop teasing me," she stammered breathlessly.

"I didn't realize that was what I was doing," he chuckled.

"You're just saying those things to get a rise out of me," Laurie declared hotly.

"Why? I've told you before that I thought you were beautiful." His eyes moved slowly over her bare skin, sending flaming color to her cheeks. "Sexy bikini. I like it. A lot."

The conversation unnerved Laurie completely. "I think I'll take a dip before it gets too cool."

She started to lean forward, expecting Rian to move back and allow her to get to her feet, but he stayed put. She succeeded only in getting much too close to him, finding the sensual curve of his mouth had a hypnotic effect.

"Please let me up, Rian." The trembling in her voice betrayed her inner turmoil.

"Every time I get close to you, you run away. Why is that?" His voice was a caressing whisper. "Are you afraid you might like it?"

As Rian moved closer, Laurie sank farther back against the cushions. Her breathing tightened as the outcome of their encounter began to seem inevitable.

"Why are you doing this?" she murmured, the agony of wanting him almost more than she could bear. "I mean nothing to you."

"On the contrary, you're my fiancée." His tone was teasing, and it bothered her.

"Do you have to keep bringing that up?" Laurie protested weakly, her shimmering blue eyes taking in his rugged features. "Our engagement is a farce."

"Hey, the ring on your finger didn't come from Woolworth's, and you put it there yourself." A wicked gleam lit his dark eyes.

"What's your point? I did that for only one reason—your aunt, Vera Manning. It doesn't mean you own me," Laurie declared, firmly controlling her yearning for his touch.

"Maybe not, Laurie," Rian said quietly, "but I do want you. I'm completely serious."

"You're twisting what I say for your own purposes!" Despair rang in her voice as she tore her gaze away from his face.

"You act as though I have sinister designs on your virtue." Impatience lent a knife-sharp edge to his words. "I've offered to marry you."

"Oh, yes. A marriage without love," Laurie reminded him bitterly.

"Is that so bad? Arranged marriages work as well as the other kind. Is love really necessary?" The last came out as a sneer.

"It is to me!" Her gaze unwillingly returned to his face.

"Why? I somehow don't think you'd really object to my caress." The look in his eyes, the burning fire in their blackness, made her heart hammer.

"I don't want you to make love to me, Rian." That at least was true. She was too afraid she might reveal how much she cared for him.

"That's what you keep saying, but your eyes tell me something different."

"Oh?" Laurie bluffed bravely. "Well, listen up. I think you're unbelievably arrogant. You just don't care about other people's emotions, do you? You chased LaRaine, gave her expensive presents, asked her to be your wife, then cold-bloodedly replaced her with me. I pity any woman foolish enough to fall in love with you. You have no compassion.''

Rian laughed softly. "Is that what you're afraid of? Falling in love with me?"

Laurie shook her head. No way would she admit that. "But you've already told me that I'm not what you're looking for in a husband. I know you want me to be warm and tender and kind, but that's a young girl's dream. You're a woman. Would you really be happy with a man who couldn't stand up to you? I don't think so."

Laurie didn't reply right away. Yes, she was in love with him. Yes, that was why she resisted him. No, she didn't want Rian to be gentle and kind, because she wanted him the way he was. She didn't want to be treated like a fragile china doll. She wanted his passion, his touch, his sensual kisses. But she couldn't say that.

"Please—" A broken sob rose in her throat.

"It's time you made up your mind, Laurie." Rian's head moved closer to hers, his mouth stopping a fraction of an inch away from her own. "Tell me you don't want to feel my lips against yours, and don't want me to whisper what I want to do to you into your ear. Slap my hand when I stroke your shoulders or caress your perfect breasts. Tell me again you don't want me to do any of those things," he demanded in a low, husky voice raw with desire.

With a little cry, Laurie surrendered, bringing his mouth to hers as she reveled in the searing fire of his embrace. She was his at last, her lips parting eagerly for his kiss. His lean, muscular body moved over her, but she could only glory in the nakedness of their touching skin.

Exploding shivers of ecstasy made her tremble until she lost all awareness of anything except Rian. The rough caress of his expert hands didn't stop— seeking, arousing, molding her soft body to the hard contours of his.

His mouth explored her neck, first nuzzling, then nibbling at the sensitive areas until Laurie moaned, tossing her head back to let him have his way with her. The shoulder strap of her bikini was quickly pushed aside as he caressed her shoulders, then moved to the swelling curves of her breasts, making her arch and writhe.

Rian's breathing was as ragged as hers when he returned to devour her mouth, her fingers raking the black thickness of his hair. His rising desire to possess her was becoming increasingly apparent and Laurie had lost the power to resist.

"Rian!" E. J. Denton's voice was a blast of cold air in the blistering heat of their desire.

Rian cursed underneath his breath as he straightened, silently thrilling Laurie, overjoyed that she was able to arouse Rian as much as he aroused her.

"What is it?" he snapped.

E. J. stood hesitantly on the opposite side of the pool. "There's a telephone call for a Ms. *LaRaine* Evans."

Irritation at the interruption was replaced by aloofness as Rian turned his piercing gaze to Laurie. She hadn't missed the emphasis on her cousin's name, but she couldn't imagine who would be calling LaRaine. She moved her head in a negative response, apprehensive. Had someone else found out about her masquerade? Rian rose abruptly from the chaise, gathering up his robe with a quick sweep of his hand.

"I'll handle this," he told Laurie. "You wait here."

Fifteen minutes later, Rian returned, dressed in jeans and an unbuttoned, pale silk shirt that intensified the blackness of his hair and the darkness of his tan. Laurie leaned anxiously forward in her lounge chair as he walked around the pool to her side, longing to be in his arms again.

"Who was it?" she asked, striving for calm.

"False alarm," Rian answered indifferently, picking up the sarong that matched Laurie's bikini and tossing it to her. "It was Colin calling about the Mardi Gras ball tonight."

"Oh. It completely slipped my mind," Laurie murmured, noticing Rian's reserve. "I was supposed to ask you—"

"If I was attending," he finished for her, a cynical curl to his mouth.

"I'm sorry," she said hesitantly.

"Don't apologize. Colin explained that the arrangements were made before I arrived in Mobile, then adjusted to include me. Thoughtful guy."

Laurie flinched at the sarcasm in his tone. "Colin's been great. He escorted me to the Mardi Gras festivities and invited both of us to the final ball." Her awkward defense seem to amuse Rian. "He's only being kind."

"And warm and tender," he jeered.

"Will you stop bringing that up!" she snapped angrily, wrapping the sarong around her waist and knotting it. If only she knew what had brought about the change in Rian from ardent lover to taunting stranger! "I hope you said no politely."

"Did I say no?" An eyebrow arched contemptuously.

"Are you going?" A quick frown knitted her forehead, as she stared up at him in bewilderment.

"Uh, no. I told Colin I had business to attend to."

"I don't understand." Her voice faltered.

"You and Colin can go alone. You can't miss the social event of the year," he said scornfully. "I know you'll be the belle of the ball."

"You're allowing me to go with Colin?" Her eyes rounded in disbelief.

"Isn't that what I just said?"

"Yes, but—" Laurie stopped in hopeless confusion. "But you've repeatedly warned me to stay away from Colin." She wanted to say that she didn't want to go without Rian, but his coolness made that impossible.

"Have I?" he asked indifferently.

"You know you have," she retorted.

"If you don't want to go, Laurie, simply call the man back and tell him," Rian said coldly, frowning. "It doesn't matter to me one way or the other. Go or stay—it's up to you."

So his attraction to her was nothing but physical. His freezing tone made that clear. "I'm going to the ball with Colin," she said quietly, salvaging some of her pride and independence.

"He'll pick you up at nine-thirty this evening." There was a patronizing nod of his head. "I have some calls to make." And he pivoted on his heel and was gone.

Utter torment at his sudden rejection rocked her, body and soul. He'd learned she was his any time he wanted her by now. She'd been betrayed by her aching need for his possession, though she knew only too well that Rian was ruthless, autocratic, completely lacking in human compassion.

With a broken sob, Laurie realized that she still loved him—and that it would only bring her heartbreak and misery. But it was too late. If Rian was only capable of giving one-tenth of the love she felt for him, she would marry him. Half an hour ago, in his arms, she would have agreed without hesitation.

Now she would have to choose between an empty marriage to Rian or the misery and loneliness of a life without him. In her agony of loving him, Laurie couldn't decide.

Her ingrained pride and self-respect prevented her from collapsing under the weight of her emotions. With dogged determination, she resolved to look her best tonight so that Rian would never guess how much he had hurt her by palming her off on Colin for the evening.

Laurie spent an hour in a bubble bath to relax her jangled nerves, then another hour in front of the mirror painstakingly applying her makeup. She arranged her hair in several different ways before choosing a Grecian style with trailing white ribbons for an utterly feminine look.

She stepped into her evening gown, pleased to see that it fit her perfectly. The sleeveless dress was a column of gleaming white satin, ankle length, with a mock train. The neckline dipped demurely in the front and plunged in back, revealing her golden tan. The classically simple lines of the gown were enhanced by seed pearls artfully scrolled under the bodice to her slim waist. The final touch:

elegant, long white gloves that extended beyond her elbows.

There was a satisfied sparkle in her sapphire eyes as she studied her reflection in the mirror. No jewelry—the gown was perfect just as it was. Without vanity, Laurie acknowledged the beauty she saw, finding self-assurance that would be effective armor.

There was a light rap on the door. "Colin's here, Laurie," Vera told her after Laurie told her to come in. "Honey, you look lovely! You'll be the envy of every woman there. It's a pity Rian isn't free tonight. I know he would be proud to show you off. Still, it was considerate of him to allow you to go with Colin so you wouldn't miss the festivities."

Once again, she felt a pang knowing that Rian couldn't care less whether she took part in the Mardi Gras celebration. For a moment, it was impossible for Laurie to speak. She smiled politely at his aunt's words and reached for her beaded evening bag. She turned for one last look in the mirror.

"I'll tell Colin you'll be right down," Vera smiled.

Laurie waited a few minutes, wanting for the first time to make an entrance. She'd seen LaRaine do it so often that her actions were almost instinctive as she walked quietly in the carpeted hall, gliding silently down the stairs to the landing. There she stopped, spying Colin at the base of the stairs looking extraordinarily handsome in his evening suit while he exchanged a few words with Vera.

Rian was deep in discussion with E. J. Denton several feet away near the front door. One gloved hand rested lightly on the newel post as she silently

willed Rian to look at her. But it was Colin who
noticed her first, the shimmering white of her gown
catching his eyes against the background of gold
flocked paper.

"My God!" Colin breathed, drinking in her
beauty.

"Am I very late?" Laurie smiled, noticing the
way Rian's head jerked up at the sound of her
voice, feeling his intense gaze on her as she glided
down the steps to Colin.

"You look ravishing!" Colin exclaimed. "Exactly
like a Greek goddess."

He captured a gloved hand and held it gently
with both of his while Laurie basked in the glow
of his admiration. It was the boost her ego needed.
She allowed her hand to linger a bit longer than was
necessary before she gently withdrew it, sending a
sidelong glance at Rian from beneath her lashes.
His expression was aloof, as if he didn't care about
the attention Colin was paying to his fiancée.

"Vera said this was a formal affair," she said to
Colin. "I hope the gown isn't too much." She was
deliberately hinting that she could be overdressed,
the way she'd heard her cousin do many times
before.

"Too much!" Colin laughed, unable to take his
eyes off of her. "I'd consider myself a lucky man
to have one dance with you."

"What do you think, Rian?" Laurie purred, turning to face him, then floating gracefully to his side.
Her bright eyes sparkled up at his expressionless
face. "Do I look all right?"

"Nice gown," he commented blandly, dismissing
E. J. with a nod of his head.

"Is that all?" Laurie tilted her head back in a

coquettish challenge, hoping that he might even refuse to allow her to go to the ball without him.

"What do you want me to do?" His sneering voice was lowered so only she could hear his words. "Hold your hand like Hartford did?"

Hurt anger flared immediately in her eyes. "Yes!" she challenged him.

As her arm began to raise, Rian caught her wrist. The pressure of his grip turned her towards Colin.

"Enjoy yourselves," Rian drawled, his mocking smile resting momentarily on Laurie's face.

"I'm sure we will," Colin nodded, quickly turning his admiring gaze to Laurie.

"Here, honey." Vera handed her the matching satin stole Laurie had left in her room. "It might get a little cool later on. Have a nice time."

"Yes, thank you," Laurie murmured, letting Colin drape it over her bare shoulders before he led her towards the door.

Hot, bitter tears burned the back of her eyes. Once Rian had said she belonged to him, but right now she had the impression that he'd happily given her to Colin.

The sound of laughter, clinking iced drinks, and the music of a dance band reigned supreme at the Mardi Gras ball, one of several held that night. A constant stream of strangers paused to chat with Colin, and Laurie never lacked a dance partner, politely refusing as many offers as she accepted. Still she found no enjoyment in the evening. The men, made bold by too much alcohol, paid her fulsome compliments that meant nothing to her since they didn't come from Rian. When Colin suggested they leave several hours later, Laurie nearly sighed with gratitude.

Colin didn't question her silence during the drive home, no doubt chalking it up to the excitement of the evening. Laurie thanked him with as much warmth as she could for escorting her when he stopped the car in front of Vera's house.

"My pleasure," he assured her.

As he helped her out of the car, the chill of the night air swept away some of Laurie's numbness and brought her senses to life. Colin took her hand at the door, gallantly raising it to his lips.

"Have a nice night, Laurie," he murmured, hesitating as if he wanted to say more before releasing her hand and stepping back.

"Good night, Colin," she answered softly, opening the front door. As she walked into the hallway, she heard the sound of his car engine revving to life. Laurie slid the bolt on the door quietly into place and turned to tiptoe to the stairs. The silence of the house was soothing after the din of the ball and she paused to let its peace flow over her, a weary sigh breaking from her lips.

"Reflecting on all your triumphs?" Rian's voice came from the darkness near the stairs.

Her muscles constricted as Laurie stood still in rigid surprise. The last thing she had expected was for Rian to stay up until she returned. The thought angered her after the way he'd handed her off to Colin.

"Don't tell me you waited up for me," she said sarcastically when Rian stepped out of the darkness into the dim light of the hall. "How touching."

"No, I didn't wait up." His eyes flashed with anger. "I've been working. You could have been home hours ago for all I noticed."

His words stabbed at her heart. "I'd forgotten

you existed, too,'' Laurie answered sharply, the lie restoring some of her pride.

"I'm sure you tried to," Rian jeered.

"It wasn't too difficult," Laurie declared airily, looking away so he couldn't see the pain in her eyes as she swept off the satin stole. "Colin was a *very* attentive escort."

"I don't doubt it—with the goddess Aphrodite on his arm," he murmured complacently behind her. "Wasn't she married to the god of fire?"

Laurie froze for a split second before turning towards Rian with an arch smile demurely dimpling her cheeks. "Was that before or after her affair with the god of war?"

"She got around," Rian said cynically. "So am I supposed to believe that you and Colin are fooling around behind my back?"

"Hardly behind your back. You encouraged him," she corrected.

"I find it hard to believe." A derisive chuckle emphasized his disbelief. "Colin's sense of honor wouldn't allow him to take advantage of a friend. The old Southern code of chivalry still applies. The Judge wouldn't have dreamed of touching Vera once she was married, even if she'd led him on. Like father, like son."

"I'm afraid you don't know Colin very well," she lied. "We didn't come straight home."

The corners of his mouth curled into a mocking smile. "Liar," Rian said smoothly. "You don't have the look of a woman who's been made love to—I should know."

A crimson color filled her cheeks, then faded to pink. "Really?" she mocked. "How?"

She failed to get a rise out of Rian. The arrogant look in his eyes didn't change.

"Pity you're engaged to me, not Colin."

"I couldn't agree more," she said bitterly. "If I never saw you again, I'd—"

"You can't avoid it. Remember our engagement party is this Saturday night."

Laurie's dark head raised with a jerk. "You aren't serious!" she gasped. "You can't go through with this farce!"

"I am serious, and it's no farce," Rian declared. "I told Vera to go ahead and make the necessary arrangements. We'll make a public announcement that evening to the press."

"No!" Her denial was intensified by the horrified expression in her eyes. "This fake engagement has gone too far already. It has to end."

"Our engagement ceased to be fake the day I arrived here and discovered your impersonation," he ground out savagely. "That same evening you agreed to wear my ring. You're my fiancée, Laurie!"

"No!" Her protest was weak.

"And you're about to become my wife."

"But there's no love between us, Rian," she pleaded.

There was a black fury, tightly controlled, in his eyes. "My work takes up a lot of my time. We won't have to suffer through too many hours of each other's company."

"What if I refuse to marry you?"

"You won't. You've deluded everyone into believing you're madly in love with me. I'm holding you to the promises you made."

Her temples throbbed with pain as Laurie realized that the combination of Rian's domination and her love for him had overwhelmed her. That thought led her to the answer to the question she had been puzzling over.

As long as Rian didn't care for her, she could never marry him, no matter how much she loved him. Even the thought of bearing his child someday would never make up for loveless hours in his arms. If her feelings for him were going to destroy her, then she didn't want Rian around to see.

"I hate you, Rian Montgomery!" Laurie declared, brushing past him to the stairs, wishing all the while that she did.

CHAPTER TEN

Her sleep was leaden and Laurie awoke with her nerves as raw and taut as the night before. The decision had been made. At the earliest opportunity, she would leave. Rian had never asked for her return airline ticket, which was tucked away in the bottom of her purse. It would get her back to Los Angeles, and that was as far ahead as Laurie could think at the moment. She didn't doubt Rian would stop her if he learned of her plans. The toughest part would be to convince him that she intended to carry on the pretense of being engaged as he had ordered.

One look at her reflection and the stark apprehension mirrored in her eyes told Laurie it was going to be a difficult task. The strain of her decision was visible in the harsh lines of her face. She shuddered at the consequences if Rian figured out the reason for her haunted look, although it might not occur to him that she would attempt to thwart his plans. She had given in so easily before, agreeing to his commands with only token protests. She'd given him no cause to believe that it would be any different this time, and that was on her side.

Encouraged, Laurie made her way down the stairs to the breakfast area, wearing a coral top that gave color to her face. Her hair was down, loose and waving to soften the harsh lines of strain, but she was too tense to have anything more than toast and coffee. Luckily Vera wasn't there to prompt her to eat more. The cook told Laurie that she had already gone riding, and repeated Vera's instructions that Laurie was to sleep as long as she wanted.

The front door opened and closed and Laurie braced herself as footsteps sounded in the hall. Reluctantly, she glanced towards the open door leading from the hall to the peacock blue and gold dining room where she sat sipping the last of her coffee. The muscles of her stomach constricted tightly as she prepared herself to see Rian. But it was E. J. Denton who started to breeze past, then caught sight of Laurie and paused in the doorway.

"Good morning," he said cheerfully. "You look pretty good for someone who stayed up late. Did you enjoy the ball last night?"

"I had a great time," Laurie nodded.

"Is there more coffee in the pot?"

"Nearly half full. Would you like some?"

"I certainly would," E. J. sighed wearily. He took a clean cup from the sideboard and poured it full of black coffee. "I need a stimulant and as they say, while the cat is away, the mouse can put his feet up."

"Is Rian gone?" Laurie held her breath, not believing that she could have that kind of luck.

"Yes. I just came back from taking him to the airport," he nodded, removing his dark-rimmed glasses to rub his eyes. "I'll be glad when Trevors is back to handle these minor crises."

"When will Rian be back?" She kept her tone deliberately neutral.

"He's booked on a return flight from Miami this evening." E. J. drained his cup and refilled it. "I'll take this with me. The correspondence and paperwork in that study must be ten feet high."

The instant she heard the study door close, Laurie hurried upstairs to her room and rummaged through her purse for the airline ticket. With the precious paper in her hand, she called the reservation office from the phone on her night stand. When she hung up, her seat on the flight leaving that afternoon had been verified. There was plenty of time left to pack, write Rian a note, and catch a cab to the airport. By the time Rian returned, she would be safely in Los Angeles.

The suitcases lay open on the bed while Laurie rushed to fill them, not in the least concerned with how neatly her clothes were folded. Over an hour later, she made a last-minute search of the dresser drawers and cupboards for anything she might have overlooked before closing the lid of the first suitcase and locking it.

"There you are, Laurie. I was look . . ." Vera Manning's voice trailed off as she saw the suitcases on the bed, her startled gaze rushing to Laurie's suddenly stricken expression. "You aren't leaving?"

"Yes," she whispered. Her well-thought-out

explanation deserted her in the face of Vera's hurt and bewildered look.

"Why?" the older woman asked. "You look as pale as a ghost, honey. Is something wrong? Has something happened?"

Laurie gestured helplessly at the telephone, forcing the words through the constriction in her throat, "I ... I received a phone call earlier. There's been an accident. My ... mother's in the hospital. I have to fly home right away."

"Oh, Laurie, no wonder you look so upset!" Vera moved quickly to her side, taking the younger woman's trembling hand between her own. "Is there anything I can do?"

"I've already made flight reservations and finished packing. I don't believe I've forgotten anything," Laurie shrugged. Her genuine agitation only made her white lies more convincing.

"What a time for Rian to be gone!" Vera shook her head sadly. "Do you want me to contact him? I know he'll rush right back."

"No, no, don't do that," Laurie said quickly. "I've probably made it sound more serious than it is," she continued more calmly. "You know, the shock and all of the phone call. Mother broke a leg and suffered a mild concussion, but they assured me she wasn't in any kind of danger."

"Well, that's a relief," Vera smiled consolingly. "But you want to be with her anyway and I can understand how you feel."

"I was going to write Rian a note explaining everything as soon as I'd finished packing." Laurie took a deep breath. "I probably won't be able to make it back for the engagement party you'd planned for this weekend."

"Don't give it another thought," Vera ordered. "It was a spur-of-the-moment idea anyway. Our friends will understand why it has to be canceled. It's nearly lunch time. Would you like some soup or a sandwich to settle your stomach? Carla said you only had toast for breakfast."

"Vera, I really couldn't eat a thing. I'm sure they'll serve a snack or a meal on the plane. It's a cross-country flight."

"I'll send Sam up for your bags. He'll drive you to the airport whenever you want to leave. Everything will turn out just fine, Laurie."

"Oh, Vera . . ." Her chin trembled traitorously. "You've been so good to me. I hate to leave like this." The warm-hearted woman made Laurie wish she had stolen out in the middle of the night rather than deceive Vera again with more lies.

"So do I," Vera nodded, tears shimmering in her own blue eyes. "But neither one of us had any control over it, did we?"

After Vera had left, Laurie sat down and composed the note to Rian. She kept it terse, not allowing her heartache at leaving him to be revealed. She told him that she was leaving and in no circumstances would she ever consent to marrying him, that he might as well take her decision as final and not attempt to follow her. She placed the note, the sapphire engagement ring, and the bracelet in Rian's bedroom, telling Vera that she had left his note there.

Two hours later Laurie was on board the plane streaking across the sky towards Los Angeles. But she didn't draw a secure breath until her luggage was safely in the trunk of a taxi cab at the airport and she'd climbed in the rear seat, giving the address of the apartment she shared with LaRaine to the cab driver. She had forgotten how little money she had with her until they reached her destination and she spent nearly all of it on the fare.

Asking the driver to carry the bags inside the lobby of the building, Laurie walked on through the glass doors. Her expression curved into a weary but happy smile as she saw that her favorite security guard, Tom Farber, was on duty.

"How are you today, Mr. Farber?" she greeted him.

"Well, you sure are a sight for sore eyes. What are you doing back here?" he grinned. "Not that I'm not glad to see you, because I am."

"Why shouldn't I be back?" Laurie asked, a puzzled frown on her forehead. "I live here."

A look of apprehension stole over his face. "I thought something was wrong," he said hesitantly. "I'm sorry, Ms. Evans, but your cousin canceled her lease on the apartment and moved out a week ago."

"That can't be!" she gasped.

"She left her parents' address and said to forward her mail. And she said you wouldn't be back," Tom Farber nodded grimly. "Perhaps you should call your aunt."

"Yes, I guess I'd better," Laurie agreed absently, taken aback by the discovery that she had no place to stay.

"You're welcome to use the phone here," he offered, motioning to the phone on the counter.

With a dreadful feeling of unease, Laurie dialed her aunt's number. The phone was answered on the second ring.

"Aunt Carrie, this is Laurie," but she got no further than that.

"I didn't think you'd have the nerve to call here," her aunt's shrill voice declared. "After what you did to LaRaine, I'm surprised you'd even dare to show your face!"

"After what I did to LaRaine?" Laurie echoed.

"Yes! My poor baby was just torn apart when she discovered you'd stolen her fiancé right from under her nose. Do you even care how badly her heart was broken? Your uncle and I sacrificed to raise you as our own and now you pay us back like this! It's horrible!"

"You didn't have to sacrifice," Laurie was close to tears. "My father left enough money to take care of me."

"And you squandered that, too!" Carrie Evans cried. "Well, don't think we're going to support you anymore! Get your wealthy fiancé to take care of you, and stay out of our lives! You've done enough damage already!"

The line went dead. Her aunt had hung up on her. It was obvious that LaRaine hadn't told her parents the truth about how Laurie had happened to be in Mobile instead of her. Heaven only knew what spiteful lies her cousin had told after Rian had ended *their* engagement. But the end result was that her aunt and uncle wanted nothing more to do with her.

The full weight of her predicament made her heart sink. She turned a lost look to the kind face of the uniformed guard.

"They tossed you out on your ear, did they?" he said gruffly, feeling nothing but sympathy for the young woman with nowhere to go.

"What am I going to do?" Laurie sighed, then gave a bitter laugh. "I don't even have enough money for a place to stay tonight."

"I could lend you some," he offered gently.

"No, no, I couldn't let you do that," she protested sadly with a firm shake of her head. "I'll get by."

"Would you consider the offer of a place to sleep tonight?" he asked, hurrying on before Laurie had a chance to interrupt. "My wife and I have a real nice guest bedroom in our home. It wouldn't be any trouble at all and you could stay until you decide what you're going to do."

"I know what I'm going to do. I'm going to get a job," Laurie smiled weakly. "But I really wouldn't feel right about taking any more charity." Her aunt's harsh words still rang in her mind.

"It wouldn't be charity," Tom Farber insisted with a perceptive understanding of the reason behind her refusal. "As soon as you find yourself a job, you could pay us whatever you felt was fair for your room and board."

It was a very tempting offer, but Laurie hesitated.

"Tell you what, you think it over," he smiled. "Sit down here on the couch, have a cup of coffee, and relax. Ed Jenkins will be here in about fifteen minutes to relieve me so I can go home. If you decide you want to leave, I'll give you a lift wherever you want. If you want to come home with me, then that would be just great. How about it?"

"Sounds good to me, Mr. Farber." His cajoling expression coaxed a genuine smile from her.

"I'm Tom to my friends."

"And Laurie to mine," she smiled, taking the hand he held out to her.

A quarter of an hour later, Tom Farber was loading her red luggage in the trunk of his car. Of the two alternatives he had offered her, only one seemed sensible—to stay with Tom and his wife. Laurie refused to even consider contacting Rian. As much as she loved him, she would rather starve than marry a man who didn't love her.

When Tom crawled behind the wheel of the car, Laurie glanced hesitantly at his cheerful face. "Tom," she began, then paused to phrase her words, "if someone comes looking for me at the apartment, could you . . . would you tell them you don't know where I am?" If Rian did come after her, Laurie wanted to be sure he couldn't find her and manage to charm her into marriage.

"Are you in some kind of trouble?" he asked gently.

"No, not really. There's a man who might want to speak to me, but I don't want to see him," Laurie replied in a tight voice.

"Then he'll never find out where you are from me," Tom declared with a wink.

Betty Farber, Tom's wife, turned out to be as warm and friendly as her husband, waving away Laurie's apologies for disrupting their household and declaring she would be glad to have a woman around the house to gossip with. Exhausted by her hurried flight from Mobile, hurt by her aunt and uncle's rejection, Laurie had trouble sleeping that night. Her mind insisted on reliving each memory of the moments spent with Rian. The knowledge that she must never see him again only intensified the pain. Her pillow was damp when she finally fell asleep.

The next day Betty insisted that Laurie rest up

from her trip, allowing her to do no more than circle help-wanted ads. Despite the woman's perpetual chatter, Laurie felt the hours dragging by and wondered how she would ever get through a lifetime without Rian.

At the supper table that evening, Tom Farber eyed her curiously, taking in the slightly puffy eyelids, the sadness in her expression, and the absence of her usually ready smile. When the dessert had been eaten and the coffee poured, he cleared his throat. Blank blue eyes glanced up at him reflexively.

"Were you referring to that Montgomery man yesterday?" he asked, masking his interest by staring into his cup.

"Was he at the apartment?" A piercing sadness mixed with the apprehension in her expression as Laurie avoided a direct answer.

Tom nodded, "Yes, he was. At first I thought he was looking for LaRaine and I told him she'd moved back with her parents. But he told me in no uncertain terms that he was looking for you."

"What did you tell him?" she whispered, imagining the thwarted anger that must have compelled Rian to fly all the way to Los Angeles to find her.

"The truth, but not the whole truth. I said you arrived at the apartment yesterday afternoon, found out your cousin had broken the lease, made a phone call, and left."

"Did he believe you?"

"I think so," the man nodded. "He said you were his fiancée."

Laurie blanched, touching the faintly white circle where the sapphire ring had adorned her finger. "I was, but it's all over."

A silent message was exchanged between husband and wife that Laurie missed, and the subject was deftly changed to some inconsequential happening that didn't require her attention. A few minutes later she mumbled a request to be excused and walked swiftly to her room, where not even the tears could assuage the twisting pain in her heart.

After only a few days of job hunting, Laurie was hired as a legal secretary trainee by a large law firm. Concentrating on the unfamiliar legal jargon kept her attention centered on her work, and forced the haunting thoughts of Rian to the recesses of her mind.

The daylight hours passed swiftly during the week, but not the miserable nights and the empty loneliness of the weekends. The heartache remained, striking with piercing swiftness as an odd word would bring back some memory with vivid clarity.

Never once in three months did Tom or Betty Farber bring up the subject of her broken engagement, and Laurie couldn't talk about it either. The first month after she found work, she made a half-hearted attempt to find an apartment. Few were in the price range that her meager salary would cover. The prospect of sharing an apartment didn't appeal to her either. And Betty and Tom were so set against her going out on her own that Laurie finally gave in and agreed to stay on with them.

One Monday evening after the supper dishes were done, Laurie sat at the oval dining room table, leafing through the newspaper. One look at the top of the page froze her into immobility as she stared at the virile, dark-haired man in the center of the picture.

The blurry newspaper photograph didn't hide the arrogant tilt of Rian Montgomery's head as he gazed down at the girl at his side. Unwillingly Laurie shifted her attention to the dark-haired girl looking up at him provocatively. It was LaRaine, her one and only cousin.

Swallowing back the sob in her throat, Laurie read the caption beneath the picture. "Hotel owner and entrepreneur Rian Montgomery was seen escorting the rising young star LaRaine Evans at a recent Hollywood party. Rumor has it there's a dark-haired fiancée in Rian's life. Could this be the one?"

Laurie tried to be glad that Rian and LaRaine were back together. She tried, but she kept remembering the way his dark eyes looked at her, searching her face, sparking that flame of desire that heated up every moment they spent together.

All the memories that she had fought so hard to push to the back of her mind came racing back. It might as well have been yesterday that she'd left him, so sharp and fresh was the pain of her love. Laurie didn't even realize she was crying until she saw the wet drops smearing the newsprint. Quickly she scrubbed the tears away, closed the paper, and walked to her room, not noticing the questioning gaze from the kind old man in the easy chair.

Laurie's powers of concentration had deserted her. Liberal use of concealer hid her undereye circles, evidence of too many sleepless nights. Tired eyes skimmed the page Laurie had just printed out, almost crying as she realized she had typed Rian's name in place of the client's name that belonged in the legal document. The glaring error would have to be corrected and the printer was jamming. Laurie wanted to weep with frustration as she removed the shredded paper from the machine's innards, bit by bit.

Footsteps sounded beside her desk and Laurie cringed in anticipation of Mr. Jennings's wrath when he discovered the document wasn't ready. A quick apology formed on her lips.

"I'm sorry, I haven't finished it yet. I only have one page left—" The apologetic words died in her throat as Laurie glanced up. Her mind was playing tricks on her, making her see Rian's face when he wasn't even there. She blinked once, then again, but he didn't go away.

"Hello, Laurie," Rian said grimly, his obsidian-dark eyes staring at her with unrelenting harshness.

"What are you doing here?" she whispered. She glanced around anxiously, seeing the interested looks on the faces of the other women in the room.

"That's obvious, isn't it?" was his only reply.

Laurie wasn't able to meet his mockingly severe look and turned to stare at her computer screen. "Go away, Rian." It was more than she could bear to have him so close to her and not be in his arms.

"Tired of playing hide-and-seek yet?" he asked harshly.

"Please, leave me alone," she begged in a whispering voice that threatened to break.

"Ms. Evans, do you have that agreement printed out yet?" A harried man with disheveled hair bustled over to her desk, his preoccupied air preventing him from noticing the tall, imposing man already standing there.

"Not yet, Mr. Jennings," Laurie answered tightly. "I need it immediately."

"Would you mind," Rian interrupted with the autocratic tone of someone accustomed to making others wait, "I'm talking to Ms. Evans."

"See here—" her employer began indignantly, turning an outraged face towards Rian. But his outrage slowly receded as he met the full force of the other man's gaze. "Aren't you—" Mr. Jennings began.

"Montgomery, Rian Montgomery," he supplied, offering no apology for keeping Laurie from her work.

"Of course, I thought I recognized you," Mr. Jennings smiled, his pale eyes lighting up at the name. "What can we do for you, Mr. Montgomery?"

"I'd like to talk to Ms. Evans alone. Somewhere private." Rian ignored her gasp of dismay.

"Ms. Evans?" the man repeated blankly, gazing down at her as though he had forgotten she was there. "Yes, of course. There's an office right over there you can use."

Rian's dark gaze rested on Laurie again, challenging her to refuse to see him alone. That was exactly what she wanted to do. The shock of seeing him again after so many months had shattered her defenses. He read the hesitation in her eyes, the half-formed decision to protest.

"Would you prefer to have our discussion here?" Rian asked, a derisive glance taking in the roomful of women. "In front of an audience?"

Reluctantly Laurie rose from her chair, surprised

to find her legs were capable of supporting her, and followed Mr. Jennings to the office two doors down the hall. Rian followed her, anticipating her desire to bolt and successfully shutting off her escape.

Inside the office with the door closed behind them, Laurie glanced anxiously towards Rian, whose long strides had carried him to the window. The sunlight streaming in gave the room a cheerfulness he didn't seem to feel.

"Did you think I couldn't find you, Laurie?" he asked at last.

"I didn't think you would try." Laurie edged the softness of her voice.

"Then why were you so careful about covering your tracks?" Rian demanded.

"I didn't . . . or at least, not deliberately," she amended lamely. "I went back to the apartment, then discovered that LaRaine had moved out. I didn't have any money, so when Tom—Mr. Farber—offered to rent me a room in his house, I accepted."

"Then you made sure he told no one where you were. Too bad the second guard, Jenkins, wasn't so closemouthed. Your aunt and uncle were half out of their minds with worry about you."

"That's a lie! Aunt Carrie told me not to set foot—" Her angry words died at the sudden glint that appeared in Rian's dark eyes. "It doesn't matter." She shrugged, then hugged her arms about her to calm her nerves. "Why did you come looking for me? Why can't you just leave me alone?"

"You're my fiancée." There was an uncompromising hardness in his expression and tone.

"Not anymore," Laurie said fervently, lifting her

hand, bare without the sapphire. "I'm not wearing your ring. I put it on and I took it off. There isn't any more engagement."

"Really? You left my aunt with the impression that you were nursing your sick mother. You didn't mention any broken engagement," he pointed out.

"How could I?" Laurie asked. "What was I to do? Tell her that I hated her nephew?"

"So you left it to me. I know you don't want to hear this, but Vera still believes we're engaged." His mouth curved into a sarcastic smile.

"Is that why you had to find me? So you can make me remember what a fool I was? You have no idea how much I regret the day I arrived in Mobile!" Her statement ended in a choked sob.

"Guess you're not looking forward to your return trip."

"I'm not going back," Laurie retorted.

"Oh, yes, you are," Rian said. "Vera wants you at her wedding!"

"Wedding? Do you mean . . . Is she marrying the Judge?" A tiny glow of happiness brought a sparkle to her eyes.

"Yes," he snapped. "And she expects my fiancée to be there."

There was a small pause as Laurie wished secretly that she could be there as a friend. "It's impossible," she said aloud, knowing she could never stand up under the prolonged strain of being with Rian and not letting him see she loved him. "Invite LaRaine. It's time she met your family, anyway."

"LaRaine can go to hell! It's you that Vera is expecting!"

"Make up a story, or tell the truth," Laurie

pleaded, her feet involuntarily moving closer to him. "We just can't keep up this pretense any longer."

"There was no pretense." His piercing gaze unnerved her. "I offered to marry you."

"Why? There were no feelings between us," she protested. Not until she saw the sudden tightening of his jaw did she realize her hands were resting against his chest in a beseeching gesture. They lowered quickly to her side as the silence pounded as loudly as her heart.

"There was always something between us." Rian's voice vibrated with barely controlled emotion. The glitter in the depths of his eyes compelled her to meet his gaze even as Laurie tore herself away, more shaken by his steel-hard magnetism than was safe.

"No." The single word of denial severed the thread that had held Rian in check.

The iron grip of his fingers closed on her arms, and he pulled her swiftly against his powerful body. Yet there was no fear in her blue eyes as she gazed with aching desire into his beloved face.

"Do you know the hell you've put me through?" Rian said softly. There was the slightest lessening of the pressure of his fingers around her arms before he opened one hand and stroked her hair, his touch so sensually arousing that Laurie's eyelashes fluttered down to hide the heat waves he was sending through her. "You've haunted my days and my nights until I was nearly crazy with wanting you," he declared hoarsely. "And then you say there was nothing between us."

His mouth closed over hers. The glorious words Laurie had just heard were still ringing in her ears as she returned his kiss with all the passion she possessed. In the next moment she was crushed against his chest, Rian's lips burying themselves in the dark cloud of her hair.

"I won't let you go, Laurie," he vowed hungrily. "I can't let you go! You're mine and, God help me, I can't live without you!"

"Rian, Rian," she whispered, filled with unbelievable happiness as she nestled against his chest. His heart was thudding as wildly as hers beneath his shirt. "Are you telling me you love me?" she asked breathlessly.

"Yes," he groaned bitterly. "Yes, I love you. I worship you. The first time I touched you—at the pool, when I thought you were LaRaine—something strange happened to me. I blamed the anger I felt on your deceit. But I kept wanting to touch you again, to hold you in my arms. You had no idea how much I wanted you—"

"Rian, stop!" Laurie cried, unable to bear the torment in his voice any longer.

"You had me on my knees," he said, staring down into her agonized eyes. "Didn't you know that?"

Mutely she shook her head in denial.

One moment Laurie was crushed against him, in the next she was free and Rian was standing with his back to her staring out the curtained window, wearily rubbing the back of his neck.

"Will you come to Mobile with me?" he asked quietly.

"I'll go to the North Pole with you, Rian," she answered just as quietly. "Or anywhere else."

There was a moment of stillness when Rian froze

at her words; then he turned swiftly around, staring at her in stunned disbelief. "What did you say?"

"I said I love you, Rian Montgomery," Laurie replied, letting all her pent-up emotion shine for him alone. Then she was in his arms again, locked in a possessive embrace, returning the fire of his kiss with the white-hot passion of her own.

Sometime later, Rian held her away from him, tracing a fingertip over the lips he had kissed so thoroughly and so well.

"As much as I would like to see you walking down the aisle of a church to me, I think we should get married before we fly back to Mobile," he decreed.

"Yes, Rian," Laurie agreed meekly, aglow with the blissful knowledge that he really did love her.

"Laurie, why did you leave?" Even as he asked the question, his dark eyes studied her, as if reassuring himself of the love he saw in her eyes.

"Because I thought you didn't care for me," she answered honestly, only now realizing how wrong she had been. "You kept saying I had to marry you, yet you handed me over to Colin. If you loved me then, Rian, why did you practically force me to go to the ball with him?"

He took a deep breath before answering. "That time at the pool before Colin called—do you remember?" A crimson blush filled Laurie's cheeks as she remembered the way she'd abandoned herself to Rian. "Yes, well," he continued, "believe it or not, that was when I lost control of my heart. And everything else. If E. J. hadn't come out when he did—" His gaze raked over her, knowing she had filled in the rest. "I knew then what was happening and like any normal, red-blooded male, I bolted. I wasn't going to let any woman put a ring through my nose.''

That statement drew a lilting laugh from Laurie. As if Rian could ever be led.

"What about that photo in the newspaper of you and LaRaine? I thought you'd gone back to her.'' Sobering, she remembered the pain she had felt.

"I was trying to find you, honey. That was the only reason I saw her. Jealousy is a terrible thing, Laurie. I wanted you to go with Colin that night to prove that you meant nothing to me. It was the most agonizing night I've ever spent—except for these last months when I didn't know where you were.''

"I'll never leave you,'' she vowed, seeking the warmth of his embrace. "Not ever again.''

"You won't want to,'' Rian murmured against her mouth. "I'm about to make you the happiest woman on earth.''

A LAND CALLED DESERET

CHAPTER ONE

A hot wind blew red-brown dust through the opened windows of the old Jeep, coating everything inside. The fine grit clogged the pores of LaRaine's skin, particles clinging to the gloss on her lips until she could taste it in her mouth. She couldn't breathe without the dust filtering into her lungs. The dry, earthy smell of it overpowered the scent of the expensive perfume she wore.

Depite her amber-tinted sunglasses, her dark eyes smarted from the dust and she could see no relief ahead. The raw, harsh land stretching around her was marked with jutting mesas and slashing arroyos. Yellow grass dug tenacious roots into the inhospitable earth and the stubby, gnarled trees offered very little shade.

The Jeep bounced over the rutted track that passed for a road. Above the roar of the engine she heard the groaning, thumping rattle of protest it made. LaRaine clutched the armrest of the passenger door to keep from bouncing all over the seat, the scarlet sheen of her long fingernails contrasting vividly with the beige upholstery.

"I'm surprised somebody hasn't given Utah back to the Indians," she muttered.

The man driving darted a glance at his raven-haired passenger. His attention couldn't be spared for long from the road as the ruts tried to wrench the steering wheel from his hands. Sam Hardesty saw LaRaine wipe her throat and neck with a handkerchief and saw her grimace at the dirt that perspiration had gathered. The mirrorlike finish of his sunglasses hid the glitter of amusement that danced in his eyes.

A gust of wind sent a choking cloud of dust into the interior of the vehicle. LaRaine coughed and covered her mouth with one hand while the other waved the handkerchief to clear the air. It didn't do much good.

"How much farther do we have to go?" she demanded, her voice choked with dust and impatience.

"McCrea's ranch can't be far now." Sam Hardesty successfully hid a smile at LaRaine's obvious discomfort.

"That's what you said twenty minutes ago." She coughed again and futilely wagged the handkerchief in front of her. "I'm going to choke to death on this dust before we get there!"

"Roll the window up if it's getting to be too much for you," he suggested without sympathy.

"Excellent idea, Sam," she agreed sarcastically "With the window up, this rattletrap turns into a furnace."

"You asked to come with me," he reminded her. "Nobody twisted your arm."

"I never dreamed it would be like this. I thought you'd take one of the limousines, or, at the very least, an air-conditioned car. Instead you take this." There was no mistaking the contempt in her voice for their mode of transportation. Her slashing glance at the driver caught the silent twitch of laughter at the corners of his mouth. "And stop smirking! It isn't funny."

"Can you imagine any of the cars from the studio traveling over this?" He gestured briefly to the rough road ahead of them before grabbing the wheel with both hands again. "Springs, shocks— the whole bottom of those cars would be torn out before they could get a mile. Besides, you could have changed your mind when you saw I was taking the Jeep."

"I wish I had," she insisted tightly.

"No, you don't." Amusement colored his dismissal of her statement. "When you found out about McCrea, you would have walked to get to his place. The minute you heard the words 'local rancher,' all your antennae came out. Is he single? Is he rich? Is he handsome? When the feedback was positive, you decided then and there to be the first member of the cast to meet him. You intend to establish your claim on him before anyone else finds out he's around."

It was on the tip of LaRaine's tongue to deny his allegation, but Sam knew her too well. She would never be able to convince him that she was just along for the ride. His words did wound, though. He made her sound so mercenary, but in a sense, she supposed she was.

"I wouldn't care if McCrea were fat, bald and eighty," she stated, as if to deny that she felt some sense of guilt. "Any man would do in this godforsaken wilderness!"

"Then go get him, girl." Sam briefly met her look of surprise. "I'm serious. You need to find yourself a rich husband because you don't have any future as an actress. The only part you can get is when you play yourself. There aren't that many roles that call for a greedy, grasping bitch."

LaRaine paled at his vicious jab, but she doubted that her dust-coated face revealed it. She had become an expert at concealing her true feelings, such an expert that she sometimes wondered if she felt anything anymore.

"Your bitterness is showing, Sam," she replied coldly, and stared out of the window. "I didn't realize it still bothered you that I turned down your marriage proposal. You're only a struggling young assistant producer. Basically, you can't afford me."

"I was a fool to think I could." Sam's response was sardonically dry as he pushed lank brown hair from his forehead. "But I was blinded by your beauty like a lot of others. I didn't realize that you were only using me to make sure you landed this part in the film."

"I needed the role." Financially and in every other way, her career had been in a downward spiral. "And I'm grateful for all the support you gave me."

"Yeah, right." His mouth was grim as he shifted the vehicle into a lower gear.

"Did you expect to get paid for your help? Maybe you thought I'd go to bed with you?" Her volatile temper flared. "I may be guilty of a lot of things, but using the casting couch isn't one of them!"

"No, you just dangle suckers like me until you get what you want, then you cut the line," Sam muttered. "The word is out. You aren't going to find many more suckers you can hook. You were a fool, LaRaine, to ever let Montgomery slip out of your fingers."

"I dropped him," she lied.

"And he fell right into your cousin's hands, didn't he?" taunted Sam.

"She's welcome to him," LaRaine insisted haughtily. The Jeep bounced in and out of a pothole and she narrowly missed hitting her head on the ceiling. The rough ride was bruising. "I hope it'll all be worth it when we reach the ranch," she murmured the thought aloud.

"It'll be worth it, believe me," was the faintly smug reply.

But her thoughts were already refocusing on a previous comment from Sam. Rian Montgomery had possessed all the attributes she had sought in a husband: wealth, power, ruthless good looks. The mere fact that she'd attracted his attention and worn his engagement ring was the reason she'd been offered her first supporting role in a movie.

Foolishly she had grabbed at the part, confident of her ability to maneuver Rian Montgomery. LaRaine had never believed for a minute that he loved her, or that she loved him. They had suited each other's purposes. He had been looking for a trophy wife, someone to entertain his business associates and maintain a beautiful home, someone who would make no demands on him and who would be satisfied with a lavish lifestyle instead of affection.

That arrangement had been acceptable to La-Raine—until she'd been offered the movie part. She had seen the chance to get glamor and fame in her own right, so she took it. She had the looks and a killer figure. By the time she discovered she didn't have the talent to be a success, Rian had learned about her deception in accepting the initial role and concealing it from him. He'd broken off their engagement and married her cousin.

LaRaine's mother, who had raised both LaRaine and her cousin Laurie, had accused Laurie of stealing Rian from her daughter, but LaRaine didn't blame her, even though she had often envied her cousin during their early years. Neither of her parents had expected Laurie to excel in anything, but they had practically demanded that LaRaine be the best at everything—get the highest grades, wear the best clothes and be the prettiest girl, the most sought-after girlfriend, the most popular one in her class.

Since that first movie and the broken engagement to Rian, LaRaine had been offered a handful of other roles, each one smaller than the last. A half-dozen starstruck men had proposed to her, but their prospects for the future looked no brighter than her own. LaRaine's upbringing had forced her to believe she deserved the best. It was too deeply ingrained for her to settle for less.

Some, and Sam Hardesty was among them, had accused her of being too deeply in love with herself to love anyone else. It wasn't true. If the accusations hadn't hurt so much, they would have been funny. She had been tagged as a cold, calculating bitch, and she had begun to act the part with more finesse than she had ever displayed on the screen.

This movie now being filmed on location in Utah would probably be her last job in the industry. The critics were crucifying her performance in her most recently released movie with Jake Chasen. She wasn't exactly a hot property at the moment—unless she wanted to work in Z-grade horror movies.

The thought of Jake Chasen brought a painful, self-deprecating smile to her scarlet lips. She had actually believed that she had a chance of catching him. She had even imagined declaring to the world that she was giving up her acting career for him—when in truth there had been no career to give up.

LaRaine was desperate. Her parents, especially her mother, were angry with her because she didn't fight to take Rian Montgomery away from her cousin and upset because she was doing so poorly in her career. She had no friends. A marriage seemed to be the only way she could save face. But it had to be someone outside Hollywood, someone who wouldn't know of her reputation or her humiliating rejections by Rian Montgomery and Jake Chasen. Who better to dazzle with her status as an actress than a wealthy Utah rancher? At least, that was LaRaine's fervent hope.

The four-wheel-drive vehicle bounced over a ridge and rolled to a stop. LaRaine glanced around, looking for some indication that they had reached their destination. There wasn't a building in sight, only more vast stretches of wasteland. She hadn't expected the country to be so desolate, which was how it seemed to her.

"Carl was right," Sam mused aloud. "This'll be a great backdrop for the ranch sequences."

"This?" LaRaine looked around once again, unable to see it through his eyes. "But there's nothing here."

"Exactly." He started the Jeep forward.

A wheel briefly spun into the dust, sending a gritty cloud through the open window. LaRaine coughed. "How much farther?"

"Just over the rise. You can see the roofs of the buildings." Sam pointed, a half-smile curving his mouth.

"Thank God," LaRaine murmured. She opened her bag and took out a hand mirror. "I look awful!"

The wind had played havoc with her curling black hair, tousling it into provocative disorder. Dabbing at her face, she took care not to ruin the makeup that highlighted her striking bone structure.

"I wouldn't worry, LaRaine," Sam observed. "You're the only woman I know who can look stunning with a dirty face."

LaRaine wasn't sure if he meant that. "Thanks," she returned, but her voice was as dry as her throat. She added a fresh touch of lipgloss and decided that was the best she could do under the circumstances.

As the vehicle crested the rise, her anticipation soared. She had expected to see a modern, sprawling ranch house complete with stable and barn and immaculate white-fenced corrals, and her brown eyes widened in shock at the ranch buildings before them.

The massive house was an old, two-story affair. The hot sun had long ago blistered the paint from the boards. The flat gray color added years to the structure's age. Both the barn and a small shed seemed on the verge of falling down, their siding equally bereft of paint. A late model pickup truck was parked near the shed, its color hidden by the thick coating of dust.

The single corral was constructed out of leftover posts, boards and logs, a conglomeration of materials that made it appear less substantial than it was. A windmill creaked noisily in the gusting wind, adding to the feeling of total dilapidation.

"Surprised?" Sam's voice mocked her expression as he stopped the Jeep in front of the house.

LaRaine removed her sunglasses to turn her dark, accusing eyes on him. "You knew it was going to look like this, didn't you?"

"Carl gave me a pretty good description of the place," he admitted.

"And you led me to believe this rancher had money!" Frustration throbbed in her voice, mixing with anger.

"I never said he had money." Sam opened his door and stepped out. "I said he was well-to-do. Like most ranchers, McCrea is rich in land and cattle, but kind of strapped otherwise. Why else would he sell the rights to film on his land? He needs the cash."

Pushing open her door, LaRaine stepped out. She brushed at the dust that powdered the ivory silk of her blouse; the action sent puffs of dust in the air. A closer look at the buildings didn't improve their appearance.

"I hope you're planning to pay him enough to buy some paint," she declared, disappointment tasting bitter.

"I'm sure we will," Sam answered, but his thoughts were elsewhere. Behind the sunglasses, his gaze had narrowed to inspect the premises. "This place could be used to film the opening scene. I'll have to make sure he doesn't paint anything until we decide."

"Typical arrogance. You producers give a man money, then tell him when he can spend it," she retorted with biting softness.

Sam merely smiled and walked to the porch. LaRaine didn't follow; she doubted that the porch floor would hold the weight of two people. She waited beside the Jeep, wiping at the dust on the soft fawn leather of her split riding skirt. The screen door rattled when Sam knocked on it. The swirling wind billowed the light blue windbreaker he wore as he waited. He knocked again.

"Doesn't seem to be anyone home," he said, and walked off the porch. A chicken scratched the dirt in his path and clucked in protest as it was forced to move out of his way to join the others.

"Did you tell him that you were coming by this morning?" LaRaine asked. "Or did you just expect him to be here when you showed up?"

"No, that's something you would do," Sam retorted. "You always expect people to be around when you want them. I called McCrea last night to tell him I'd be by this morning." He pushed back the elastic cuff of his windbreaker to look at his wristwatch. "Carl warned me about the road, so I told McCrea not to expect me until around eleven. It's a couple of minutes before that now."

His passing remark that she expected people to be at her beck and call had hurt, and LaRaine tried to get back at him. "I'd laugh if he's changed his mind about letting you film on his land."

"You wouldn't laugh for long," he told her as he walked around to the driver's side. "Any more delays would mean budget cuts. Your role isn't all that essential. You might remember that, La-Raine."

"Are you threatening me, Sam?" For all the laughing challenge in her voice, LaRaine was inwardly intimidated by his statement. "I didn't realize what a sore loser you were."

"Revenge might be sweet," was the only response he made as he reached inside the opened window of the vehicle to honk the horn.

The blaring sound sent the chickens scurrying, wings flapping, to the rear of the house. LaRaine felt sick and frightened, but she wouldn't let Sam see that. Her downcast gaze took in the dust on her knee-high boots. The handkerchief had been used to wipe everything else; she decided she might as well use it on her leather boots.

Resting a toe on the bumper, she bent to wipe away the dust from her boot. A swipe of the linen cloth brought out the polished sheen of the fine leather, a darker, complementing shade of brown to the riding skirt she wore. With one boot free of dust, she shifted her attention to the other.

"That must be McCrea coming now," Sam announced.

LaRaine glanced up to see a horse and rider approaching the ranchyard. She held her pose, one foot on the front bumper of the Jeep and an elbow resting casually on a raised knee. Her attitude of indifferent interest was feigned as she studied the horse and rider coming toward them.

The muscled conformation of the mahogany bay horse was flawless. LaRaine was a novice when it came to ranches and cattle, but she did know good horseflesh, and the horse the man was riding was no ordinary nag. As they came closer, LaRaine realized that the horse was not only powerfully muscled, but tall as well, standing easily sixteen hands high. Its running walk ate up the ground with effortless ease.

When she got a better look at the rider, she saw that the horse had to be big in order to carry the man on its back. Anything smaller than the bay and the rider would have dwarfed his mount, making a combination as incongruous as an adult on a Shetland pony.

The man was very tall with a broad chest and shoulders. Despite his size, he rode with effortless grace, relaxed and at ease as if born in the saddle. LaRaine could see little of his face beneath the brim of his sweat-stained cowboy hat. What was visible was mostly strong jaw and chin.

Saddle leather creaked as the horse and rider entered the ranchyard. A red calf was draped across the saddle in front of the rider. It hung limp, showing no sign of life, when the horse was reined to a stop in front of the barn.

Gathering the calf in his arms, the rider stepped down from the saddle. As yet, the man had not acknowledged their presence with more than a look. Sam walked forward to meet him, but LaRaine waited.

"Hi, I'm Sam Hardesty from the movie studio." He introduced himself, not bothering to extend a hand since the rancher's arms were holding the calf. "I called you last night."

The calf wasn't as small as it had first appeared. LaRaine guessed that it easily weighed over a hundred pounds, but the rancher carried its limp weight with ease.

"Sorry I wasn't here when you arrived, Mr. Hardesty." The man's voice was pitched low, with a pleasant drawl despite the business tone. "Do you mind if we hold off our talk for a few minutes? This calf is in bad shape. I have to tend to him first."

"Not at all," Sam replied with the faintest trace of impatience creeping into his answer.

LaRaine removed her boot from the bumper and moved a couple of steps to bring her in line with the path the man was taking to the house. She tipped her head at a provocative angle, letting the black cloud of her hair drift to one side.

"Did I hear wrong or is that a touch of Texas in your voice?" she questioned in a deliberately playful challenge.

The man stopped. His brown eyes inspected LaRaine with almost insulting indifference to her feminine beauty. Meeting him face-to-face, she noticed the wings of gray in his otherwise dark hair. Even though he carried the calf, she could tell that the broad shoulders tapered to a slim waist and hips, giving a deceptive impression of leanness. And it was deceptive. She was petite, but she felt even smaller next to him.

"Yes, I'm from Texas originally," he admitted, and turned his gaze to Sam.

The look prompted an introduction. "Mr. McCrea, this is one of the supporting actresses in our film, LaRaine Evans. She came along to get an idea of the lay of the land." His sly innuendo wasn't wasted on LaRaine. Sam had meant that she was checking the rancher out.

She had the suspicion that the rancher knew exactly what Sam meant. It was an unnerving feeling. She had expected him to be something of a country bumpkin, unsophisticated, someone who could easily be tricked. She caught a hint of worldly sophistication in those glittering brown eyes, despite his obvious brute strength.

"LaRaine, this is Travis McCrea," Sam finished the introduction.

"It's a pleasure, Miss Evans."

"Please, call me LaRaine," she insisted with a wide smile.

"Thank you." His head dipped in acknowledgement, the hat brim concealing the glitter of mockery she briefly glimpsed in his eyes. "Excuse me, I have to take care of the calf."

Travis McCrea moved past her onto the porch, which surprisingly supported the combined weight of him and the calf. It didn't sit well with LaRaine that this man found her subtle flirtation amusing. He had been impressed by neither her looks nor the fact that she was an actress, two things she had been counting on. She had struck out, and Sam was smirking at her.

As she started to follow the two men into the house, her gaze swept the weathered boards of the house. The appearance of the house didn't match its owner. Her previous disappointment in the surroundings had faded when she had seen Travis McCrea for the first time. He didn't strike her as the kind of man who would be content to live in this hovel. So why was he?

It was a puzzle and one she couldn't solve until

she had more answers to the questions buzzing in her head. Sam was holding the screen door open for her. LaRaine put a tentative boot on the porch floorboards. They were more solid than they appeared and she walked forward. The interior of the house might be totally different from the outside. Then the thought crossed her mind—how different could it be if Travis McCrea was taking a calf inside?

CHAPTER TWO

The porch door opened into the living room. In LaRaine's estimation, it was furnished with Salvation Army rejects. A couch and chair were covered in a hideous maroon with a thin gold stripe. An overstuffed recliner in cheap vinyl leather was in front of a smoke-blackened fireplace. An area rug covered the linoleum floor. LaRaine guessed that the rug might have once possessed an Oriental pattern, but it was so threadbare, the color and design had faded into meaningless combinations.

There were water stains on the ceilings in both the living room and the hallway leading into the kitchen. Both areas had the same wallpaper, yellowed with age, its seams curling away from the wall. The few pictures that had been on the wall resembled old calendar covers that had been framed. LaRaine looked around with disdain. If possible, the interior of the house was worse than the outside.

A darkened staircase branched off the hallway to the second floor. LaRaine shuddered at what might be in the rooms above. She followed the men's voices into the kitchen. There, the linoleum floor had cracked in several places, exposing black seams splintering across a scuffed, yellow-splattered pattern. The wood cabinets were finished in a cherrywood stain.

Gray tile rose halfway up the walls where a band of brick-patterned wallpaper separated the tile from the upper half of the wall, painted a sickly shade of green. The wooden table in the center of the room looked as if it had fifteen coats of brown paint on it. The surrounding chairs were all in different styles, from an armed captain's chair to a severe straight-backed chair.

Everything about the house made LaRaine want to cringe. The only thing that could be said in its favor was that it was clean. Even that couldn't make up for the deplorable lack of taste used in decorating it.

The red calf had been set down on a braided rug in a cleared area of the room. Travis McCrea was kneeling at its head while Sam hovered nearby, watching. LaRaine's intense dislike for the house didn't extend to its owner. She walked around the ugly brown table to stand near them.

"What happened to the calf?" she asked to make conversation.

"He got a faceful and noseful of thorns," was Travis's response as he continued working near the calf's head without glancing up. "He tangled either with some cactus or a patch of briars."

Travis moved and LaRaine noticed the tweezer-like instrument in his hand and glimpsed the swollen and festering sores around the calf's nose and eyes. It was a repelling sight, but she forced herself to remain indifferent.

"How did it happen?" She found it difficult to believe that even a dumb animal could have something like that happen to it.

"I wouldn't even begin to guess." Travis shrugged to indicate the "how" was immaterial at this point. "Maybe something frightened it into stampeding into the thorns."

Although LaRaine didn't have a clear view, she could tell that he was pulling out some of the thorns and cutting out others that had worked themselves in too deep. Despite the obvious pain Travis had to be inflicting, the calf didn't make a sound or struggle.

"Is it alive?" She was beginning to doubt it. She glanced at its rib cage to see if she could tell whether or not it was breathing. The movement was very faint.

"He's alive, but just barely. It must have happened a couple of days ago or more," Travis explained. "He hasn't been able to eat, maybe not even able to drink, since then. He's very weak."

"Will he live?" It was Sam who put forward the question.

"I don't know." The grim mouth quirked briefly. "I'll tell you in a couple of days." Raising his head, Travis cast a glance sideways at LaRaine. "There's antiseptic and some swabs in the cabinet by the back door. Would you get them for me?"

She hesitated for a fraction of a second, then walked to the cupboard he had indicated. The bottle of antiseptic and swabs were exactly where he had said they were. She carried them to where he knelt beside the calf.

"Is the calf worth saving?" Sam asked.

"He's worth saving, if for nothing else, than to butcher as beef for my own use." A note of dryness crept into Travis's otherwise patient voice. With a nod of his head, he indicated that LaRaine should kneel beside him. When she did, she was made aware again of how powerfully muscled his shoulders and arms were. Amidst the animal smells clinging to him, she caught the tang of his aftershave. "Your hands are cleaner than mine. You apply the antiseptic and I'll hold the calf's head still."

LaRaine stared at the swollen and now bloodied face of the injured calf, stunned by the request Travis had made. So many of the wounds were close to the eyes, nose and mouth. She had heard or read somewhere that antiseptic could be fatal if swallowed. She had never treated a sick creature in her life, and the thought kept running through her mind that she could accidentally kill it in her ignorance.

"I . . . I can't," she stammered out her stunned refusal, shoving the bottle toward him and recoiling.

"It's very simple. You just—" Travis began to explain with taut patience.

"Save it," Sam interrupted, his voice laced with scorn. "I'm sure LaRaine doesn't want to risk staining her leather skirt with the medicine. Useful she definitely isn't."

There was a suggestion of contempt in the dismissing glance Travis gave her. "My mistake. I should have realized you wouldn't dirty your clothes. Move to the side." It was an order, not a request. It all happened so quickly that LaRaine didn't have a chance to refute Sam's statement. "Would you mind holding the calf's head, Mr. Hardesty? He's been pretty quiet up until now, but I don't want to take any chances."

"Glad to help. What do you want me to do?" Sam moved closer while LaRaine shifted out of the way and rose to her feet.

She watched as Travis showed Sam what he wanted. She could have done that, but she hadn't been asked. LaRaine kept silent. Why on earth should she regret not being able to help an animal? It was stupid and silly. She should be glad she didn't have to touch that smelly, infected creature.

"Look where you found the antiseptic—there's a black container with a syringe inside," Travis told her. "Would you get that for me, and the vial of antibiotics in the refrigerator?"

LaRaine located the syringe right away, but she had to look for the vial in the refrigerator. She brought both of them to Travis as he finished disinfecting the wounds. Sam looked away as Travis jabbed the needle into the calf. LaRaine had never been squeamish about such things as shots or the sight of blood. She watched all the rancher's ministrations to the calf with a curious fascination.

"You can let go of him," Travis told Sam.

The calf weakly kicked out with a hind leg when Sam relaxed his hold and straightened to his feet. It seemed to be breathing more easily. LaRaine wondered if the swelling had affected its nasal passages. Poor little thing, it looked so helpless lying there on the rug. She resisted the impulse to kneel beside it and pet its matted red hide. Sam would only make fun of her and silently accuse her of doing it to impress Travis McCrea. Instead, she hooked her thumbs in the waistband of her riding skirt, pretending an indifference she didn't feel.

"What will you do with the calf now?" she asked. "You aren't going to turn it loose, are you?"

"Right now I'm going to mix up some mash and calf milk to see if I can get some nourishment down him. Then I'll put him in one of the stalls in the barn until he's up and around again before I turn him loose." Behind the blandness of his tone, La-Raine had the impression that Travis was mockingly inquiring whether or not his plan met with her approval.

It irritated her. "I see." She looked away, aware that there was anger in her eyes. "Tell me, do you always treat your sick animals in the kitchen?" The audacious question slipped out before she could get control of her irritation.

"Not all the time. Some of the animals I can't get through the door. In this case, it seemed easier to bring the calf to the equipment than to bring the equipment and medicine to the calf. Why, do you object if I treat *my* animals in *my* kitchen?"

LaRaine shrugged. "Of course not. I was just curious."

"And I always thought curiosity killed the cat," Sam murmured, and LaRaine wanted to hiss at him like a cat after that remark.

She couldn't resist one playful claw at her former boyfriend. "Just ignore him. He's bitter because he asked me to marry him and I turned him down." She watched Sam turn red with anger and gave him a tiny feline smile.

Sam grabbed her arm and half turned her so

that her back was to Travis, who seemed to find the interplay between them beneath his attention. LaRaine didn't like being ignored any more than she liked being the butt of some secret joke.

"Dammit, LaRaine," Sam muttered beneath his breath. "This is a business meeting. I said you could come along, but that doesn't mean McCrea has to hear personal stuff."

"You started it, darling." She ran her fingernails lightly across his shaven cheek in a mock scratch, then disdainfully twisted her arm free of his hold. In a louder voice, addressed to both men, she said, "Since you have business to discuss, I think I'll get some fresh air."

Neither man made a single protest as she walked from the kitchen. LaRaine was in one of those moods where even that angered her. Out of sheer politeness they could have pretended that she was welcome to stay.

In a burst of temper, she let the screen door slam loudly shut. Walking off the porch, she kicked at a rock. It bounced over the ground and sent a chicken squawking for cover. The bay horse stood in front of the barn, the ends of the reins dragging the ground. Under other circumstances, LaRaine might have wandered over to it. It wasn't her horse, so why should she care if it was still saddled and standing in the sun?

Nothing had gone the way she planned it. The ride here had been a miserable, bone-jarring, bruising experience. The ranch was a despicable place and Travis McCrea had not fallen at her feet, figuratively or literally, when he'd met her. She felt close to tears, which was ridiculous. She never cried. She stared at the distant horizon and blinked at the smarting moistness.

The screen door opened, the sound followed by heavy footsteps on the porch floorboards. LaRaine didn't turn around to look at Sam or Travis McCrea.

"Well, that business discussion was short but sweet," LaRaine said, to let them know she was aware they had joined her outside.

"It isn't over." It was Travis who responded to her comment. "I came out to bed the calf down in one of the stalls."

"Oh." Her tone was indifferent. She wanted them to know that she didn't care what either of them did.

Out of the corner of her eye, she could see Travis only a few feet away. The calf was in his arms. This time it was making an attempt to hold its head up, purple splotches of antiseptic on its white face.

"Are you admiring the view?" Travis asked.

"Yes," LaRaine agreed rather than turn to look at him. She was afraid that the brightness of unshed tears might be in her eyes and she didn't want him to see. A further comment seemed to be expected from her and she searched for one. "It's a vast, beautiful . . ." The lie stuck in her throat. She couldn't find anything beautiful about the desolate country. "Nothing," she finished with cold, blatant truthfulness.

"Hm." Travis seemed to consider her reply. "You could be right."

LaRaine felt his gaze dwelling on her. Heat rushed through her as she realized he was applying the description to her instead of the land, a beautiful nothing. She pivoted to glare at him, proud and defiant, her dark eyes flashing, her volatile beauty coming to life.

"On the other hand, maybe one of us isn't seeing it all," Travis qualified his previous statement.

His sun-browned features revealed nothing. Neither did his eyes. LaRaine was confused, unsure whether there was a double meaning to his comments or whether she had imagined it. Travis moved off toward the barn before she could decide.

LaRaine watched him go, with Sam following. She saw him say something to Sam, evidently about the bay horse, because Sam gathered the reins and led the horse inside the barn after Travis had slid the door open. An hour ago she would have smiled at that, aware of Sam's dread of horses. At that moment, the thought didn't even register.

When they came out of the barn they were discussing the proposed use of Travis's ranch as a location for the movie. Sam was doing most of the talking, explaining which sections of the ranch would be used and the approximate length of time it would take to film the location sequences. They discussed price and who would be responsible for what. The two men remained outside, standing on the porch, and LaRaine overheard it all.

When they came to terms, Sam shook Travis's hand. "It's a deal, then, McCrea. I'll have the legal papers drawn up so you can review the agreement with our attorney. Our film crew can come out here next week if it's all satisfactory."

"Sounds good," Travis agreed noncommittally.

"I'll make some calls and get the ball rolling." Sam excused himself, and entered the house.

His departure left a silence in its wake. LaRaine wandered with seeming aimlessness toward the porch where Travis stood, a shoulder leaning against one of the upright posts supporting the roof. His hat brim shadowed the upper part of his face, but she felt his gaze on her.

"You could have asked for more money," she told him. "You would've got it. Everyone on the production staff wants your ranch for the location shots now that they've seen it."

"I'm satisfied with the price and the terms. Seems fair to both sides." His tone indicated that it was none of her business.

"I was just trying to be helpful." LaRaine shrugged, but she felt defensive and on edge.

"Thanks, but I'm old enough to make my own decisions," he said dryly.

"And how old is that?" she blurted, her gaze flickering to the streaks of white hair at his temples.

"Forty last month, and how old are you?" Travis countered without hesitation.

"No gentleman asks a lady her age." LaRaine would have guessed that he was in his late thirties. She veiled her surprise at learning he was older than that. He didn't look it. There was so much vitality about him, so much untapped strength.

"I'm not a gentleman." But his answer implied that she wasn't a lady, either.

"I'm twenty-five, going on twenty-six." She wished she hadn't put it that way. It reminded her of a child who had to tack on the approaching year to appear older.

Sam chose that moment to return. "Okay, we're good to go," he told Travis. "I'll be back in touch with you in the next day or two."

"Fine."

"I know you have work to do, so we won't keep

you. Besides, we have to be heading back.'' Sam shook hands with him again. ''We'll be seeing a lot of each other over the next month or two, so I won't say goodbye.''

''It was a pleasure meeting you, Mr. McCrea,'' LaRaine offered with studied formality. Strangely enough, she was just as eager to leave the company of the rancher as she had been to seek it. It wasn't like her to fluctuate in her wishes.

''You, too, Miss Evans,'' was his bland response.

The Jeep had crested the rise, leaving the ranch-yard behind, before Sam directed a remark to La-Raine. ''McCrea didn't turn out to be the pushover you thought he would, did he?'' he said with smug satisfaction. ''Don't try to twist him around your little finger.''

''Who said I wanted to?'' LaRaine would rather have died than admit differently to Sam.

It was an extraordinarily long and silent drive back to the motel in Delta that served as head-quarters for the cast and crew. LaRaine was glad when Sam let her out at the entrance and went to report on his meeting with Travis McCrea.

As she walked down the hallway to her room, a door near hers opened. Susan Winters, who had a supporting role in the film, stepped into the hall. She was a slim, attractive girl with honey-brown hair. An eyebrow lifted in recognition when she saw LaRaine.

''You're back,'' she announced.

The statement was so obvious that LaRaine simply nodded and slipped the key into the door lock. She wasn't in the mood for conversation. The only thought in her mind was to shower away the grit and dust from the rough ride.

"You should've told someone where you were going." Susan followed LaRaine into her room, unconcerned that she hadn't been invited. "Andy Pandy was upset when he couldn't find you," she said, using the cast's nickname for their director. "Luckily someone saw you leave with Sam or your name would have been mud."

"You mean it isn't?" LaRaine retorted cynically. The director's opinion of her had seemed to be pretty low since she arrived here. "Besides, it wasn't any of his business where I was. My free time is my own. I checked the shooting schedule and there was nothing posted for me today."

"That was before Chuck cut his leg and had to be taken to the hospital for stitches. They had to abandon that scene and rearrange the schedule," Susan explained.

"What heroics was Chuck performing this time?" She derisively referred to the leading man and his penchant for macho behavior.

"It was a totally stupid accident. He stepped on a rock, twisted his ankle and fell, cutting his leg on a piece of glass lying on the ground."

"I'll bet that isn't the story the press release will give," LaRaine commented, knowing it would be one to enhance the star's image. She sat on the edge of the bed and began tugging off her boots.

"What made you decide to go with Sam today? I thought you two were bitter enemies." Susan had an emery board in her hand and began filing at her nails.

"He's bitter. I'm not." She tossed the boots in a corner and began unbuttoning her blouse. "He was going out to the new location to see if it met with his approval and asked if I wanted to come along. I wanted to get out of this dreary hole." Her gaze swept the room with disdain.

"What's the verdict on the new location? Did Sam tell you?" Susan moved to half stand against and half sit on the low chest of drawers.

"Looks like we'll be shooting out there next week." LaRaine took off her dirty blouse and tossed it carelessly on the bed.

She was accustomed to someone picking up after her. When she was younger, it had been her mother. Later, her cousin Laurie had cleaned up her messes, then maids or cleaning ladies. Her disregard for such things had become a habit.

"This whole project has been chaos from the beginning," Susan declared. "No one is organized. Really, LaRaine, changing locations in the middle of filming proves it right there. No wonder everyone keeps talking about the budget and delays."

"From what Sam said, the change of locations won't require any reshooting." LaRaine stepped out of the fawn leather riding skirt and left it lying on the floor.

Walking to the small closet, she took out her two robes, one a red caftan and the other a velour that zipped up the front. She hesitated in her choice before selecting the red. She flung the other across the lone chair, not bothering to hang it back up. After slipping the caftan over her head, she walked into the adjoining bathroom and turned the water on in the tub.

"The new place is on somebody's ranch, isn't it?" Susan called, raising her voice to make herself heard above the running water.

"Yes." LaRaine returned to the bedroom and began winding her shoulder-length black hair into a bun on top of her head, securing it with a comb and pins.

"I heard the guy that owns it is a bachelor. Did you meet him or just look around?" Susan eyed her curiously.

"We looked around and we met the owner." LaRaine answered the question and volunteered no more.

"And?" Susan prompted. "What was your impression?"

"You have to see the place to believe it." She looked around the hotel room, mentally comparing it to the ranch house and deciding the room was a palace.

"Who cares about the place?" Susan dismissed that as totally unimportant. "I want to know about the man."

"You'll meet him yourself next week." LaRaine had no desire to discuss Travis McCrea.

"What does that mean—hands off, you saw him first?" the girl laughed with a trace of sarcastic challenge.

"It means . . ."—LaRaine walked to the bathroom door—"that I'm going to take a bath—in private."

Alone in the bathroom, LaRaine heard the hotel room door close, signaling that Susan had left. It wouldn't matter what she told Susan about Travis. The word would have spread that she was out to snare the rancher. Everyone expected her to go after any available bachelor that came along, especially the wealthy ones. It was true, wasn't it? So why did it bother her?

CHAPTER THREE

It was almost two full weeks before the movie company moved onto the McCrea ranch. Gossip had spread throughout the cast and crew, linking LaRaine with the rancher, even though she hadn't seen him since their first meeting.

LaRaine ignored it. As intrigued as she had been with the man, Travis McCrea did not meet her standards. Just thinking about the house made her shudder. In her mind, she crossed him off her list. The problem was that there was no one left on her list who could be regarded as potential husband material.

Her future beyond the conclusion of this film looked bleak. Twice she had come close to catching the ideal man, only to lose him both times to someone else. She was afraid of another failure. Her confidence was shaken, although no one on the outside had guessed.

But then no one liked her, so they never bothered to find out how she truly felt about anything. That was the way she wanted it, she told herself. Who needed them anyway?

The film company was taking a noon break for lunch. The cast and crew intermingled, clustered in little groups around the film set. The director and his assistant were huddled with the screenwriter, going over more proposed script changes. A tangle of electric cords snaked along the ground, running from the lights and sound equipment to the generator truck.

LaRaine was alone, sitting on a flat rock apart from the others. Her back was turned to the luxurious motor homes parked to the side, provided for the leading actors in the film. Inside the large vans there were soft, cushioned chairs and couches, plus air-conditioned comfort. She didn't need to be reminded that she would never attain that status in her career.

The styrofoam cup in her hand contained iced tea, but the sun had warmed it to tepid. She swirled it uninterestedly. The remains of a sandwich and its wrapper were on the ground near her feet, cast aside half-eaten.

It seemed like such a short time ago that she had shared an apartment with her cousin Laurie. At the time, LaRaine had been sure she could conquer the world. Now it seemed that the world was threatening to conquer her. Thick and long curling lashes touched to blink at the stinging moisture in her dark eyes. But her artfully made-up features retained their smooth, unemotional expression.

The drumming rhythm of hoofbeats opened her

eyes. A horse and rider were approaching the film set. LaRaine recognized the easy-riding man in the saddle immediately: Travis McCrea. She noted the slight checking of the reins that slowed the bay horse from a canter to a trot and finally a walk.

She got to her feet, discarding the cup on the ground. The tea spilled onto the thirsty soil. Her senses came to life, no longer dulled by the unhappiness of her thoughts. There was a faint quickening of her pulse as she watched him rein in at the edge of the set, not thirty feet from where she stood.

His gaze touched on her in silent recognition. LaRaine was drawn toward him, compelled by something she neither understood nor questioned. Others were aware of his arrival, but she didn't notice. As she walked forward, she admired his fluid dismount. Despite his height and muscled build, his movements held an animal grace, the suggestion of lightness almost catlike.

"Look what the wind blew in!" Her voice was tinged with mockery and a trace of arrogance. "If it isn't our long, tall Texan!"

"Ms. Evans." Leather-gloved fingers touched the dusty brim of his brown hat in a respectful greeting, yet she didn't like that knowing complacency in his look. "Why are you all by yourself?"

Instantly LaRaine was on the defensive. "I was having lunch. I prefer to eat alone," she stated, her spine straightening rigidly.

"I thought you might have been waiting for me." The corners of his mouth deepened in amusement, but the half-smile seemed to taunt.

"But I didn't know you were coming." She kept her tone calm while she bristled inside.

"I thought your boyfriend might have mentioned it." Travis gave the impression of shrugging indifferently.

"My boyfriend?"

"Sam Hardesty," Travis said.

"He isn't my boyfriend." Her correction was cool and swift.

"That's right." He nodded briefly, remembering. "You said you dumped him, didn't you?"

Which was almost literally what she had done once she was assured she had a small part in this film. She had been accused of it before, but, coming from this man, it was a condemnation that hurt.

"No, I said that he asked me to marry him and I refused." She rephrased it to take out the sting of his sentence.

But the look in his dark brown eyes said that he assumed she'd probably led Sam on. Maybe she had, but LaRaine would only admit that to herself. She rationalized her actions with the excuse that she needed the job. She had been desperate—and still was.

"I believe you did say that," Travis agreed, but his expression didn't change.

"Hello, Travis." Sam Hardesty hustled forward to shake his hand. "It's good to see you again."

"You left a message—said you wanted to talk to me? Here I am."

"Yes, I did," Sam replied. "We have a scene coming up next week that calls for cattle. I wondered if you'd rent us about thirty head of your stock."

Neither man paid any attention to LaRaine standing beside them. She waited for Travis to snap up the offer, guessing that he was probably desperate for money considering the state his ranch buildings were in.

But he didn't. "What will you use the cattle for?" he questioned instead.

"We just need a small herd grazing in the background, with maybe a couple of cowboys working them," Sam explained. "We won't be stampeding them or anything like that."

"In that case, I can gather thirty head for you," Travis agreed.

"Good, and the scruffier they look, the better," Sam added.

"All I have is blooded stock," Travis told him. "If it's rough-looking range cattle you want, you'd better check with one of the other ranchers in the area."

"I see." Sam looked thoughtful, mulling over this information. "Maybe they'll work, anyway. I'll talk it over with the others," he said. "In the meantime, why don't you come over where the others are and I'll introduce you around?"

Travis hesitated as if he had more important things to do, then agreed, "All right."

"Do you want a cup of coffee, a sandwich or anything?" Sam offered. "The mobile canteen is here."

"Nothing, thank you," he refused.

LaRaine walked along with them. She noticed the way heads turned as the lunching cast and crew noticed Travis walking through, leading his big bay horse. It wasn't just because he was a stranger. It had something to do with that air of quiet authority about him, a presence that made itself felt. She couldn't help thinking that it was a pity he wasn't rich. "How is the calf?" She sought his attention because it was something she sensed the other women there would like to have. "Did it live?" She remembered how pathetically weak it had been.

His cool gaze swung to her, taking in the made-up perfection of her face. "Yes, it lived," he answered, and looked straight ahead. "It's blind in one eye, but it's getting around all right."

"If it's blind, you won't turn it loose, will you?" The thought of the helpless calf wandering about the wasteland that surrounded them made La-Raine frown.

Again he inspected her face, amused by her response. "The calf lost the sight in only one eye. He'll make out all right," he assured her.

"That's heartless!" LaRaine declared in a tautly controlled voice.

Sam had been listening in on the conversation. "Coming from you, LaRaine, that's rich," he laughed.

"Nobody asked your opinion, Sam." She shot him an angry look, the insult stinging because it had been made in front of Travis. She didn't understand why that mattered. Hadn't she decided she wasn't interested in him?

Sam directed their path to where a couple of members of his staff were seated, and LaRaine stood to one side as he introduced Travis. She noticed how at ease Travis seemed in surroundings that must be strange to him. As far as she could tell, he wasn't in awe of those around him. She remembered when he'd met her, how indifferent he'd been to her supposedly glamorous profession. In some ways, it was a consolation to discover that he treated the others the same way he had treated her.

The bay horse stomped at a fly buzzing around its hocks, its head bobbing down to its knee to brush it off with its nose. The sleek, mahogany hide shivered to chase away the flying pests. LaRaine admired its conformation again and the rippling muscles in its chest and hindquarters.

"What's the matter?" she murmured, and stroked her hand along its neck and withers. "Are the flies bothering you, mmm?"

The horse turned its head to rub its forelock against her shoulder. Smiling at the action, she took a step away to scratch the spot on its forehead. The horse inhaled her scent and blew softly through its nose.

"You like that, do you?" LaRaine crooned. "You're a big, beautiful brute. Do you know that?" The horse bobbed its head, but it was to chase away another fly and not a response to her low question. LaRaine chose to pretend that it was, playing a childish game in her mind.

"Aren't you afraid he might hurt you?" The question from Travis made her suddenly aware that he was watching her. "He outweighs you by several hundred pounds."

"No, I'm not worried." It was easier for LaRaine to keep looking at the horse than to glance at Travis. "I like horses. What's his name?"

"Dallas."

"Is that where you're from? Dallas, Texas?" This time she did look at him, her glance curious, but when she met his gaze, a crazy sensation raced through her nerve ends, a tingling awareness of his rugged virility.

"No, I bought him from a Mormon rancher. He named him, I didn't," Travis answered.

"He's a beautiful animal. I'd like to ride him sometime." LaRaine wasn't angling for an invitation when she said it, but she realized afterward that it probably sounded as if she was.

"Sorry, he's a working horse." Travis turned her down gently but nonetheless firmly.

"Which means you think he's more than I can handle," she concluded. "I'm not a novice. All the same, I can understand why you won't let just anybody ride him. If he were mine, I wouldn't either."

"I'm glad you understand my reasons," he said.

Sam interrupted their conversation to include Travis in a discussion he was having with one of the staff. LaRaine continued to stroke the bay horse while covertly watching Travis. She became fascinated with the powerful line of his profile, strong and bold. His skin was stretched tautly over his bones like a tanned hide, and was almost the same color.

The smoothness of his sun-hardened features was marred only by crinkling lines around his eyes and the grooves running from nose to mouth. In an actor, LaRaine would have suspected the silver streaks in his hair had been professionally dyed. But there seemed nothing artificial or fake about him. Travis McCrea was all man.

As she studied him, she noticed his gaze narrow. He seemed to be looking beyond the small circle of men, and she glanced around to see what had attracted his attention. Susan Winters had just walked by, but other than that, everything looked the same as it had only minutes ago.

LaRaine looked back at Travis and realized his gaze was following Susan. His expression changed from piercing scrutiny to frowning disbelief and then wary recognition, one right after the other. LaRaine glanced at Susan. Did Travis know her? How?

In the next second Travis was walking past her, his long strides taking him after Susan. His abrupt departure from Sam and his group left them in stunned silence. Like LaRaine, they stared after him, puzzled and surprised.

"Natalie?" Travis called out the name in a questioning voice. As he drew closer to Susan, he repeated it with more certainty. "Natalie!"

LaRaine realized he was referring to Susan by that name, but Susan continued to walk on, unaware that anyone was trying to get her attention. She yelped in surprise when Travis caught up with her and grabbed her arm to turn her around to face him.

"Natalie, I—"

"What are you doing?" Susan struggled against the grip he had on her shoulders and tipped her head to look up at him, her honey-brown hair swinging away from her face.

Travis didn't complete the sentence he had started. LaRaine could almost see the poised stillness come over him. It lasted only as long as it took him to examine Susan's face. Abruptly he released her and took a step away. His features hardened into granite to control his expression so it wouldn't reveal what he was thinking or feeling. "Sorry," he apologized curtly. "I thought you were someone else."

"You're sorry? You scared me to death!" Susan laughed, a trifle breathlessly, but she was talking to air.

Travis had already pivoted away and was striding back to where LaRaine stood beside his horse. Silence dominated Sam and his group. His rock-hard expression kept anyone from joking about his mistake. It also kept them from saying anything.

The reins had been left to drag on the ground. When Travis reached the group, he scooped the dangling reins up in his gloved hand. LaRaine's fingers curved inside the cheek strap of the bridle, instinctively holding the bay horse.

Travis's gaze swung to the group, specifically to Sam. "I have to get back to work. Let me know if you decide you want to use my cattle."

"Sure thing, Travis." Sam was plainly intimidated.

Travis didn't wait for the response as he looped the reins over the bay's head and slipped a toe into the stirrup to swing into the saddle. LaRaine still had hold of the bridle. She checked his attempt to rein the horse away from the group. She wasn't intimidated. Her curiosity was too thoroughly aroused to let it go unsatisfied. His hooded gaze slid to her.

"Who did you think Susan was?" she demanded.

"Susan?" There was initial blankness before he realized she was referring to the girl he had thought was someone named Natalie. His mouth thinned. "Isn't it obvious?" His question was almost a jeer. "I thought she was someone else," he snapped. This time he touched a spur to the bay's ribs. The horse jumped out of LaRaine's hold, spinning around on its hindquarters. It took one bounding leap forward before its rider checked its speed to a running walk.

LaRaine watched him go, his back ramrod

straight. As he rode off the set, a murmur of voices began to swell. Everyone who had witnessed the scene was talking about it. Travis's answer hadn't satisfied LaRaine, only whetted her already aroused curiosity. She resolved to find out what it was all about someday, and to find out who this Natalie person was.

When Susan came up to her, LaRaine was still watching the horse and rider growing steadily smaller. She barely glanced at Susan. Her interest was completely captured by the departing figure.

"Who was he?" Susan questioned. "Don't tell me he's the man who owns this ranch?"

"Yes, he is," LaRaine admitted. As he disappeared from sight, her preoccupied gaze swung to Susan.

"No wonder you kept your opinion about him such a deep, dark secret," Susan commented. "What's his name?"

There was no reason to withhold the information. Susan could find it out from someone else easily enough. It took a couple of seconds for LaRaine to say it, though.

"Travis McCrea."

"Travis." Susan repeated the name as if testing the sound of it. "I wonder who he thought I was."

"Somebody else, obviously." LaRaine used his answer, her voice as dry and biting as his had been.

"Yes, but I wonder who?" Susan repeated the question, her expression thoughtful.

"Maybe you looked like his sister." She was suddenly impatient with the questions, the very same questions that were running through her own mind.

"No, not his sister," Susan replied with certainty.

"The way he was looking at me before he discovered I wasn't this Natalie would have melted any woman's bones. Whoever Natalie is, she isn't his sister."

"So? Maybe she's an old girlfriend." LaRaine shrugged as if this Natalie's relationship to Travis was of no interest to her, when in reality she was dying to know.

"I'll tell you one thing—I wish I had been Natalie," Susan declared.

"You aren't, so what's the sense in going on about it?" LaRaine retorted.

"Because that Travis McCrea is a hunk. I thought you had the inside track on him." The brown-haired girl measured LaRaine with a look. "But I don't think you do. I think I have a better chance with him than you do."

"Why? Just because you look like someone he might have once been in love with?" LaRaine challenged with a brash air of unconcern. Inwardly, she was afraid that Susan was right.

"Sure. Why not?" Susan reasoned. "I know I got his attention. I think I'll invite him to the party we're having next weekend. I'll bet he accepts."

"You're too late. I've already invited him," LaRaine lied.

"You have?" Susan frowned, her disappointment showing. "Is he coming?"

"What do you think?" she retorted, making it deliberately sound positive before she turned to walk away.

Susan caught her arm. "Is he really coming with you?" she demanded.

"If you don't believe me, ask him yourself the

next time you see him." LaRaine returned the girl's skeptical look with one of cool reproof.

"You always have to go after every new man that comes along, don't you, LaRaine?" Susan accused.

"Hm. The pot calls the kettle black," LaRaine mocked. "You've just admitted that you're going to chase him."

"There's a big difference between you and me. I want to go out with Travis McCrea because I like him, but you want to see what you can get out of him. Do you think a Utah rancher is going to get you a part in some movie? You won't be able to trick Sam again, that's for sure."

"Has Sam been crying on your shoulder?" La-Raine pretended that the remark hadn't bothered her.

"He's talked to me about you, yes," Susan admitted.

"Then I hope he told you that I never asked him to get me this job," she retorted.

"Maybe not, but you gave him the impression that you wanted it so the two of you wouldn't be separated."

"If that's what he thought, too bad. It wasn't true," LaRaine said.

"I'm sure it wasn't." Sarcasm crept into Susan's voice. "So what's going on with you and Travis McCrea?"

"Oh, just keeping in practice until something better comes along," LaRaine offered.

Anger reddened the other girl's face. "If he's stupid enough to be taken in by you, I don't want him." Susan turned and stalked away.

LaRaine's gaze followed her. People were so easily manipulated sometimes, she thought. With just a few well-chosen words, she had eliminated her competition. Susan had gone from wanting to invite Travis to a party to handing him back to LaRaine.

Why had she claimed that Travis was going to the party with her? LaRaine sighed. Had it been because she saw someone else wanted him? Sometimes she didn't understand her motives, if she had any. Even now she didn't understand why she was doing all this soul-searching.

Either way, she had committed herself to persuading Travis McCrea to go to the party with her next week. He might not be husband material, but neither was anyone else around here. However, he would certainly be a diversion. LaRaine decided that she had been taking her life a little too seriously. Maybe it was time she had some fun.

Travis McCrea could be quite a challenge. Again, she wondered who Natalie was. From what Susan had said, it must have been someone he cared about a great deal. Obviously he still did, if his reaction when he had mistaken Susan for her was anything to go by.

If he were still in love with someone else, then he wouldn't want to get serious. LaRaine shied away from possessive men who didn't have anything to offer in the long run. Sam Hardesty had become a bore, what with his broken heart permanently on display.

Maybe she could establish some kind of casual relationship with Travis McCrea. Until this moment she hadn't considered going to the party next week. But if she could persuade Travis to go with her, LaRaine had a feeling she would be the envy of every woman there.

Just for a minute, LaRaine felt her spirits droop. What difference did it make if they envied her? None of them liked her. If she fell on her face, they would all cheer and congratulate the one who knocked her down.

Why was she suddenly wishing it weren't that way? LaRaine breathed in deeply and released a long sigh.

CHAPTER FOUR

Two nights in a row, LaRaine tried to call Travis to invite him to the party the following week. The phone rang and rang, but no one answered. La-Raine knew she would just have to find another way to reach him. She wasn't about to give up.

Her name wasn't on the day's shooting schedule. Skirting the film set, she walked to the horse vans where the actors' horses were kept in readiness. The remuda boss was sitting on a bale of hay in the shade of one of the vans.

"Hi, Don." She was wearing the same split riding skirt and blouse that she had worn the first time she had met Travis. "Is anybody using the palomino today?"

He tipped his hat back and looked up at her. "Nope."

"Good. I thought I'd take him out for a ride.

The palomino needs the exercise almost as much as I do," LaRaine said.

"You know I'm not supposed to let anyone take these horses out," Don reminded her, his cheek bulging with a wad of tobacco.

"I know the whole insurance routine," she nodded. "I promise I won't sue the company if I get hurt. If a horse throws me, it's probably my fault anyway. So what do you say, Don? Will you let me ride the palomino?" A flat-crowned hat, protection against the sun while she was riding, dangled down her back.

"If it were anyone else but you asking, I'd turn them down," he said, and turned his head to spit out a stream of tobacco juice. The remuda boss was a former stunt man; his career ended when an accident crippled his leg.

"Don't tell me that you trust me, Don," LaRaine laughed. "That makes you a minority of one around here."

He smiled briefly at that and pushed himself to his feet.

"I don't know as how I'd trust you with my money, but I do trust you with my horses."

"I don't understand your logic. But as long as you're going to let me ride the palomino, I don't care whether or not it makes any sense," she declared.

"You wait here and I'll bring him," Don ordered, and limped away.

Fifteen minutes later, LaRaine was astride the palomino and riding off in the direction of the ranch two miles away. The horse was spirited and eager to cover ground, but responsive to its rider's commands.

Picking up the rutted trail, LaRaine followed it to the ranch, cantering the horse where the terrain was relatively smooth and slowing it down to a walk or trot where it was rougher. She doubted that she would be lucky enough to find Travis at the house.

The place looked deserted when she rode in. She walked the palomino to the house, dismounted and tied the reins around a porch post. She knocked at the door, but there wasn't any answer.

Leaving the palomino tied, she walked to the barn. The wide double doors stood open, sunlight invading part of the darkened interior. As she entered, her boots made a rustling sound on the straw-covered floor. From one of the stalls, a calf bawled. LaRaine followed the sound to a stall closed in with a gate.

It took a minute for her eyes to adjust to the dimness. Then she saw the red calf curled up in the straw. Its white face turned to her, marred with purple medication spotting its white hair. She glimpsed its injured eye, but the calf still looked considerably better than it had the last time she had seen it. It made a low, bleating sound at the sight of her.

"At least he hasn't turned you loose yet, little guy." Her mouth quirked in the semblance of a smile. "Where did he go? Do you know?"

The calf continued to stare at her. Sighing, La-Raine turned away from the barn and walked back into the sunlight of the outside. She slipped her hat off, letting it hang down her back, held by the rawhide thong around her throat. She wondered where Travis might be.

Trying to find him in this desolate country without knowing where to look would be ridiculous. It

would be too easy to get lost. It all looked alike to
LaRaine—sage and grass-covered land bounded
by juniper-studded mountains with a multitude of
canyons and deep valleys. LaRaine paused, shading
her eyes with her hand. There didn't seem to be
a sign of life anywhere. She walked to where the
palomino stood and untied the reins. Mounting,
she turned it away from the house and hesitated.
Maybe if she made a sweeping arc around the
ranchyard, while staying within sight of the house,
she might catch a glimpse of Travis. It was worth
a try, she decided.

Urging the palomino into a canter, she started
out, making a wide circle away from the buildings.
Her gaze skimmed the landscape, unimpressed by
the wild terrain. A long-eared jackrabbit raced
alongside her for a while and then made a lightning-
quick right angle turn to disappear into the sage.
LaRaine ignored it, as she ignored the chukar that
took flight at the palomino's approach.

She had almost decided that her attempt to find
Travis would be fruitless when she caught a movement out of the corner of her eye and reined the
palomino to a stop. It pranced in protest while she
tried to locate what had momentarily caught her
attention.

Far back in an arroyo she saw the distinctive red
color and then the shape of Hereford cattle taking
form in the sage and brush. They were ambling to
the mouth of the arroyo, as LaRaine was about to
ride on. Then she saw the horse and rider driving
the dozen or so head of cattle. It was Travis. She
felt she would recognize him anywhere.

A smile curved her mouth as she turned the
palomino and started it down the incline that

would take her to the valley floor and eventually to the mouth of the arroyo. Once down the slope, she had to wind her way through the thick stands of brush, relying on her sense of direction to guide her to her destination. It proved fairly reliable. Travis was just riding out of the mouth when she intersected his path and reined her horse alongside his. Surprise flickered briefly in his eyes.

"Hello." There was triumph in her greeting. The taste of successfully finding him was sweet.

"Are you lost?" Amusement glittered in the sideways look he gave her.

"If I were, I'm not anymore. You've found me." LaRaine gave him a smiling look.

"What are you doing out here?"

"I was looking for you," she replied truthfully.

"Oh?" The simple word asked for an explanation.

A mottled gray dog with a black face barked at a straying cow and chased it back with the others. The palomino danced nervously at the swift shadow of the cattle dog.

"I wanted to prove to you that I could ride," she answered after easily bringing her mount under control and slowing it to a sedate walk beside his horse. This time he was riding a buckskin. It was almost the same size as the bay, but it lacked the finer points of conformation that the bay possessed.

"I believed you," said Travis.

"Did you? You looked skeptical when I told you," she said, but without malice. "Who's your friend?" She nodded to the dog.

"Blue is my working partner, a blue heeler." When Travis spoke his name, the dog looked around, its ears pricking. Deciding there wasn't going to be any command, the dog returned to its business of keeping the cattle grouped and moving forward.

"Do you run this ranch by yourself?" she asked, a finely arched brow lifting.

"No, I have a hired hand, the younger son of one of my neighbors. A hard-working boy."

"Boy?" LaRaine questioned the term.

"He's nineteen. From my view, that's young," Travis explained dryly.

"I'd forgotten how old you are," she mocked. "Is that your bones I hear creaking, or the saddle?"

"This time it's the saddle." A cow threatened to elude the dog and take off into the sage. Travis reined his horse to pursue it, but the dog turned it back with the others.

"The buckskin isn't as good a horse as the bay," LaRaine observed, unconsciously attempting to show off her knowledge of horses.

"Not in looks maybe," Travis conceded. "But he's strong and dependable, and tough as nails. Looks alone don't count for much out here." His gaze was on her when he said the last. LaRaine had the feeling the comment was directed at her.

"Did you buy him here?" Uncertain how to take the remark, she kept the conversation centered on the horse.

"In Utah, yes," he nodded.

"From the same man who sold you the bay?"

"No, I've only had the buckskin a year. I bought the bay two years ago when I moved here," Travis answered.

"Two years ago?" She eyed him curiously. "You mean you've only owned this ranch for two years?"

"That's right." Travis never let his attention become diverted for long from the cattle.

"Did you have a ranch in Texas?" LaRaine had difficulty visualizing Travis working for someone else.

"No. I managed ranches. I finally decided it was time I put in all those long hours on a place of my own. So I took my savings, came here, and bought this ranch, such as it is. But it's mine." There was a quiet pride in the statement.

"Why did you come here? Why didn't you stay in Texas?" LaRaine thought she knew the answer, but she waited to hear what he had to say.

"I felt there was more opportunity here." His look dared her to challenge his answer.

For the time being, LaRaine didn't. "Where did you work in Texas?" she asked instead.

"Do you want my life history, is that it?" His slanted smile seemed to taunt her, but he answered, "I was born in the Texas Panhandle and worked on one of the ranches there after I graduated from high school. Then I moved to a ranch in the Hill Country outside of San Antonio. After a few years I took over the management of that ranch." He seemed to hesitate. "A friend of mine was hurt in a plane crash, so I ran his place in West Texas until he recovered. Then I came here."

"Oh. Your friend who was hurt, was his wife's name Natalie?" LaRaine asked, positive that his faint pause, and the tightness of his voice, had given it away.

He glanced at her and smiled slowly. "Cord's wife is named Stacy."

"Well, who's Natalie?" she persisted in treading on what she guessed was forbidden ground.

"She's a woman I know," was all he would say.

"And you loved her?" LaRaine asked.

His look was hard and impatient. "I love her," but his voice was calm.

LaRaine noticed that he didn't use the past tense. "What happened?"

"That's none of your business," he said flatly.

And she knew it was foolish to try to make him say more. She let both hands rest on the saddle horn, the reins loose around the horse's neck.

Travis looked straight ahead at the red backs of the cattle, while LaRaine let her gaze rest on the golden head of her horse as it bobbed back and forth in rhythm with its walking stride.

"You wouldn't happen to have some water in your canteen, would you?" she asked. "I'm thirsty and I forgot to bring any."

"Never go riding in this country without it," Travis stated, and reined his horse to a stop. "You never know when it might save your life."

LaRaine stopped her horse. "I'll remember that the next time."

With a hand signal, Travis gave a command to the dog, and LaRaine watched with fascination as it circled the cattle and forced them to stop without spooking a single one. There was plenty of yellow grass growing amidst the clumps of sage. The Herefords were content to graze.

When she glanced at Travis, she discovered he had dismounted and was removing his canteen from the saddlebags. LaRaine started to dismount, then changed her mind when she saw Travis walking around his horse to her left side. She realized he was going to do the gentlemanly thing and help her down.

It was an opportunity that she didn't intend to pass up. She swung her right leg over the saddle horn as his large hands reached up to span her waist. Kicking her left boot free of the stirrup, she placed her hands on his broad shoulders for balance. He lifted her as easily as he had carried the calf.

When her feet touched the ground, LaRaine swayed toward him. Her hands, instead of gliding down his chest, curved around his neck. As she tipped her head back and to the side, a sultry, enticing look darkened her eyes. She offered the glistening sheen of her lips to him. Every move was deliberate and calculated to invite an embrace.

Travis's hands rested loosely on her waist, neither holding nor rejecting. He looked down at her upturned face. His expression revealed an aloof kind of dry amusement as he made no move to accept her invitation.

LaRaine had expected this initial, passive resistance. She slid her fingers into the thickly curled black strands of hair at the back of his neck to force his head down. Travis submitted to the pressure, but it was a slow descent.

The touch of his hard lips on hers was warm and undemanding. Her pulse quickened in excitement. Travis was proving to be as susceptible to her practiced charm as others had been. His mouth moved experimentally over hers, yet there was nothing tentative about the kiss.

Slowly, LaRaine let herself begin to relax against him. It was like leaning against a stone statue warmed by the sun. Her intent was to deepen the kiss and introduce a seductive passion to the embrace. But before her lips could make their demand on him, his leather-gloved hand moved to capture her chin and hold it still.

The initiative had been hers, but now Travis was taking over. He was in control of the intensity of the kiss now, and he chose to avoid passion. His mouth continued its exploration of hers, with a firm pressure that was subtly teasing, frustrating LaRaine with its promise of satisfaction that was not fulfilled.

She was not free to respond but only to feel. A multitude of sensations began crowding into her mind. The hot sun had dampened his skin with sweat, intensifying the odors that clung to his shirt. The smell of leather and horseflesh mingled with a lingering whiff of aftershave, then intermixed with his own male scent to form a potent combination.

Her arms around his neck made LaRaine aware of the even rise and fall of his solid chest. The large hand resting at her side encompassed both the curve of her waist and her hip bone, its grip relaxed and unrestrictive. The hand cupping her chin was firm, implying a strength that could snap her like a toothpick. Most of all her sensitive nerve ends were aware of the male length of him, from the sinewy hard columns of his long legs to the muscled brawn of his chest and shoulders—masculinity in its perfect state, virile and powerful.

There was a fluttering weakness in her stomach. For the first time in her life, LaRaine wanted to respond naturally to a man's kiss. It was no longer a part of some scheme to get a man to give her what she wanted. The irregular beat of her heart drummed the discovery into her mind.

This unexpected longing quivered through her.

It was a slight movement, barely discernible, yet Travis must have felt it. For a fraction of a second his mouth was motionless in its possession of hers. Then he was slowly lifting his head and relaxing his hold of her chin. Her long, curling lashes drifted open. Confused disappointment was in her dark eyes for Travis to see, but his shuttered look revealed nothing.

Unwinding her arms from around his neck, he brought them down and held them to make a space between them. Shaken by the sensuous experience, LaRaine lowered her gaze to her hands; her wrists were lost in the loose hold of his gloved hands.

"Are you bored, LaRaine?" His voice taunted. "Looking for fun? Hoping to fool around with a local cowboy to pass the time?"

She drew her wrists free of his hold and turned, taking a step away. That had been her plan. Only now, everything seemed to be turned upside down, but the veiled attack was just what LaRaine needed to regain control of her confused senses.

"I don't know." Her initial response was truthful. "Maybe I am." Over her shoulder she cast him a look filled with coy arrogance. "If I were, what would you say?"

Amusement twitched the corners of his mouth, as if he found something about her challenge humorous. "That there are still men around who prefer to do the chasing."

"Sometimes men are so slow," LaRaine shrugged. "A girl can get tired of waiting for one to catch up with her."

Travis didn't respond to that. Slipping the canteen strap off his arm, he unscrewed the lid. "Do you still want that drink?'' His tone doubted that she had been thirsty in the first place.

"I do, yes." She reached out to take the canteen from his hand.

Tipping her head back, she lifted the canteen to her lips and let the warm water trickle down her throat. While she was drinking, Travis removed his dusty brown hat and hooked it over the horn of her saddle. With his fingers he combed the springing thickness of his black hair and smoothed it into the silver wings at the side.

Finished with the canteen, LaRaine handed it back to him. "This is the first time I've seen you without a hat," she observed. Except for the white at his temples, there wasn't a trace of gray anywhere else in his dark hair. "I was beginning to wonder whether or not you were bald."

His mouth twisted into a half-smile, the canteen poised midway. "Do you always say what's on your mind?"

"Gee, I thought that men liked honest women." She studied the hand holding the canteen. It was covered with a work-worn leather glove, but it didn't disguise its size. She wondered what it would be like to be caressed by his hands, whether they could arouse her in that same strange, new way that his kiss had.

"Who told you that?" Travis had taken his drink and was recapping the canteen.

LaRaine shrugged. "It's something I learned through personal experience and observation. I don't know if it's really true. But I do know that I'm never ignored."

"As long as you don't forget that a little goes a long way." He put his hat back on, pulling the brim down low in front. Walking to the palomino's head, he took hold of the bridle and glanced at LaRaine. "Are you ready to move on?"

"I guess so," she agreed, and walked over to mount her horse.

His hand gripped her elbow to help her aboard. Then Travis was passing her the reins and walking over to mount his buckskin. He whistled to the dog lying alertly on the ground near the grazing cattle. Within seconds the rider and dog had the cattle moving.

"Where are you taking them?" LaRaine questioned.

"To the corral by the barn. Sam decided it would be more feasible to use my livestock than pay another rancher to bring his in," he explained.

"He needs more than these, doesn't he?" Making a rough count, LaRaine doubted if there were two more than a dozen.

"Blue and I will drive these in and get another bunch." His gaze swung from the small herd to her. "Why aren't you working? Aren't they filming today?"

"Yes, but I'm not in any of the scenes we're shooting. My part isn't very large." Which was putting it mildly.

"Are you waiting to be discovered?" he inquired lazily.

"I've already been discovered." LaRaine found herself answering his question with unusual honesty. "The trouble is that the same time they discovered me, they found out I wasn't another Julia Roberts. I can't act my way out of a paper bag."

"How did you get this part?"

"Through Sam," she admitted. "He used his influence to get it for me."

"Because he loved you," Travis stated dryly.

She faced him, her chin held high in defiant challenge, pride stamped in her features. "Yes, because he loved me. It sounds like a dirty trick, doesn't it? But I needed a job—I needed it desperately. I never lied to Sam, though. I never told him I loved him or promised him anything." She couldn't tell what he was thinking. His expression was masked. She looked straight ahead. "I always dreamed of being famous. When I was offered my first movie role, I grabbed at it. Because of that, my fiancé broke our engagement and ultimately married my cousin. Now I'm just hanging on. I'll probably never be famous, but so what?"

"What will you do when this movie is over?"

"Find a rich man and marry him." After she had said it, LaRaine laughed. Her dark eyes danced with mischief when she glanced at Travis. "If you'd been rich, I would have married you."

"Why are you telling me this? Don't be too honest." There was amusement in the look he returned to her.

"No." She considered her answer before she gave it. "There are some men that you can't hide things from. They find out anyway. I think you're one of them. If I didn't tell you, you'd guess. You might as well know where I stand."

"I see," he murmured noncommittally.

"Do you? Good, because there's a party next week that some of the cast and crew are having. I'd like you to come with me," she invited.

"No." His tone was curt.

"Oh." She let out her breath in a sigh. "I have a problem, then."

"What's that?" Travis eyed her warily.

"I've already told everybody that you're taking me," she admitted without a hint of regret.

Travis chuckled in disbelief. "What is this? Are you trying to trap me into taking you so you won't be caught lying?"

"It's more a case of putting my foot in my mouth. It's a recurring thing with me. So will you help me out?" LaRaine knew it was an audacious tactic, but she sensed that boldness was the only thing Travis would appreciate.

The ranch buildings were in sight. Travis reined in his horse and whistled a signal to the dog. When the cattle had stopped moving, he looked across his shoulder at LaRaine. She waited as his inscrutable gaze skimmed her face.

"Seems like I've always been easy prey for women who are in trouble and need help," he said at last.

Somehow, LaRaine had the feeling his thoughts weren't on her. He was thinking about Natalie, whoever she was. She thought she caught a glimmer of pain in his faraway look.

"Then you'll take me to the party?" she breathed out the question.

"Yes, but don't try to use me, LaRaine. You won't get away with it," he warned.

"Good." LaRaine bit at her lower lip to contain her bursting triumph. "I'd better be getting back. Technically, I'm not supposed to be riding this horse." She told him which day it was and what time he could pick her up and where.

With a wave of her hand she started toward the dirt road beyond the ranch buildings. Travis left the herd with the dog and rode to open the corral gate. Before she was out of sight, LaRaine saw the horse and rider and dog driving the cattle into the enclosure.

CHAPTER FIVE

The meeting with Travis had surpassed her wildest expectations. Outside of those unsettling moments of his kiss, she had controlled everything. Travis had not proved as formidable as she had thought he might, but he hadn't attempted to match wits with her, either.

Don't underestimate him, LaRaine told herself. She ran her fingers over her lips, remembering how his mouth had felt when it had explored them. How seductively he had mastered her and made her respond differently physically than she had with any other man. In many ways, Travis was still an unknown element. She had to feel her way.

The palomino quickened its pace as it crested the hill and saw the horse van ahead and the other horses. LaRaine didn't try to hold him back, letting him canter in. She was in such a good mood that when she saw Sam walking forward to meet her, she waved and smiled. He didn't return it. In fact, when she stopped her horse near him, Sam was glowering.

"I might have known you were out riding," he accused.

"What's the matter, Sam? Were you worried about me?" she joked, and swung lightly out of the saddle.

"No, I wasn't worried about you," Sam said. "I wouldn't waste my time that way."

LaRaine laughed, a throaty, practiced sound. "You sound angry about something, Sam. What is it?" She stroked the palomino's neck, patting its sleek coat, only faintly warm from the ride.

"I'll tell you what it is," he began, only to be interrupted by a strident male voice issuing a demand.

"Where have you been, Ms. Evans?"

Turning, LaRaine saw the director puffing toward her. His jowly face was livid with rage. She was sure he was going to burst a blood vessel in his neck any minute.

"I went for a ride, Mr. Behr." Her tone was respectful, not mocking him the way she did Sam. The cast and crew called the director Andy Pandy behind his back, but never to his face.

"Who gave you permission to take that horse?" he demanded.

"No one. I wanted to go riding, so I checked to see which horse wasn't being used today and took him." LaRaine didn't say it had been the remuda boss who had given her that information.

"It so happens we rewrote the scene and needed that horse. Only you'd taken it!" the director accused angrily. "Without asking anybody! Without telling anybody where you were going or when you'd be back!"

Obviously Don, the remuda boss, hadn't told him that he'd saddled the palomino for her. If she expected him to do any more favors for her, LaRaine knew that she didn't dare tell the director otherwise.

"No, I'm sorry. I didn't," she lied, and remained calm and cool in the face of his anger

"You're sorry!" he exploded. "You're not only a lousy actress, you're a disruptive influence as well. You pull another stunt like this and you'll find out what sorry means!" He flashed a look at Sam and snapped an order, "Bring that horse, Hardesty."

Turning on his heel, he puffed his way back toward the area where the cameras were set up. Sam watched him go, his mouth open in empty protest. LaRaine smiled, knowing how much Sam hated any animal bigger than an alley cat.

"Here, Sam." She offered him the reins to lead the palomino.

He closed his mouth and turned around, eyeing her coldly. "He means it, LaRaine. Cross him one more time and you'll regret it."

"If that happens, don't worry, Sam. I'll make sure he doesn't blame you for getting me this part," LaRaine said with false indifference.

While he seethed impotently, she pressed the reins into his hand and walked away. She knew she was walking a fine line with the director. Twice now she had been indirectly responsible for upsetting his schedule, once when she had gone with Sam to the McCrea ranch and this time.

Andrew Behr was the kind of man who tolerated no excuses, however legitimate or justified they were. LaRaine had to be extra careful from now on. She couldn't risk the humiliation of being thrown off the set.

Soberly, LaRaine walked away. She wasn't in the mood to hang around the film set. She didn't want to risk accidentally incurring the director's wrath again by being underfoot in the wrong place. She saw Susan off to one side in costume and makeup. Fixing an uncaring expression on her face, she walked over to the girl.

"Hi, Susan. May I borrow your car? I thought I'd go back to the motel. You can catch a ride with somebody when you're through, can't you?" she reasoned. LaRaine's own car had been sold several months ago because she'd needed the money more than the transportation.

"What's the matter? Are you afraid Andy Pandy might bite instead of snarl if you stay around here?" Susan guessed accurately.

"Andy is a pussycat if you know how to handle him," LaRaine lied. "It's too boring around here, that's all."

"My keys are in my bag over in Makeup. Tell Anna I said it was okay for you to take them," Susan gave in.

LaRaine drove the battered VW Jetta back to the hotel. It was hardly luxury transportation, but under the circumstances, LaRaine was grateful for it.

There was mail waiting for her when she stopped at the desk. She leafed through it as she walked to her room—mostly bills and her bank statement. In her room, she opened the statement first. There was a slip inside, informing LaRaine that her account was overdrawn.

Sighing, she stared at the notice, then picked up the telephone on the stand beside the bed. LaRaine dialed slowly and placed a long-distance collect call to her agent. She heard the ring of impatience in his voice when he accepted the charges.

"Hi, Peter. It's LaRaine," she identified herself unnecessarily. She forced herself to sound cheerful. Not more than two hours ago after leaving Travis, she had been flushed with victory, but her money problems put an end to her good mood. "How's the weather?"

"Smoggy. I hope you didn't phone me to discuss the weather, LaRaine," he sighed.

"Business, business, business—that's all you think about, Peter," LaRaine laughed, but it sounded hollow in her ears.

"Please get to the point. I'm busy," he said wearily.

"Of course I didn't call to talk about the weather," she said. He wasn't making this easy. "I have a slight problem."

"Let me guess," her agent said dryly. "You need money, don't you?"

She swallowed hard, but spoke calmly enough. "Not very much," she admitted.

"How much is not very much?" he demanded.

"My bank account is overdrawn. If you could advance me a couple of thousand dollars—"

"Two thousand!" He held back his temper with an effort. "I just gave you money before you left Los Angeles. How could you possibly have spent all of it? What do you do? Give it away?"

LaRaine dropped all pretense of blithe unconcern.

"I didn't call to hear you lecture me about money. Can you advance me the money or not?" If he didn't, she didn't have the slightest idea where she would get it.

"Hey, if I do, consider the money you're getting for this movie already spent. You won't have any more coming."

"Yes, I realize that," she admitted curtly.

"Okay, I'll transfer the money into your account, but don't ask me for another cent," Peter warned.

"But darling," she stressed the endearment with cloying sweetness, "you are my agent. Who else would I call?"

"Don't remind me." The line went dead as he hung up.

Biting her lip, she stared at the phone before finally placing it back in its cradle. She glanced at the bank statement with its overdrawn notice and the bills scattered on the bed. The money wouldn't last very long. Peter was right; she really should be more careful with her money. But she'd never had to pay attention to prices and budgets. They were completely alien to her.

"You just can't teach an old dog new tricks," LaRaine sighed aloud. "I've got to marry someone with money. And soon!"

With the crisis weathered, it was only a few days before she forgot all about it. Her financial straits crossed her mind fleetingly once when she bought a new dress for the party. She rationalized the purchase by convincing herself it might be the last new dress she could afford for a long time.

It was a beautiful red, with a scooped neckline and long sleeves. The material was featherlight, softly draping her figure. The scarlet hue was the perfect color to set off her brunette hair and flashing dark eyes. LaRaine applied a matching shade of red lipstick to her mouth with a tiny brush, carefully outlining the curves and then filling them in.

There was a knock at her door. LaRaine set the lip brush down and went to answer it. Travis stood in the hallway. Wearing a suede jacket that molded the breadth of his shoulders and tapered to his waist, he looked casual and ruggedly handsome.

"I'll be ready in a minute." LaRaine stepped out of the doorway. "Come in and sit down."

His dark gaze skimmed her from head to toe once, then twice. "You look fine."

"Give me a few minutes and I'll look better," she promised. She liked the way the dress swirled silently around her legs as she turned to walk back to the vanity mirror. "I'm sorry the accommodations don't include an in-room bar or I'd offer you a drink while you're waiting."

"That's all right."

Instead of sitting on the lone chair in the room, Travis followed her to the mirror. Unbuttoning his jacket, he slipped his hands into the pockets of his pants and leaned a shoulder against the wall to watch her.

Usually LaRaine didn't mind people watching her, including men, but Travis's study made her uneasy. With the red carefully applied to her lips, she powdered them, blotted that off with a damp cosmetic sponge and added gloss. Her hand trembled slightly as she penciled short, feathery lines to increase the fullness of her naturally arching eyebrows.

She was grateful she had already applied her makeup base and the various makeup coloring sticks to contour her face. A subtle blend of three eyeshadows covered her lids as well as a discreet amount of charcoal eyeliner. A few coats of mascara made her lashes longer and thicker than normal. She had spent almost an hour on her hair. If Travis had watched her doing that, she doubted that she would have achieved this perfect effect.

Before she was completely satisfied, LaRaine added a touch more blush to her cheekbones. She studied the result in the mirror, then glanced at Travis.

"How do I look?" she asked, knowing the answer couldn't be anything but positive.

A slow smile spread across his strong mouth. "Fine." Which was the same thing he had said before.

There was something about his expression that LaRaine didn't like. "Why are you smiling?" It was a half-demanding and half-laughing question.

"I was trying to decide whether I was looking at a little girl playing grown-up with her mommy's lipstick or a grown woman hiding from the world behind a painted mask." Travis continued to watch her reaction with lazy interest.

His answer made LaRaine study her reflection in the mirror. It implied that something was wrong. But she couldn't see where she had been heavy-handed with the makeup.

"What's wrong?" Her dark eyes were wide and confused. "Don't you think I look beautiful?"

"Yes, you look beautiful." Travis agreed on one hand, and took it back with the other. "Like a photo of some fashion model. So perfect that you don't look real. Everybody else has moles while models have beauty marks."

LaRaine was irritated. "Isn't that just like a man?" she said to no one. "I spend hours getting ready, styling my hair and putting on my makeup just to look beautiful to you. And what's your reaction? You accuse me of not looking real or being a little girl playing with lipstick."

"Why did you leave out a woman hiding behind a painted mask?" he asked, alertly catching her omission. "Do you wear all that makeup so people can't see how scared you are inside?"

LaRaine pushed away from the table. "Oh, please! I've never heard anything so ridiculous in my life! I wear makeup for the same reason that every other woman does—because I want to look good." Rising to her feet, she walked to the door and paused when Travis didn't follow her. "Are you ready to go?" she demanded impatiently.

Travis straightened from the wall. "I thought you might want to wait a little longer before you make your entrance at the party."

"In another minute I might change my mind and decide not to go at all." The fuse of her temper was sparking with fire.

"We can't have that happen." With long, easy strides, Travis crossed the room to open the door for her. "If we didn't show up, everyone might think you were lying when you said I was bringing you to the party."

It was an unwelcome reminder of the ploy she'd used to obtain his agreement. LaRaine pressed her lips tightly closed, not making any reply to his mocking words. His hand was at her back to guide her down the hallway to the hotel exit. The body heat emanating from his touch seemed to burn through the thin material of her dress. She was rigidly conscious of his brawny frame, tall and rugged, shortening his strides to match hers. She felt small, and not just because his height emphasized her petite build.

How had this happened? she asked herself as he walked her into the parking lot. She had handled him so easily the other day when they'd been riding. Everything had gone so well. Why was he taunting her now, saying all those things about her?

When they approached the entrance to the private hall that had been rented for the party, she felt Travis looking at her, but she wouldn't glance at him. She would show him. No one treated her like that and got away with it.

"Are you going to pout all night?" his low voice asked, making her suddenly self-conscious of her lower lip. So she was sulking. So what?

"I'm not pouting," she retorted.

"I hurt your feelings, didn't I?" His question mixed curiosity and amusement.

"Nothing you could say could possibly hurt my feelings," LaRaine flashed, striking back by emphasizing how unimportant she considered him to be.

His mouth curved in a complacent smile that mocked her words as Travis reached in front of her to open the door. LaRaine fumed silently, but this was not the time to be trading angry words.

Inside the party was in full swing. The music from a sound system blared through the long room; its pulsing beat filled the air.

As partyers glanced around to see who had arrived, LaRaine linked her arm with Travis's and smiled as if she hadn't a care in the world. She guessed how hypocritical he would think she was when, not two seconds ago, she had been snapping at him.

They made their way across the room toward the makeshift bar in the corner, with LaRaine laughing and calling out greetings. She knew what she was doing. She was showing off, making certain everyone saw her with Travis. Happy and bubbling, she clung to his arm, laughing up at him but avoiding direct eye contact.

There was a cluster of people at the bar. Most of them already had drinks in their hands and were just standing around talking.

"What would you like to drink?" Travis asked.

"Whatever you're having, honey," LaRaine answered, loud enough for everyone to hear.

Travis turned to one of the crew who was acting as bartender and ordered, "Two beers."

A cast member was leaning against the bar. When he heard the subsequent order, he hooted, "Beer! I thought you never drank anything but Cosmopolitans, LaRaine." He laughed and everyone around joined in.

She hated beer. "Whoever told you that, Mike?" She laughed in denial, and lied, "I like beer."

"If you wanted something else, you should have asked for it," Travis told her quietly, a cool challenge in his look as he pressed a cold bottle of beer in her gesturing hand.

"This is fine," she insisted with false brightness, and tried not to gag when she took a sip from the bottle.

It was disgusting; she knew she would never be able to drink it all. She had to find a diversion. A new rock tune began to play. LaRaine set the bottle on the bar and reached for Travis's hand.

"Let's dance," she urged.

"No, I don't dance," he refused.

"It's easy. I'll teach you." Tipping her head to one side, she looked up at him through the alluring sweep of her long lashes and gave him a coaxing smile.

"No." He was unmoved by her charming attempt at persuasion. "If you want to dance, you'll have to find someone else."

His indifference to the embarrassment he was causing her by rejecting her invitation in front of everyone surprised her, an emotion that was quickly replaced by anger.

"Do you think I can't?" she hissed so only he could hear. His dark brows arched briefly in unconcern. She whirled away from him, her skirt billowing like a shimmering red cloud. She tapped the shoulder of the nearest man. "Dance with me, Mike," she ordered, and took the drink from his hand, setting it beside hers on the bar.

He was trying to protest as she led him to a cleared area of the room where there were others dancing. Once there he gave in and began moving with the driving rhythm. LaRaine cast a smug look in Travis's direction, but he wasn't paying any attention to her. Angered again, she centered all her interest on her dancing partner, smiling and flirting with him outrageously in revenge.

When the song ended, Mike pleaded exhaustion. LaRaine started to walk back to the bar with him. The sight of Travis, his dark head bent attentively toward the tall blonde from Wardrobe, made her change direction. She snared another unattached male cast member and dragged him onto the dance floor for the next song.

After that song he was still with the blonde. They had been joined by Susan, another girl from Wardrobe, and one of the stunt men. LaRaine found another partner, and so it went. She kept waiting for Travis to claim her in between dances, but it was as if he had forgotten all about her, as if she never existed and he had never brought her to the party at all. Beneath her raging anger she was close to tears.

Her fury got her through three more dances. LaRaine kept looking to see where Travis was or whom he was with, unable to ignore him the same way he was ignoring her. Finally she ran out of partners and was forced to leave the floor. She glanced around the room for Travis, intending to boast about how much fun she was having and let him know he hadn't hurt her feelings at all.

There was no sign of him in her first sweep of the room. LaRaine looked again, wondering how she had missed him. Travis was so tall that she had been able to spot him instantly all the previous times. A tiny frown creased her forehead when her second search was equally unsuccessful.

Working her way around the crowded room, LaRaine continued to look for him. A painful suspicion was beginning to form in her mind. Then she saw Susan talking to the tall blonde Travis had been with earlier. If he hadn't gone somewhere with either of them, where was he? Her frown of uncertainty deepened.

"Looking for someone?" Sam Hardesty was at her elbow.

LaRaine erased the frown from her expression and forced a bright smile. "Travis. Have you seen him?"

"He's gone home, back to the ranch," he told her, swaying unsteadily and lifting the drink in his hand to his mouth.

She laughed off his answer. "Oh, stop trying to be funny, Sam. Have you seen him or not?"

"I'm not joking, LaRaine." He shook his head and smiled, taking delight in the frozen look stealing over her face. "He said to tell you he'd had enough."

"Do you mean he just walked out and left me here?" she demanded. Humiliation burned through her veins, reddening her face. "He can't do that!"

"He did. He's gone." Sam continued to smile with satisfaction. "Look around for yourself. You've already done that, though, haven't you?" he mocked.

LaRaine was trembling with fury. "He isn't going to get away with this!"

Her teeth were clenched to keep her chin from quivering. "Let me borrow your car, Sam." When he hesitated, she added a taut, "Please."

"Sure." Sam fumbled through his pocket and handed her the keys. "It's the burgundy Lexus parked at the corner."

Just for a second LaRaine let herself be sidetracked by his announcement. "Lexus?" He'd been driving a Camry the last she knew.

"Yeah, brand new." There was an unnatural glitter in his eyes. "Maybe you shouldn't have been so quick to turn me down."

She hesitated, then replied, "If you had a million dollars, it wouldn't change a thing."

She suspected that she just might be telling the truth. In more rational moments it might have been a shocking discovery, but right now she was too obsessed with going after Travis.

CHAPTER SIX

The powerful car sped out of town onto the main highway. A full moon illuminated the rough countryside with silver light. LaRaine's foot was heavy on the accelerator as she raced the car through the night. She almost missed the unmarked gate and the dirt road leading back to the ranchyard.

Making the turn, she drove as fast as she dared over the winding track. On a curve, her headlight beams briefly caught the glowing eyes of a wild animal before it slunk away into the darkness. It didn't really scare her. Her only thought was of Travis and the things she intended to say to him.

It seemed to take forever before she crested the rise and saw the dark outlines of the ranch buildings silhouetted against the moonlit sky. There was a light on in the house. LaRaine stepped on the gas to speed over the last hundred yards. The tires skidded and slipped as she braked to a halt in front of the house.

A dog came racing out of the barn to bark at the intruder. LaRaine ignored it as she stormed out of the car and onto the porch. Not bothering to knock, she jerked open the door and sailed into the house. Travis was halfway across the living room, wearing the same clothes. His cream shirt was completely unbuttoned and hanging open. He stopped cold at the sight of LaRaine sweeping toward him.

"How dare you!" She confronted him, her hands doubled into fists held rigidly at her side. "How dare you walk out and leave me! Nobody treats me like that!"

"Maybe it was time somebody did." Travis didn't raise his voice to meet the angry pitch of hers, but kept it calm and cool.

Her hand lashed out to strike at his cheek. With lightning reflexes, Travis caught her wrist, his strong fingers completely circling its slenderness. LaRaine strained to pull her wrist free of his hold, but it was no use.

"I was never so humiliated in all my life!" she stormed. "I had to find out from Sam that you'd left—you didn't even tell me yourself."

"I warned you that I wouldn't be used." His eyes narrowed into coal-black slits. "You asked me to take you to that party to save your precious pride. I did. Five minutes after we walked through the door, you went off on your own to have fun with your friends."

"You weren't exactly bored while I was gone," LaRaine accused. "I saw you talking to Karen, from

Wardrobe, and Susan. You weren't interested in where I was or what I was doing.''

"Did you expect me to go off in a corner alone because you weren't with me?'' The sardonic line of his mouth quirked to show her how ludicrous that thought was.

"I didn't expect you to go off and leave me there by myself!'' she snapped. "I thought you were a gentleman. Obviously I was wrong.''

"It's funny you should make that mistake.'' There was a hard glitter of amusement in his look. "I guessed all along that you weren't a lady.''

Stung by his insult, LaRaine raised her free hand, nails curled to claw at his face. It was as easily captured as the first. When she attempted to struggle, she was hauled roughly against his chest, her arms twisted behind her back to make her a helpless captive. Her raven-black hair swung about her shoulders as she tipped her head back to glare at him.

"You dirty rotten b—''

His mouth crushed down on her lips, making her swallow the curses she longed to hurl at him. With his shirt opened, she was arched against his bare chest. His fiery body heat seemed to burn right through the thin material to envelop her in its blazing warmth.

Smothered, LaRaine couldn't seem to catch her breath. Everything seemed to be reeling. The force of his kiss overwhelmed her. She had been drawn into the vortex of his anger, and realized that she wasn't all that eager to escape his arms.

A series of thudding sounds penetrated her consciousness. At first LaRaine thought it was the drumming of her heart. When a knock rattled the screen door, she realized what she had heard were footsteps on the wooden floor of the porch. His mouth ended its crushing possession of hers as her arms were untwisted from behind her back, but Travis kept hold of her. His expressionless face was turned toward the door. LaRaine took a shaky breath and tried to fight free of the haze that enveloped her senses.

The screen door rattled again. "Travis?" a young male voice called. "Is there anything wrong? I heard the car and—"

"Nothing's wrong, Joe," Travis answered.

LaRaine was amazed at how quickly he controlled his anger. Of course, the unexpected kiss had driven out her own anger, so maybe it had done the same for him, providing a release.

The man on the porch hesitated and then there was the thud of footsteps on the boards. LaRaine's pulse had still not settled down to its normal rate when the footsteps could no longer be heard. She stared at Travis's chest, not ready yet to meet his gaze.

"Who was that?" she murmured.

"My hired hand."

"Where was he?" It seemed easier to talk about him.

"He sleeps in the shed," Travis answered.

"In the shed? That broken-down old building near the barn?" LaRaine couldn't believe it was the one he meant.

"It's sturdier than it looks," he informed her dryly. He turned her around and pointed her toward the door.

"What are you doing?" she protested.

"You're leaving," Travis said, and marched her to the door.

"What if I'm not ready to go?" LaRaine pulled back.

"This happens to be my home," he reminded her. Opening the door, he pushed her onto the porch. "I didn't invite you here. You just barged in."

"And now you're telling me to get out," she concluded tightly. His hand on her elbow kept her from tripping down in the porch steps.

"You could put it that way," Travis agreed, and walked her to the car as if he wanted to make certain she left.

"Why don't you ride with me as far as the highway?" LaRaine said sarcastically. "That way you can make sure that I'm off your property."

He opened the car door and pushed her inside behind the wheel. Holding the door open, he looked down at the rebellion flashing in her eyes.

"You're a spoiled, selfish brat," he said flatly. "You want everything your way and you don't care who you hurt getting it. Life doesn't work that way, and it's time you learned that. I hope tonight was the first of many lessons."

He slammed the door shut without giving her a chance to respond to his accusations. LaRaine shivered at the freezing scorn that had been in his voice. Tears burned her eyes, but she kept them at bay as she turned the ignition key. The front fender of the luxury car narrowly missed grazing Travis as she made a sharp turn to take the dirt road back to the highway. Once she left him behind, tears streamed down her cheeks. She kept wiping them away, but it only seemed to make room for more.

She drove recklessly back to town, speeding, half blinded by tears. She kept telling herself that she didn't know why she was crying and that she didn't care about his opinion of her.

The parking space on the corner was still empty, although LaRaine noticed that the space right behind it was occupied by a highway patrol car. She sniffed and wiped the tears from her face one last time as she carefully parked the Lexus in the same spot she had taken it from. The last person she wanted to face was Sam, so she left the keys under the floor mat rather than give them back to him in person.

As she climbed out of the car, she noticed that the patrolman behind her did also. She was certain she hadn't done anything illegal. She ignored him and started to walk to the hotel.

"Wait a minute, miss." It was unmistakably an order.

She hesitated, then stopped. After all that crying, she probably looked a mess, but there was nothing she could do about repairing her makeup now. Gathering all her poise, she turned.

"What is it, Officer?" she demanded.

A rotund man was puffing after the approaching patrolman. When he recognized LaRaine, he stopped short beneath a streetlight and his face turned a blotchy red.

"You!" he sputtered finally. "You're the one who stole my car?"

"Your car?" LaRaine repeated, staring at the director with a sinking heart. "But I thou—"

"Do you know this woman?" the officer asked Andrew Behr.

"Unfortunately, yes," he said as he expelled an angry sigh. "She's an actress, a lousy actress."

Her feet seemed to be rooted to the pavement. It hadn't been Sam's car. It belonged to the director, yet Sam had let her believe it was his. He had given her the keys. Now she was being accused of stealing it.

"You weren't aware that she'd taken your car?" the uniformed officer questioned.

"No," the director denied, glaring at her. "I came out here to get in my car and it was gone. If she took it, it was without my permission."

"But—" LaRaine began weakly, only to be drowned out by the patrolman.

"Did you leave your keys in the car?"

"I told you I don't remember," Andrew Behr answered impatiently. "I might have."

Light flashed from the building behind the two men as a door was opened and closed. LaRaine noticed a man standing in the shadows of the overhang. It took her a second to recognize Sam. She took a step forward to ask him to explain to the officer and the director that he had loaned her the car. Then she realized that he would deny it. He had done it deliberately, hoping to get her into trouble. He had succeeded.

"Do you intend to press charges against her?" the patrolman asked. "You do have the car back. There doesn't seem to be any damage to it."

LaRaine spoke up in her own defense. "I didn't steal the car—I borrowed it."

The director paused before answering. He seemed to do it deliberately to let LaRaine dangle over the heat of the fire, hoping she would cry out for mercy.

"No," he said finally, his voice ominously low. "I won't press charges. I'll handle this my own way. Sorry to bother you."

"That's what I'm paid for." The patrolman touched his hat in a one-fingered salute before returning to his black-and-white.

Andrew Behr walked to the middle of the street where LaRaine stood. She offered no apologies or explanations; she knew she would be wasting her breath. When he reached her side, they walked in unison to the sidewalk.

"Want me to spell it out?" he asked when they stopped at the other side.

"Go ahead," LaRaine answered brazenly. "If nothing else, then just to make it official."

"You're through, finished!" he snapped. "I don't want to see you or hear from you again. I want you packed and gone in the morning."

"By morning?" she smiled sweetly. "I'm surprised you're giving me that long."

"Keep that up and I might change my mind," he threatened.

"Excuse me." LaRaine kept her saccharine smile in place. "I have a lot of packing to do."

Turning her back on the man, she walked to the hotel, not stopping until she reached her room. She walked to the vanity table and sank into the chair. Staring at her reflection in the mirror, she noticed that other than her mascara being smudged, her face looked okay. Numbly she set about repairing the slight damage.

Halfway through, she began laughing. The world had fallen in around her head and she was fixing her makeup. She realized she was on the verge of hysteria and sobered. What was she going to do?

She walked to where she had left her purse and counted out her money. She sank onto the bed in quiet shock. Where had it all gone? There was barely twenty dollars in her billfold. Most of it had gone to pay bills and cover her overdrawn account, she realized. The rest she had squandered on the dress she was wearing. She remembered her agent's lecture and wished she had listened for once.

Hope flickered briefly. Maybe Peter would loan her some more money. No—LaRaine shook her head. The minute he learned she had been fired, he would probably wash his hands of her. Her parents? She'd had a postcard from them a week ago. They were vacationing somewhere, a long ocean cruise, LaRaine thought, but she couldn't remember where and she'd thrown the card away.

There was a knock at her door. LaRaine ignored it, hoping whoever it was would go away. But the knocking persisted. She scooped up the contents of her purse and dumped them back in the bag. After running a smoothing hand over the midnight black of her hair, she walked to the door and opened it.

Sam was leaning against the doorjamb, a knowing smile on his face. "Hi, LaRaine. I thought I might find you here."

His voice was a little slurred, but he looked more sober than he had at the party. For a minute La-Raine toyed with the idea of asking him for help, but something in his expression told her that was what he was waiting for. He wanted revenge, wanted to turn her down, the way she had rejected him. She wouldn't give him the satisfaction.

"What do you want, Sam?" she demanded instead.

"The old man kicked you out, didn't he?" His mouth twisted into a cruel smile.

"If you want to gloat, you're wasting your time." LaRaine walked away from the door. "I've had it with this place. I'm glad I don't have to stay around here any longer."

He followed her into the room and closed the door. "You wanted the job bad enough a couple of months ago," he reminded her.

"Things change. People change." She shrugged. "Look at you—good, kind, sweet Sam. This was all your doing. You set me up deliberately. You gave me the keys, let me believe it was your car, and probably told Behr it was gone."

"I did warn you not to cross him," Sam told her.

"Then you made sure that I did, didn't you?" LaRaine asked.

"I guess I did," he admitted.

"I know you regret helping me get this job," she said. "But I would have had a lot more respect for you, Sam, if you'd had the guts to fire me yourself instead of tricking someone else into doing the dirty work for you. You've just given me one more reason why I'm glad I never agreed to marry you."

"Is that right?" He seemed utterly untroubled by her harsh words.

"Yes, that's right." Spinning on her heel, LaRaine walked to the vanity table where she picked up a brush and began running it through her hair.

"So you think it was a mean, dirty trick I played on you?" Sam asked.

Her hair crackled with electricity. LaRaine felt charged by it, too. "It was," she snapped.

"You've done it all your life," he accused. "You tricked your cousin into impersonating you so you could make your first movie without Montgomery ever discovering it. Later I heard about the way you tried to trick Jake Chasen's girlfriend into believing that you and Chasen were having an affair. You've tricked others, more successfully. I was one of them."

"You're a sore loser, Sam." LaRaine set the brush down and fluffed her raven hair with her fingers, pretending a total indifference to his words.

"No, I'm a wise one. And I just hope that after tonight you know what it's like to be a victim of a dirty trick. It's a painful experience to go sailing along and have someone pull the rug out from underneath you when you're not looking."

Her pale complexion grew whiter as Sam explained his motivation. He knew just how far and how hard he'd brought her down, because he knew how badly she had needed this job. He studied her stricken look with satisfaction.

"I hope it hurts, LaRaine," he said. "You've always wanted to believe that you belonged on a pedestal. Well, you don't." He walked to the door, opened it and paused. "I won't wish you good luck. I'll save it for the next poor sucker you latch on to."

With the closing of the door, something inside LaRaine crumpled. She stared after him for several minutes. Then mechanically, she began undressing and changing into her nightgown. Crawling into bed, she stared at the ceiling. Sam's words kept mixing with what Travis had told her—that he hoped tonight would be the first of many lessons. It was a long, long time before she slept.

A knock on her door wakened her the next morning. LaRaine didn't want to wake up, preferring the oblivion of sleep to the problems she faced. She pulled the pillow over her head to try to shut out the persistent knocking.

Finally, groggy from sleep that had brought her no rest, she climbed out of bed and tugged on her robe. Not bothering to tie it closed, she held it shut with her hand. She walked to the door and opened it a crack to look bleary-eyed at the desk manager of the hotel.

"Heard you're leaving this morning," he said. "I wondered what time you intend to vacate the room."

LaRaine ran a hand across her eyes and tried to think. If she left, where would she go? But she had to leave. Even disregarding Andrew Behr's orders for her to be packed and gone, she didn't have the money to pay for a hotel room.

"I . . . I haven't packed yet," she stalled. Which was true. "As a matter of fact, you just woke me up."

The manager didn't apologize for that. LaRaine could well imagine what the director had probably told the man about her. She didn't have a chance of appealing to the manager to let her stay another day.

"Twelve noon should give you enough time to pack your things," he told her.

"Noon, yes, that will be fine." She smiled wanly. What else could she say?

The man nodded curtly and turned to walk down the hallway toward the lobby. LaRaine closed the door and leaned her shoulder against it. The room was a mess, clothes scattered everywhere. And she was supposed to pack and be out by noon.

Sighing heavily, she walked to the bathroom. First things first. She would shower, get dressed, put on her makeup, then pack. If she were a few minutes late, then it was just their tough luck.

The shower did her a world of good. She felt refreshed, more able to battle whatever was to come. Going through her crowded closet, she selected her outfit with care—a faded pair of tight jeans and a yellow knit T-shirt. It was simple, down to earth, and exactly the image she wanted to portray.

Next came the makeup. The base and contouring color sticks were standard routine. But LaRaine used less eyeshadow and chose a tawny combination of shades with a light brown eyeliner. The mascara, too, she was careful not to overdo. Instead of red lipstick, she applied a more natural color that tinted her lips. Brushing her raven hair until it shone, she let it swing free about her shoulders, its style loose and casual.

The hard part was next—packing. The closet was jammed with clothes and so was the dresser. Outside of weekend trips, LaRaine had never done any major packing in her life. There had always been someone else to do it—a maid or her mother or her cousin.

Dragging the suitcases out of the closet, she opened them on the bed. Without following any natural order, she began folding garments and putting them in. She ran out of room before she ran out of clothes. Her brief attempt at neatness was abandoned as she began cramming clothes and cosmetics into any and every available hole.

Closing and locking them became the next problem, solved when she sat on them. It took all her strength to drag the bigger cases off the bed and set them on the floor. Normally LaRaine would have called to have a bellhop carry her luggage to the lobby, but that would mean tipping. The few dollars she had could be better spent on other things.

It took her three trips before all her luggage was sitting in the hotel lobby. Her arms ached with the effort. She glanced at the clock above the desk. It was half past eleven. She had made the deadline, she thought triumphantly.

The manager was looking at the computer screen behind the counter. LaRaine walked to it and dropped her key on the top. He turned at the sound. His gaze flicked past her to the suitcases she had piled near the door.

"All packed, I see," he commented.

"Yes," she nodded. "I was wondering if you knew someone I could hire to drive me where I want to go."

"How far were you going?" he questioned. "The bus stop is just a few blocks—"

"I'm not going to the bus station," LaRaine informed him. She didn't have the price of a ticket to Los Angeles.

"Where, then?" he frowned.

There was only one place she could go and one person who might help her. None of the cast or crew would assist her. LaRaine knew that without asking. Once she would have believed that Sam might have, but after last night she knew better.

"The McCrea ranch, outside of town," she answered.

CHAPTER SEVEN

Laraine held on tightly as the old pickup truck bounced over the dirt road to the ranch. She was afraid to look through the back window at her expensive leather suitcases sliding from side to side in the rusty bed of the truck. The crusty old man behind the wheel seemed to have a death wish, considering the speed he was driving at. It was no wonder the springs no longer could absorb the shock of the ruts and chuckholes. It was a worse ride than the one Sam had made over the same road.

As they crested the rise and the ranch buildings came into sight clustered on the mesa, LaRaine almost sighed aloud in relief that they had made it in one piece. The man hadn't said two words to her the entire trip. Not that she particularly wanted to talk, or even think.

"Don't look like no one's home," the old man

observed as the truck hiccuped to a stop in front of the house.

"That's all right. I'll wait," LaRaine told him, and climbed shakily out of the cab of the truck.

The door didn't want to close. "I'll get that. There's a trick to it," he informed her, and walked over to kick the door shut with his boot.

"The trick is sheer brute force." LaRaine shrugged.

"But only if you kick it in the right place." Moving the rear of the truck, he began dragging her suitcases to the tailgate.

"Please be careful!" She winced at the treatment he was giving them. There were already scratches on the sides. But he paid no more attention to her now than when he had loaded them in the truck. He stacked them on the ground.

When they were all out, he turned to her and held out his hand. "We agreed on five dollars."

"Yes." She opened up her purse and took out the bill. "Thank you." She gave it to him.

"You're welcome." He tipped his hat and walked back to the truck.

It backfired as he reversed up the dirt road. The chickens scratching in the yard scattered in a blur of dust and flying feathers. LaRaine coughed and waved a hand to clear the air in front of her.

Glancing at the suitcases piled on the ground, she wished she had asked him to carry them to the porch. He would probably have charged her extra, she thought wryly. Picking up the largest with both hands, she lugged it to the porch.

When all of them had been moved, she sat down on the strongest one to wait for Travis. She briefly contemplated going into the house where she would be out of the dust and sun, but she remembered Travis's reaction when she'd walked in uninvited the last time. She needed his help desperately; she could not risk offending him.

Directly overhead the sun grew hotter and hotter. LaRaine wished for a drink of cold, cold water. Then the sound of cantering hooves made her forget the thirst. Rising quickly to her feet, she walked to the corner of the porch and shaded her eyes. Two riders were coming in. One was Travis and the second had to be his hired hand.

Her hand was resting against the corner post, tension running through her nerve ends, stringing them taut. The riders were approaching the rear of the barn, which meant she was out of sight.

Then LaRaine saw Travis slow his horse and change its angle so he could see the house. She guessed that he had caught a glimpse of her. She waved, wanting desperately to speak to him alone. It would be embarrassing if she had to tell her story in front of the young hired man.

She heard Travis call something to the other rider, but the distance made the words unclear. Reining his horse away from the barn, he guided it directly to the house. The bay horse trotted into the yard, slowing to a stop in front of the porch.

Studying his rugged features, LaRaine tried to find a clue to his reaction to finding her there, but his expression was unreadable. His dark gaze raked her, then moved to the suitcases stacked on his porch.

"What are you doing here?" he asked in a quiet voice.

LaRaine felt pinned by his intense gaze. "I'm in trouble, Travis."

He hooked his right leg across the saddle horn and leaned on it. She realized he was waiting for an explanation of that statement. Moistening her dry lips, she completely forgot her rehearsed speech, blowing her lines as she had done so often in front of the camera.

"I was fired," she admitted. "I lost my job and was evicted from the hotel."

"Why?" Just the one word.

"Because"—LaRaine took a deep breath—"the car I drove here in last night belonged to the director. I thought it was Sam's. He gave me the keys, but he didn't tell Andy Behr. When I got back to town last night, Behr was notifying the police that someone had stolen his car—me. He didn't have me arrested, but he fired me and ordered me to pack up and leave."

"Sam didn't explain?"

"No." She laughed without humor. "Do you remember what you said last night about the lessons I needed to learn? Well, Sam gave me lesson number two. So I would know what it felt like to be tricked."

"None of this explains why you're here," Travis stated.

"I'm broke. All I had was twenty dollars, and I had to give five of it to the man who drove me out here. I couldn't think of anyone who might help me." Her voice cracked on the last, the desperateness of her situation creeping through.

"What makes you think I'd help you?" He eyed her narrowly, not moving out of his relaxed pose, leaning on the knee hooked around the saddle horn. Yet he was alert, unnervingly so.

"Because I"—LaRaine faltered—"I remembered what you said about being an easy mark for women in trouble."

She saw the silent laugh Travis breathed out before he looked away and shook his head. His dark eyes glittered with sardonic amusement when they refocused on her. The line of his mouth was hard and unrelenting.

"So you expect me to give you some money," he drawled in a voice that didn't admit whether he would or not.

"Yes." LaRaine held her breath.

"How much do you need?" The bay horse stamped at a fly and the saddle creaked beneath Travis as his mount shifted.

That sounded promising. She widened her eyes, hardly daring to hope. "A thousand?" At the lift of his eyebrow, she added hastily, "I could get by with five hundred."

Travis studied the reins held loosely in a leather-gloved hand. "You're asking me to give you five hundred."

"I'll pay you back," LaRaine promised.

"I have a feeling I'd have to wait a long time." His mouth crooked cynically.

"I'll pay you back as soon as I can. You have my word on that." But the glint in his eye said he didn't put much stock in her word. She had built her hopes up so high and Travis had let her. Stung by his mocking attitude, LaRaine challenged, "Will you give me the money?"

"No."

It was a flat denial without qualification. Her eyes smarted and she pivoted away to face the wild land spreading out from the ranch buildings. She blinked furiously at the moisture in her eyes, not wanting Travis to see how close she was to crying. Where would she go now? What would she do? She didn't even have a place to sleep tonight.

"But you could earn the money you need," Travis told her, "if you're willing to work."

"Where?" She spun around, grasping at any straw.

"Here, for me." He watched her closely.

"What do I have to do? How much would you pay?" she rushed.

"I'll pay you fifty dollars a week plus room and board to take care of the house."

"Fifty dollars?" LaRaine repeated incredulously. It wasn't much, only a tenth of what she needed.

"Plus room and board," Travis reminded her dryly.

"But it would take me ten weeks to earn enough money to leave here," she protested. "Why won't you just give me the money?"

"Because I can't afford to give away the money without getting something in return for it."

"But fifty dollars?" LaRaine repeated again, and looked around before turning her imploring brown eyes on Travis. "Why can't you pay me a hundred dollars a week?"

Travis tilted his head to one side. "You came to me for help. Fifty dollars a week is my offer. Take it or leave it," he answered.

Her jaw was clenched as she met his unwavering gaze. "What's this? Another lesson?" she challenged bitterly.

"From your viewpoint, it probably is. From mine"—Travis paused—"I'm paying wages to a housekeeper so that I can devote all my time to running the ranch. What's your answer?"

"I don't have any choice." LaRaine glared at him resentfully. "I don't have anyplace to go, no place to sleep, and very little money. I'll take it."

Straightening, Travis unhooked his knee from the saddle horn and stepped down off the horse. He glanced at the barn and called, "Joe!"

A lean man stepped out of the interior shadows. "Yes, sir?"

"Will you take care of the bay for me?" It was an order phrased as a request.

The hired hand almost ran across the yard to obey. As he drew closer, the impression of youth increased. The chest and shoulders were just beginning to muscle out. There was a fresh, open quality about his features.

"Joe, this is Ms. Evans," Travis introduced. "She's going to keep house for me. LaRaine, this is Joe Benteen."

"Hello, Joe." LaRaine attempted to sound pleasant, stifling the resentment she felt toward Travis.

"Ma'am." Joe briefly lifted his black hat, grayed with dust. The action exposed the unusual red-blond shade of his hair. There was a hint of shyness in the hazel eyes, but his smile seemed natural. LaRaine remembered that he was only nineteen.

"When you're through in the barn, Joe, come to the house," Travis told him. "I'll be needing your help."

"Sure thing." He took the horse's reins from Travis and led it to the barn.

Walking onto the porch, Travis picked up the two heaviest suitcases and glanced at LaRaine. "We might as well bring your things inside."

She picked up the lightest of the three remaining pieces and followed him into the house. Her nose wrinkled in distaste at the deplorably furnished living room. Travis didn't take the hallway that led to kitchen and the closed staircase to the second floor. Crossing the living room, he walked to a door and opened it.

It was a bedroom, LaRaine discovered as she followed Travis through the doorway. She guessed that because there was a bed and a dresser and a closet. It was almost austere, with no pictures on the drab green walls to relieve its severity. Travis set her luggage on the floor at the foot of the bed.

"You'll have to wait to unpack until I can get things moved out to the shed," he told her.

"The shed?" she echoed.

"Yes, I'll be sleeping out there."

"But why? I mean, you don't have to. There are bedrooms upstairs, aren't there?" LaRaine frowned.

He studied her with amused patience. "I know it may seem to you that we're relatively isolated out here but things have a way of getting around. When people learn that I've hired a young, beautiful actress to keep house for me, they're going to talk—especially if we're sleeping under the same roof."

"So what?" She lifted her shoulders in a shrug. "I'm used to people gossiping. Doesn't bother me. I don't care what they say."

"But I care what they say. They're my neighbors, and I want their respect and trust. So you see, it isn't your reputation I'm trying to protect." Travis smiled lazily. "It's mine." Turning, he added over his shoulder, "I'll bring in the rest of your luggage."

When he came back, he set the last two pieces

of her luggage on the floor beside the others. "That's all of it," he said.

"Look," LaRaine began guiltily, "I'm sorry to be putting you out of your home this way. I really am."

"If you mean that, I'll stay here and Joe can move into one of the upstairs bedrooms, then you can sleep in the shed," Travis suggested.

Stunned, LaRaine could only look at him with horror. She couldn't imagine sleeping in that broken-down place—there were probably rats and mice running around. Then she saw the wicked glint in his eye and realized he was teasing.

"I don't think that was very funny," she muttered.

Travis chuckled and walked into the living room. LaRaine stayed in the bedroom, fighting to control her temper. She didn't like being the object of a joke. Joe came. She heard Travis give him orders to bring down an army cot from an upstairs bedroom and take it to the shed.

When that was done, the two of them exchanged the small dresser that had obviously been in the shed for a larger chest of drawers from upstairs. Then Travis emptied his things from the dresser drawers and the closet in the bedroom to make room for LaRaine's. She was unpacking when he returned to the house.

"Do you want some lunch?" He paused in the doorway.

"No, thanks." LaRaine tried to restrict her eating to one meal a day to avoid gaining weight.

A few minutes later she heard the clatter of pots in the kitchen. After that an appetizing aroma wafted into the bedroom. LaRaine steadfastly ignored it and continued unpacking. She heard the scrape of chair legs across the linoleum floor of the kitchen and the muffled voices of Travis and Joe as they sat down to eat.

She had one suitcase emptied when chair legs scraped again and there was the clink of silverware on plates. The screen door slammed and footsteps crossed the porch. But a second pair of footsteps approached the bedroom and she glanced up when Travis's brawny frame darkened the doorway.

"Do you want to leave that for a minute?" He nodded toward the second suitcase she had started to unpack. "I'll show you where everything is."

"Okay," she agreed, and tossed the blouse she was holding back in the case.

She trailed behind him into the kitchen. He walked to a cupboard and opened it. "I keep the canned goods in here. There's flour, sugar, and other staples in the cupboard by the stove," he explained. "The dishes are in the cupboards by the sink. The pots and pans, in the lower cupboards."

Her mouth slowly opened in stunned protest as the reason for his explanation began to register. But her throat seemed incapable of making a sound. Travis started toward a fully enclosed side porch off the kitchen.

"In addition to the refrigerator, there's a freezer on the porch where I keep meat," he said.

"Are you expecting me to cook?" LaRaine choked out the question.

Travis stopped and slowly turned to face her, a scowling smile on his tanned face. "You don't think I'm paying you fifty dollars a week to dust the furniture, sweep the floor, and wash a few clothes, do you? Of course I expect you to prepare the meals.''

"I can't cook," she protested.

"What do you mean, you can't cook?" His amusement was tinged with exasperation. "You must have fixed yourself a meal sometime in your life."

"If you classify slapping cold cuts between two slices of bread as fixing a meal, then I have. Other than that, I haven't even boiled water for tea!" Her voice rose on a shrill note of panic.

"Then it's about time you learned," Travis said grimly.

The contemptuous way he was looking at her made LaRaine feel stupid. She glanced away, reddening with embarrassment. Instinctively she tried to defend herself.

"I'm going to marry a man who'll be wealthy enough to hire a chef, so there was no reason for me to know how," she retorted.

"In the meantime, if you want to eat, you have to cook," he stated.

LaRaine was looking anywhere but at him. She saw the dirty dishes stacked on the counter beside the sink and knew she had just found another chore.

"I suppose I have to do the dishes, too," she grumbled in resentment, and lifted her beautiful hands and manicured nails. "They'll be ruined!"

"I'm sure they'll survive a little dishwater," Travis said dryly.

She remembered another thing he had said earlier. "And I have to wash clothes?"

"The washing machine is on the side porch."

He indicated the door behind him where he had said the freezer was.

"And the clothes dryer?" LaRaine questioned.

His mouth twitched as if he wanted to smile. "Behind the house there are poles with rope stretched between them. You hang the clothes on the rope and wait for the sun to dry them."

"A clothesline?" Her dark eyes rounded.

"Then you do know what it's called." Mockery danced in his eyes.

"Yes, I do," she snapped. "Guess you haven't heard of modern conveniences, like dishwashers and clothes dryers." She glanced around the kitchen in disgust. "I'm surprised you even have running water." Suddenly she became still, realizing that she hadn't seen the bathroom. She looked warily at Travis. "You do have a bathroom? An indoor facility, I mean, not an outhouse with a stupid little crescent moon on the door?"

"Yes, there's a bathroom," Travis chuckled softly. "It's off the porch, complete with flush toilet."

"Thank goodness," LaRaine muttered to herself.

"You can explore the place on your own after you're through unpacking. I have to get to work," he said. "Plan on having supper ready around sundown."

"What am I supposed to fix? And how?" She made an open-handed gesture of angry bewilderment.

Travis took a deep breath and walked to the refrigerator. He opened the door and pointed inside. "Do you see that package of meat on the second shelf? It's a roast." Closing the door, he walked to a lower cupboard near the stove and opened it, bending down to remove an oblong pan. "You put the roast in here and put the pan in the oven with the cover on at about three-thirty. About an hour later, peel some potatoes, carrots and onions and add them to the same pan with the roast. Do you understand that?"

"I . . . think so," she nodded hesitantly.

"I hope so." This time it was Travis who muttered to himself. To her, he said, "I'll see you later," and exited by the back door via the side porch.

When he had gone, LaRaine looked around the kitchen and wondered what she'd got herself into. But what other choice did she have? Oh, well. She shrugged her shoulders. She'd warned Travis that she didn't know how to cook. If he was willing to endure the results, she was willing to try. After a few catastrophes, he might even be willing to give her the money to leave. There was always a bright spot in every dark day.

Returning to the bedroom, she resumed her unpacking. It was after three o'clock before she remembered Travis's instructions about the roast. She hurried to the kitchen and took the package of meat from the refrigerator. Unwrapping it, she put it in the roasting pan, set the lid on it, and carried it to the stove.

The gas stove looked like an antique. Opening the oven door, she slid the pan onto the baking shelf and closed the door. She realized that Travis hadn't told her how to operate it. She studied the dials. One had graduating temperatures, so La-Raine turned it and opened the oven door to see if anything happened. Nothing. She tried each of the dials in turn and nothing happened. Catching the unpleasant smell of gas, she turned all the dials off.

"If he thinks I'm going to blow myself up playing around with this stove, he's crazy," she muttered, and walked away.

Before she reached the bedroom, she heard a pickup drive into the yard. Remembering that Travis had left in it earlier, she walked to the front door. Through the wire mesh of the screen, she saw him step out of the cab and reach back inside. Two gift-wrapped packages were in his arms when he closed the door and walked toward the house. An overwhelming and eager curiosity made La-Raine push open the screen door for him.

"I can't make the oven work," were the words she greeted him with, but she had difficulty tearing her gaze from the packages he carried.

"I suspected you'd get yourself in some kind of difficulty," he replied, and walked past her to the kitchen. "Show me what you did."

LaRaine showed him. "I smelled gas, but I couldn't see any flame," she concluded.

"That's because you have to light it yourself. With that amazing new invention, a match. It doesn't have a pilot that automatically lights the burners or the oven." He set the packages on the counter and reached for the wooden matches in a container near the stove. "I'll show you." LaRaine watched. When he had it going, Travis turned it off and handed her a match. "Now you do it."

It looked much easier when he had done it. Finally, after more error than trial, LaRaine succeeded in starting it. Travis checked the roasting pan and the roast inside.

"Didn't you season it?" he asked.

"No, was I supposed to?"

Travis glared at her. "Salt and pepper it," he ordered with exasperation. "And add some water, just enough to cover the bottom of the pan."

"I didn't know," LaRaine defended herself, and did as she was told.

When the roast was back in the heating oven, her gaze strayed to the packages on the counter. She couldn't help wondering whom they were for.

"They're for you," said Travis, as if reading her mind.

Gasping in delight, LaRaine mentally took back some of the things she had thought about him when she discovered the cooking and dishwashing that the job entailed. She reached for the smallest package first, tearing off the bow and the paper. Opening the box, she stared at its contents, a beginner's cookbook. Her wide smile grew smaller.

"I don't have time to give you cooking lessons. You'll have to teach yourself," Travis told her.

Less than enthusiastically, she offered, "Thank you."

The second and larger package contained something called a crockpot, obviously for cooking. Neither present was LaRaine's idea of a gift.

"It's an electric slow cooker," Travis pointed out. "The saleswoman assured me it was impossible for anyone to ruin food cooked in that. There's a complete set of instructions and a recipe brochure."

"Thoughtful of you," she murmured, flipping through the brochure. "This Chicken 'N Rutabagas casserole looks fabulous."

"I'm just hoping for a decent meal and doing what I can to see that I get it," he stated, and walked to door. "Don't forget to put the potatoes and the rest of the stuff in with the roast," he reminded her before closed the door.

LaRaine stuck out her tongue at his retreating back.

CHAPTER EIGHT

As far as LaRaine was concerned, the evening meal that night was such a success that it even surprised her. When Travis came in she had the table all set, complete with a relish tray with ingredients scrounged from the refrigerator. At his suggestion and with his assistance, she opened a can of green beans and heated them in a pan on top of the stove. The roast, potatoes, carrots, and onions were cooked to perfection. With every bite LaRaine silently congratulated herself. Cooking was easy, if you kept it simple and avoided rutabagas.

Joe ate with them, but he didn't say much. LaRaine had the feeling that he was silently in awe of her, which was a tremendous boost to her ego. Only two things kept the meal from being flawless: she had forgotten the coffee and there was no dessert. Travis corrected both of those by making a pot of coffee and taking some ice cream from the freezer.

Cleaning up afterward, LaRaine concluded, was a tiresome, thankless chore, and the only one with which Travis didn't offer to help. While she washed and dried the dishes, he went into the living room and did paperwork at the old desk. Joe disappeared somewhere outside.

When she was done, LaRaine soothed her hands with lotion, determined that she wasn't going to get dishpan hands. She stared with distaste at the prunelike wrinkling of her fingers and wiped excess lotion from her hands. As she entered the living room, Travis was closing his books and returned them to a side drawer. He looked up when she walked in.

"All through?" he asked.

"Yes," she nodded, and tried not to think about the state her hands were in.

Uncoiling his long frame from the chair, Travis said, "So am I. Good night, LaRaine."

"You aren't leaving?" she protested. "It's early."

"Not by my standards." He wasn't swayed by her argument. "Good night."

The house was unbearably empty after he had gone. Nighttime made the rooms even more dismal than they were in the daylight, with all sorts of creaking and groaning sounds coming from different parts of the old house. Strange noises from outside invaded the house. Something howled mournfully and LaRaine suspected it was a coyote.

It was depressing sitting alone in the house with nothing to do but try to identify the weird sounds. She wasn't all that tired, but sleep was preferable to boredom.

In the bedroom, she changed into a lacy black nightgown and climbed into bed. Immediately she rolled into the dip in the center of the bed, becoming nearly lost in the hollow. The pillow was almost as hard as a rock. She pushed it with her fist, trying to make an indentation for her head. Between the lumpy mattress and the hard pillow, it seemed to take forever before she fell asleep.

As soon as she did, it seemed that something was trying to waken her. She refused to rise to full consciousness. A hand was shaking her shoulder and she tried to shrug it away.

Dimly she heard a voice say, "Come on. It's time to wake up."

"I'm sleeping," LaRaine muttered into the mattress.

"Not anymore, you're not," the voice said. "Get up!"

When she didn't obey, she was rolled onto her back. She groaned and looked through her lashes. Travis was sitting on the edge of the bed, looking disgustingly well-rested. Beyond him was the window and a pinkish light suffusing the sky.

"It isn't even morning," she told him, and shut her eyes tightly. "I'm not getting up yet."

"Yes, you are." A large pair of hands slid under her arms to sit her up in the bed, then stayed there to keep her steady.

At first LaRaine tried to push him away, but it was like trying to push a wall. Her finders felt the flexing muscles in his arms—living steel. Slowly raising her lashes, she changed her tactics. Linking her fingers behind his neck, she arched her back in a feline gesture of tiredness.

"Please, Travis, let me go back to sleep," she coaxed with a little-girl pout to her lips.

He studied their unpainted ripeness. Without much effort, he drew her toward him. Half-drugged with sleep, it took LaRaine a full second to guess his intention. By then his mouth was tasting her lips, parting them with arrogant mastery. The kiss was a slow, insidious seduction of her senses, catching her at a moment when she was vulnerable and unprepared.

The pressure of his mouth demanded more and she found herself answering it, returning his ardor, and thrilling to the dizzying wave of strange, wonderful feelings. She arched toward him, her breasts brushing against the cotton material of his shirt, her nipples pleasurably sensitized by his body heat.

His large hands glided down her body, his thumbs barely touching the swelling curves of her breasts through the lacy material of her nightgown. LaRaine didn't understand this wild, crazy fire bursting through her veins, but it didn't seem important that she understand it.

Then his mouth was pulling away from hers. A mixed-up sigh came from her lips as she opened her eyes to look at him. Something smoldered in his eyes, and her heart skipped a few beats.

"Travis," she whispered, and tightened her linked fingers behind his neck to pull him back and show her again the magic of his kiss.

"Get out of bed." The hand that wasn't supporting her slapped her thigh.

Startled by the stinging slap, LaRaine loosened her grip. She couldn't hold onto him when he suddenly rose from the bed. She quickly braced herself with an arm to keep from falling backward.

When she didn't immediately obey his order, Travis reached out and flipped the covers off her feet.

"Come on. It's time to fix breakfast."

"At this hour?" LaRaine didn't want to think about food. Her gaze kept straying to his mouth, wondering how much of the excitement it had caused had been real and how much of it had been left over from dreams.

But she obeyed him in spite of her protest, swinging her feet out of the bed and onto the floor. Travis waited for her as she picked up the black lace robe lying at the foot of the bed and slipped it on.

"I'll show you how to make coffee before I go do my chores," he said. LaRaine followed him into the kitchen, shivering at the coolness of the floor beneath her bare feet. He took the coffee pot from its place on the counter top and carried it to the sink. "But I'm only going to show you how to do this once, so pay attention."

He was lecturing her again, like a teacher with a pupil. Some of her radiant confusion dimmed under his sternness. LaRaine watched how much water he put in the pot and how many scoops of coffee in the basket.

"Got that?" Travis asked. She nodded yes, as his gaze raked her with unnerving thoroughness. The faintly condemning light in his dark eyes made LaRaine pull the front of her robe together. "There's bacon and eggs in the refrigerator. If I were you, I'd get dressed before I started breakfast. Joe's young and he gets embarrassed easily."

He seemed to be implying that LaRaine thought nothing of parading around half-undressed in front of strange men. She bristled in anger at the unspoken accusation.

"I fully intend to get dressed." She was wide awake now. "You were the one who dragged me out of the bedroom to show me how to make coffee. It wasn't my idea. And the next time you want to wake me up, knock on the door."

"I did knock, but you didn't hear me," Travis replied evenly. "Remind me to bring you an alarm clock so there won't be a repeat of this morning."

LaRaine didn't want a repeat of this morning any more than she wanted him making insulting remarks about her. Before she could open her mouth to take back her hasty statement, Travis was walking out the back door.

Angered with herself as much as with him, LaRaine stalked back to the bedroom. Stripping out of her night clothes, she chose a pair of white pants from the closet and a black, gray and white patterned blouse. She tied a matching sash around her waist and turned to the plain, square mirror above her dresser to begin applying her makeup. The overhead light provided the only illumination in the room, which slowed her down. She was only half-done when she heard the front door open and slam shut, and footsteps walking to the kitchen.

"Where's breakfast?" Travis called.

"I haven't fixed it yet!" LaRaine shouted back, frowning as she tried to see if she had applied too much blusher in the dim light.

"Why not?" The demand came from much closer to her bedroom.

"Because I haven't finished dressing," she explained impatiently.

"You haven't finished?" Travis echoed. "I left

the house thirty minutes ago. What have you been doing all this time?'' He appeared in the doorway, a dark frown creasing his forehead.

"This light is terrible." LaRaine gestured toward the covered bulb overhead. "I can barely see to put my makeup on."

Travis stared at the collection of jars, tubes, brushes, and eyeshadow palettes on her dresser. "What is this?" he pointed.

"Lipstick."

"And this?" He went down the line, making La-Raine identify each one. Bottles of moisturizer, cleansing cream and skin freshener he set to one side along with a tube of lipstick. With a sweep of his arm he cleared the top of the dresser, dumping all the rest of her cosmetics into the metal waste-basket on the floor.

"What are you doing?" LaRaine shrieked.

"All the makeup you need is on the dresser." His mouth was drawn in a ruthlessly straight line. "No more makeup, LaRaine. No more masks."

"You aren't throwing all that away!" She grabbed for the wastebasket he had picked up. "Do you have any idea how much that stuff cost? Besides, those cosmetics are mine."

"You can have them back when you leave here," Travis informed her coldly. "In the meantime you have no use for them. There isn't anyone around here that you need to primp and paint for. And I don't intend to wait an hour or longer for breakfast every morning."

"Who do you think you are?" LaRaine demanded. "I want it all back, right now, this minute!"

"When you leave," he repeated.

"Then I'm leaving now."

"Go. I won't stop you." He shrugged.

"Very well, I will!" LaRaine pivoted away and stopped. Where could she go? How would she get there? She still didn't have any money. Travis was still standing in the doorway, watching her, knowing all along that she would have to back down. "Damn you!" Her chin quivered as she issued her taut acknowledgement of surrender.

"Start breakfast," Travis ordered.

It was several seconds before LaRaine followed him. Travis was waiting in the kitchen to assist her with breakfast; and later, Joe walked in as she forked the almost burnt bacon onto an absorbent paper towel. Without her makeup, LaRaine felt naked and self-conscious, exposed somehow . . . and it was all his fault.

It wasn't a sensation that she became used to during the next three days. At odd moments, she would touch the bare skin of her cheek with her fingertips and rail at the Travis's arrogant command but, most of her time was taken up with her job. It was all so alien to her that LaRaine was constantly struggling with frustratingly simple obstacles.

She stared at the gooey mess in the bowl and read the recipe again. Travis had suggested a cake might be a nice change for dessert. The soupy glop in the bowl didn't look at all like a cake, but she had carefully followed the step-by-step directions in the cookbook.

A fan whirred to circulate the hot air, its noise competing with the radio on top of the refrigerator blaring out a popular song. The loud music usually helped to drown out the silence of the house. In her present confusion, it was only irritating. Stalking over to the radio, LaRaine switched it off, throwing the room into unnerving silence. She brushed a straying wisp of black hair away from her cheek, unknowingly brushing a streak of flour across her skin.

A hammering knock rattled the front screen door. The unexpected sound startled her and she dropped the batter-laden spoon from her hand. Swearing softly beneath her breath, she picked up the spoon and mopped up the mess with a rag. The peremptory knock came again.

Absently wiping her hands on the front of her pants, she hurried into the living room. At the front door she stopped abruptly, stunned to see Sam Hardesty standing outside. He looked equally shocked.

Sam was the first to recover. "What are you doing here?"

LaRaine swallowed. "I . . . I live here." She lifted her head high. "If you want to speak to Travis, he said something about checking some irrigation pipes."

"I thought you went back to L.A.," he drawled, paying no attention to the information about Travis.

"I didn't." LaRaine wasn't about to explain to him why. He had enough to gloat about just knowing he'd cost her the movie part. "If you'll excuse, I'm busy. Goodbye Sam. I'll tell Travis you called." She walked away from the door, her legs trembling.

Uninvited, Sam walked in. "Are you living with McCrea?"

LaRaine would have loved to claim that level of intimacy just to watch Sam's mouth drop open, but she remembered Travis's statement about how quickly gossip traveled in this small ranch community and his desire to avoid it.

"Travis is a gentleman," she declared, not slowing down on her way to the kitchen. "He sleeps in the . . . bunkhouse." That sounded better than the shed. "And I sleep in here." But she didn't deny that there was a relationship of some kind between them.

"Why? I mean, if he's not your lover, what are you doing here?" Sam walked into the kitchen. "Holy cow! You're baking!" he laughed incredulously. "I don't believe it—a domestic LaRaine Evans!"

"Why is that so funny?" she demanded angrily, turning on him in a temper.

He stared at her, his gaze moving over her face. Confusion flickered in his eyes. LaRaine looked away, all too aware that her emotions were getting the better of her.

"You look different," Sam commented, unable to identify the cause

She lifted a hand to her face, almost protectively. Her sensitive fingertips felt the powdery streak of flour and she rubbed it away. She turned away, picking up the bowl of cake batter and dumping the contents into a greased pan. Too late to figure out whether or not she mixed it correctly. Once it was spreading across the pan she couldn't very well spoon it back into the bowl.

Sam moved closer, as if inspecting her carefully. "You aren't wearing makeup," he said accusingly.

"Is that a crime? Since when does a girl have to

wear it all the time?'' She heard the tremor in her voice.

"I don't think I've ever seen you without it,'' he remarked. "You're . . . you're beautiful.'' He seemed surprised. "What's come over you?''

"I don't know what you're talking about.'' La-Raine carried the cake pan to the oven and set it on the wire shelf.

"No makeup, baking a cake, and I'll bet you're taking care of the house and cooking meals, too.'' Sam seemed to be making a list.

"So what if I am?'' she said indignantly, feeling somehow degraded by his statements.

"Nothing wrong with it,'' he said. "I just can't see you being the little homemaker. Not the LaRaine Evans I know.''

"There are a lot of things about me that you don't know.'' There were even a few things that LaRaine was just beginning to discover about herself.

"Why? I mean—'' But Sam didn't seem to know what he meant.

"Maybe I just got fed up with that whole artificial world you live in,'' she suggested. "Maybe I decided it was time to get back to the basics of life.''

"LaRaine, don't tell me you've fallen in love with a Utah rancher? Are you really in love with him?'' he exclaimed in amazement.

"I never said that,'' LaRaine denied.

"It's the only thing that explains it. I've heard that love can work miracles, but I never believed it until now.''

"Well, it isn't true. I'm just working here because

it's what I want to do," she insisted vigorously. "There's sunshine and fresh air. And lots of breathing room."

"As I recall, you referred to this country as a desolate wasteland." Sam obviously didn't believe a word she was saying.

"People are entitled to change their minds. As a matter of fact, it's supposed to be a woman's prerogative." She gathered up the mixing bowls, spoons and measuring cups and carried them to the sink. "Did you want to leave a message for Travis or not?" she demanded, afraid of his questions and comments.

"No, I'll call this evening and speak to him myself," he said.

"Then would you please leave? I have lots of work to do." The stiff request was issued as she started to fill the sink with hot water and dish detergent.

Sam hesitated, studying the rigid set of her mouth before he finally complied with her request. From then on, everything seemed to go wrong. LaRaine forgot the cake in the oven until she smelled the acrid smoke. When she finally rescued it, it was blackened and hard. She couldn't tell whether she had mixed it correctly or not.

While preparing the evening meal, she forgot to put enough water on the potatoes and they boiled dry, and scorched. The green beans suffered a similar fate, cooked to the point of toughness. The Jell-O salad hadn't completely set, so it was like thick soup. Only the meat loaf was remotely edible.

Neither Travis nor Joe made a single comment. If there had been a hint of criticism, LaRaine was

ready to dump the food in their laps. Joe pounded
the ketchup bottle over his potatoes to cover up
the scorched taste. LaRaine attacked her meat loaf
with angry frustration, her silence almost hostile.

She remembered to tell Travis that Sam had
stopped to see him and would be back this evening,
but she didn't volunteer Sam's comments about
the change in her. Travis had simply nodded,
though he studied her quietly. LaRaine guessed
that he was wondering how much of her brooding
anger was caused by Sam.

All of it was. His visit had reminded her how
far down she had fallen. She was a poorly paid
housekeeper, nothing more. People, especially
men, had always waited on her, not the other way
around. She hated Sam for putting her in this
humiliating position by getting her fired. And she
hated Travis for rubbing her nose in it and making
her work for the money she needed.

She was washing dishes in a frozen rage when
Sam came. Travis spoke to him outside instead of
inviting him into the house. It was almost worse
not being able to overhear their conversation and
know whether or not they were talking and laughing about her.

After Sam had left, Travis came back into the
house, LaRaine was wiping the last of the silverware
dry and jamming it in the drawer. She heard Travis
walk into the kitchen, but she didn't look up.

"Well?" she said in icy challenge. "What did he
say about me?"

"Sam?"

"Of course," LaRaine snapped.

"He didn't say anything about you. He came
over to tell me that they'll be using my cattle in

the next couple of days and wanted me to drive them over to the set," he explained.

"I see." Her tone made it clear that she didn't believe him. She felt his alert gaze note her every move and refused to meet it.

"Joe and I won't be here for lunch tomorrow. Since you won't have to fix a noon meal, I thought I'd suggest that you wash clothes tomorrow," said Travis.

"Suggest or order?" LaRaine retorted sarcastically.

He ignored that. "If you'll come with me a minute, I'll show you how to operate the washing machine."

For a rebellious moment she didn't budge. Wadding the dish towel into a ball, she tossed it on the counter and turned to accompany Travis to the back porch, avoiding direct eye contact with him. Previously LaRaine had only ventured onto the porch en route to the bathroom, never bothering to notice the appliances in the small addition.

It wasn't a sleek, modern automatic washer that Travis led her to, but a big, cumbersome, old-fashioned wringer washing machine. Two gray metal tubs stood on legs beside it. LaRaine stared at the contraptions with growing dismay and anger.

"That's a mechanical dinosaur," she said rebelliously, turning the fiery brilliance of her dark gaze on Travis. "I'm not going to use that thing. You'll have to hire someone to wash your clothes."

"I have," he replied evenly. "You."

Before LaRaine could argue, he began explaining to her how to work the washer. He showed her how to hook up the hoses to the taps in the bathroom to fill the washer and rinse tubs and how to operate the wringer and move it to use with the rinse tubs. With irritating patience, he explained how long to let the clothes agitate in the washer and how to get a garment through the clothes wringer.

Finally he showed her where the clothespins were, and where to hang the washing out back. When Travis had finished, LaRaine was choked into silence by the bitterness of her fate and the futility of protest. She managed a nod to indicate that she understood his instructions.

Her first washday was a series of minor catastrophes. Clothes kept winding around the rollers of the wringer. She tore the fragile material of one of her expensive blouses trying to pull it free, and lost a fingernail in a tug of war with the gobbling cylinders over the fate of a hand towel.

Two pairs of her pants and one knit top shrank in the hot water. Two other blouses were ruined when a red T-shirt ran. The only damage to the men's clothes was the blue tint of their white underwear, thanks to the newer pairs of jeans.

Her back ached from lugging basket after basket of wet clothes out to the clothesline and stretching her arms overhead to hang them out to dry. It all had to be repeated hours later when the sun had done its part of the chore. Frustrated and exhausted, LaRaine was in tears by the time she finished.

If either Travis or Joe noticed her puffy eyes at the supper table, they didn't comment on it. Nor did they mention the new color of their underwear.

To LaRaine, their silence seemed to condemn her for not knowing how to do something as simple as laundry. If Travis had said one cross word to her, LaRaine knew she would've burst into tears. But, mercifully, he didn't.

CHAPTER NINE

Over the next three weeks, LaRaine fought a bitter war to learn how to keep house. It was more than just cooking and cleaning and washing. She had to consciously train herself to hang up clothes, to put things in their proper place when she was through with them, and to organize her time. Travis expected her to make lists of food and supplies she needed and do the shopping. He usually came along. LaRaine never remembered to write down everything she needed.

After she'd received her fourth paycheck, she felt she'd earned every dime of the money. The problem was that she hadn't been able to save it all. Because she didn't know how to care for them, some of her clothes had been ruined. She didn't want to risk the rest by wearing them while she scrubbed floors or did some other equally onerous task. So she'd used some of her money to buy jeans and cotton blouses that would stand up under the abuse. And she'd bought magazines to fill the empty evenings with something to do. At that rate, LaRaine was convinced it would take forever to save enough money to leave.

Her life on the ranch began to fall into a pattern. Sunday was her day off. Joe would attend church and spend the day with his family, but LaRaine had no place to go and no way to get there if she did. Which left her and Travis at the ranch together. As far as LaRaine was concerned, she was essentially alone since she rarely saw Travis on Sundays, or on Monday evenings, either, which Joe also spent at his parents' home. That night was set aside to be with his family, as his Mormon faith directed.

With the breakfast dishes done, LaRaine went to clean the bathroom, and stared at her reflection in the mirror. What had happened to her glamorous self? There was still something faintly regal about the lift of her head and the wing of her eyebrows, but her face looked as scrubbed and fresh as a country girl's. How long had it been since she'd had a facial and a manicure? LaRaine couldn't even remember when a stylist had touched a comb to her raven black hair.

In a burst of rebellion, she dumped the cleansers on the counter by the washbasin. She wasn't going to clean any stupid bathroom! She swept through the kitchen, hating the ugliness of the house and the emptiness of it. She needed to be around people, to be the center of attention and to be pampered and fussed over. She had spent too many lonely hours in this awful place for her to stay inside another minute.

She slammed out of the house, not stopping until she was in the center of the ranchyard. She looked for the pickup truck that was usually parked by the shed. It wasn't there. Travis was at the corral, saddling the buckskin tied to an outside rail. La-Raine crossed the ground in long, angry strides.

"I want to use the truck. Where is it?" she demanded.

"Joe has it." Travis tightened the cinch strap and began looping it around through the ring.

She pressed her lips together for an angry second, then demanded, "When will he be back?"

"He went into town to pick up some grain for the horses. He had a few other errands to run, so I don't imagine he'll be back until after lunch. You won't have to bother about fixing him anything." He unhooked the stirrup from the saddle horn and let it drop. His gaze didn't stray to LaRaine once.

"Damn," she muttered under her breath. A gust of wind blew a cloud of hair across her face and she pushed it back impatiently.

"Why do you need the truck?" he asked. "Did you forget something at the store?"

"No. I've got to get out of that house!" she exploded in frustration. "I can't stand it in there. I hate it!" One way or another, she was going to find a few minutes of freedom. "Saddle me a horse," she ordered.

Travis turned, resting an arm on the saddle. "Where are you planning to go?"

"Over to the movie set," she retorted. "I have to be around people. I've got to talk to someone before I die of boredom. I can't take this place any more—it's driving me crazy!"

"There isn't anybody there."

"Where?" LaRaine frowned. "At the movie set?"

"The last of the crew and equipment pulled out yesterday." He watched her reaction, expressionless.

She breathed in sharply at the news and looked away, her eyes smarting with tears. She would have been gone, too, if . . . There was no use finishing that thought. She had been fired. She was marooned in this godforsaken wasteland. Despair wiped out her anger.

"I'm riding out to check the cattle on the west range," Travis said. "Would you like to come with me?"

Her eyes shimmering with tears of self-pity, she looked at him, surprised by his invitation. "Yes," she agreed hesitantly, expecting him to take back his offer.

"Better get some boots on." His gaze flicked to her canvas shoes and indifferently back to her face. "And put a hat on or you'll end up with sunstroke."

"I will," she promised, and hurried toward the house.

She was escaping her prison. Excitement seared through her veins at the prospect of accompanying Travis, forgetting that he was her warden in a way. In her bedroom, she took off her shoes and tugged on her boots. Grabbing a flat-crowned hat, she dashed out the front door.

In the yard, Travis sat astride the buckskin, holding the reins to the saddled bay. LaRaine faltered for a moment, not quite believing that Travis actually intended to let her ride the big bay horse.

"You said once that you wanted to ride him sometime," he reminded her with a half-smile. "Here's your chance." He held out the reins.

LaRaine didn't need a second invitation. The height of the big horse forced her to jump to reach the stirrup. Once her toe was in, she swung onto the saddle. The stirrups were adjusted to just the right length for her to ride comfortably.

"Ready?" Travis gave her a sidelong look.

"Yes." She flashed him a smile.

At the slight touch of her heel, the big bay strode out into a canter. The buckskin matched its pace and was loping alongside within seconds. LaRaine marveled at the quickness and agility of her mount, considering its size, as it wove through clumps of tall brush. Shaking back her hair, she let the warm wind blow over her face.

The ranch buildings were far behind them when the terrain grew rough and they were forced to slow their horses. Flushed by the exhilaration of the long canter, LaRaine felt really alive for the first time in weeks. There was a sparkle to her dark eyes and a softness to her mouth.

"Thanks for asking me to come with you, Travis." She was sincere.

"We still have a long way to ride, and the same distance to cover going back. Hope you feel the same way at the end of the ride." He smiled lazily.

"I'm not worrying about getting stiff and sore." LaRaine shook her head. "I should be in pretty good shape after all the work I've done these last few weeks."

Travis took the lead up a rock-strewn ridge. As the sun marched higher in the blue sky, the air became heavy with the pungent smell of sage. The broken valley floor sprawled for endless miles, gouged by dry river beds and mounded with small hills. Against the horizon was the backbone of a mountain range, a chipped peak standing out from the rest.

"I've never seen such empty land," LaRaine commented as Travis slowed the buckskin to a walk and her mount moved forward to walk beside him.

"It's part of the Great Basin of Utah," he explained. "Thousands of years ago, this was all part of a big inland sea that covered a third of Utah. The Great Salt Lake and Sevier Lake are the saltwater remnants of it. A lot of people passed though here on their way to California and Oregon, but the Mormons were the first to settle. They called the land Deseret. It was proposed as the name of the state when it was admitted into the union, but Utah was chosen instead."

"Who was Deseret?"

Travis smiled. "Not a person. It's a word from the Book of Mormon. It means 'land of the honeybees.' The beehive is still the state symbol." He shifted into a more comfortable position in the saddle, the leather squeaking at his movement. "You've seen the highway sign in Delta, haven't you? The one referring to the Fort Deseret historical site. It's the remains of an old fort constructed of adobe and straw, built in eighteen short days to protect the local settlers from Indian raids."

"I remember the sign." She nodded, and looked around at the sprawling emptiness. "I can't imagine why the settlers ever would've wanted to fight the Indians over this land."

"Don't let the rock hounds hear you say that," Travis smiled dryly.

"Why?" LaRaine eyed him curiously.

"Topaz Mountain is to the north of here. They say it's covered with deposits of topaz, amber and other gemstones." He studied the land they rode through. "This country has a beauty all its own. It's subtle—but it grows on you."

Her gaze swept the wild, rough landscape, sensing its lasting endurance in the tenacious sage and grasses. The gnarled and twisted junipers and piñon pines survived in spite of the arid climate. She came close to understanding what he meant.

"You may be right," she conceded, but not wholeheartedly.

"Hold it!" Travis reined in his horse and signaled her to do the same. He was looking to his right, his gaze narrowed alertly. "I wasn't sure we'd catch sight of them," he murmured, a satisfied curve to his mouth.

"Catch sight of what?" She tried to look around him.

"There's a herd of mustangs." He turned the buckskin and walked it slowly forward. "We won't be able to get very close."

LaRaine could just make out the shapes of grazing horses blending against the backdrop of a brush-covered hill. When they were a hundred yards closer she could see them more clearly.

"We'd better stop here," Travis suggested.

"I've never seen a wild horse before," she whispered.

"They aren't wild in the true sense of the word, not like the deer and buffalo," he explained. "All of these horses are descended from domestic stock, so they're feral—they've gone wild."

"They aren't as big as I thought they would be."

Of the eight horses LaRaine counted, none of them was larger than a good-sized pony.

"The desert environment has bred them down to a size that can survive in this land." Travis pointed to a knoll near the grazing horses. "There's the stallion."

LaRaine spotted the mustang instantly. It seemed to be looking directly at them and testing the air for their scent. In the flash of a second the stallion was charging down the hill, neighing an order to his mares. There was a flurry of whirling horses and drumming hooves. Then they vanished, racing over the hill with a speed that took her breath away.

"That was a sight to see," she breathed. "They're protected by law, aren't they?"

"Yep. But the government has to come up with a way to control the mustang population the way they do with deer and buffalo. Right now they roam pretty much where they please, mostly on federal lands leased by ranchers to graze their cattle. So there's an ongoing controversy between ranchers and mustang supporters. Someday they'll find a compromise." He reined the buckskin around to resume their previous course. "Let's move on."

LaRaine followed, the image of the fleeting mustangs not leaving her mind. They rode in silence for a long time. Then red, curly-haired Hereford cattle began to dot the brush, their white faces lowered to the ground to tear at the grasses amidst the sage.

"I want to check the water hole," said Travis, pointing to the left.

In unison, they veered to the left. A bawling calf greeted them as they reached the water hole, shaded by a small stand of cottonwoods. The upper half of the water hole had become a mud bog. The calf was up to its belly in the center of the bog. It made a puny attempt to struggle free when they rode up.

"He's stuck!" LaRaine cast a concerned look at Travis.

He was already shaking out his coiled lariat. Swinging it once over his head, he snaked it out to let the noose settle over the calf's head. Taking a wrap around the saddle horn, he tightened the rope and turned the buckskin away from the water hole. The rope stretched taut as he began walking away. The calf bawled and struggled against the pressure pulling it to the ground.

"You're choking it!" LaRaine cried in protest.

But Travis steadily kept his horse walking, pulling the calf through the mud. The calf's eyes were ringed with white. Determined to rescue the helpless calf, LaRaine dismounted and grabbed for the rope.

"Stop it!" she ordered. "You're hurting it!"

Pulling against Travis, she tried to give the calf some slack so it could breathe. It was almost to solid ground; she could see it begin to gain footing. Ignoring Travis, she reached out to take the noose off the calf's head. At the same instant, its feet touched hard ground and it panicked, bolting forward into LaRaine before she could move out of the way. She stumbled backward, into the edge of the bog, lost her footing and fell down with a plop. Mud oozed everywhere.

After an initial cry of surprise, she sat in shock. She lifted one mud-covered hand, then the other, and tried to shake her fingers free of the clinging webs of mud. The low, rolling sound of Travis's laughter didn't lessen her fury.

"This is all your fault!" she shouted. "I wouldn't be in this mess if you hadn't almost killed that calf! I was trying to save it!"

Travis dismounted and walked to the edge of the mud. He made absolutely no attempt to disguise his amusement at LaRaine's predicament.

"Look at me!" she demanded. "Just look at me! I'm covered with mud!"

She tried to stand up, but she couldn't seem to get her legs underneath her. Her boots kept slipping in the mud. Finally she had to put a hand back in the oozing slime for balance.

"Mud never hurt anybody," Travis declared.

As she was about to stand up, LaRaine felt a boot against her backside a second before it sent her sprawling forward. She screamed. Only her outstretched arms saved her from getting a faceful of mud, but the rest of her, from chest to toe, was dripping with it. When she finally regained her footing, she was in a quaking rage, but Travis's shoulders were shaking with barely contained laughter. Her feet were weighted down with mud as she dragged herself free of the bog.

"You'll pay for that!" She stalked forward to confront him and carry out her threat.

"Why are you angry?" Travis mocked. "Don't rich women go to beauty spas for mud baths? You got yours for free."

LaRaine swung at him, but he ducked and caught her arm. She lost her balance and fell against him, covering his shirt front with mud. Automatically he circled a supporting arm around her waist, coating his hand and sleeve with the mud that clung to her. As she struck at him with her free hand, Travis dodged the blow aimed at his head, and it landed on his shoulder. She might as well have slapped a house.

Before she could hit at him again, his mouth was swooping down to capture her lips. Stilled by his sudden kiss, LaRaine was momentarily rigid in the iron circle of his arms. The searing fire of his mouth melted her against him, surrendering her to the persuasive pressure he applied. From blinding hate, she went to blazing passion. Sensual tremors quaked through her, bringing an urgency to her response that was more than matched by the devouring hunger of his kiss.

His hands slid intimately over her body, finding the soft curves beneath their layer of mud. Their touch ignited more fires until she was burning out of control. Her senses seemed to explode with the heat Travis generated. She shaped herself to the hard contours of his length, glorying in the need he echoed. His mouth began exploring her face with rough kisses, sending shivers of delight down her spine when he nibbled at her ear.

Their desires had flamed into one fire until the downward path of his mouth encountered the mud-covered skin at her throat. Travis lifted his head, wiping mud from his chin and lips with the back of his hand. His dark gaze smoldered over her face as she slowly opened her eyes to look at him. She was weak with wanting him, but the sight of his mud-streaked face made her smile.

"You look funny," she told him, and lifted her hand to wipe the smear from his face, forgetting that her hand was covered with mud. A wider patch of brown covered his jaw. "Oh!" When she realized what she'd done, LaRaine drew her hand back, covering her mouth to hold back a laugh.

Travis immediately chuckled at the mud on her lips. "We're two of a kind now," he declared, and LaRaine found herself laughing.

She shook her head in disbelief. "I'm just about covered with mud from head to toe. Why am I so happy?" she asked.

"I don't know," said Travis, but the look in his eyes made it clear that her happiness was contagious. "But it's going to be a long, muddy ride back to the ranch . . . for both of us."

"Yes," LaRaine sighed, and reluctantly unwound her arms from around him.

Travis walked her to the bay and helped her into the saddle when her boot kept slipping out of the stirrup. His hand rested for a tantalizing moment on her mud-covered thigh. LaRaine thought he was going to say something when their eyes locked for a breathless second.

"Ready?" was all he asked.

"Yes," she nodded, holding the reins in her mud-slick fingers.

When Travis had mounted, they cantered their horses away from the water hole toward the ranch. It was the most uncomfortable ride LaRaine had ever had, but her heart was singing all the way.

When they rode up to the barn, Travis said, "You'd better go and shower. I'll take care of the horses."

LaRaine glanced at his muddied front. "What about you?"

"I can get by with water from the kitchen sink and clean clothes," he told her.

Entering the house through the back door, La-

Raine undressed on the porch rather than track mud through the house to the bedroom. She went directly into the bathroom, turned on the shower, and stepped under its spray. She heard Travis come into the kitchen and the water pressure faded when he turned on the sink taps.

Clean at last, LaRaine turned off the shower and stepped out to towel dry. She was humming to herself as she slipped into the velour robe hanging on the door hook and zipped up the front of it. Her reflection in the mirror looked aglow with some hidden secret, but she didn't stop to delve into the mysteries of her emotions. She hurried into the kitchen to join Travis.

At the sight of him, she stopped. Bare-chested, he stood at the sink, his muscles rippling as he wiped his hard flesh with a towel. The desire she had known when he held her rekindled, the surging need threatening to buckle her knees. The silence of her barefoot entrance had not warned him of her presence in the room. When Travis turned to reach for the clean shirt draped across a chair back, he saw her, and the almost physical touch of his gaze sent her heart leaping into her throat.

"Hello, Rainey." His low voice was as caressing as his look.

LaRaine blinked. "What did you call me?"

Travis paused, as if unaware he had shortened her name. "Rainey." He picked up his shirt and put it on. "LaRaine doesn't seem to fit you anymore. Do you mind?"

"No." There was a breathlessness to her answer. "It's just that . . . I've never had a nickname before."

"You haven't?" One brow arched.

"No, at least none that anybody ever called me to my face." She laughed a little self-consciously and looked away.

Travis had two buttons of his shirt fastened when he stopped to walk across the room to where she stood. He crooked a finger under her chin to lift it and let his gaze run over her face.

"Travis," she whispered achingly.

In the next second she was caught up in his arms to be crushed against his chest. His mouth opened moistly over hers, taking in the softness of her lips in a devouring kiss. LaRaine arched on tiptoes, her hands sliding inside his shirt to freely explore the hard-muscled flesh of his chest and shoulders.

Her lips parted to let his possessive kiss claim her. LaRaine trembled as his fingers found the metal clasp of the zipper and her pulse raced at its release and the first exploring caress of his hands. She felt she would die with the incredible joy of it.

His mouth burned across her skin to the sensitive hollow of her throat. The loose robe slipped off one shoulder and Travis nipped sensually at the ivory perfection it exposed. Her breasts throbbed under his expert massage, their rosy peaks tingling with erotic sensation. With one arm encircling her waist, Travis lifted her slightly up, then with a half-muffled groan, he let her slide down until his mouth found her cheek and the lobe of her ear.

"You almost make me forget, Rainey," he murmured thickly.

It took her a full second to realize what Travis meant. She almost made him forget that woman called Natalie. Suddenly there was a ghost between them, summoned by his voice. The hands that had been clinging to him now strained to elude his embrace. The joy she had felt became pain. Travis overpowered her resistance, but LaRaine refused to be persuaded. At last he let her go.

Immediately she turned away, zipping up her robe with trembling fingers. It had almost been so beautiful. A tear slipped from her lashes and she hurriedly wiped it away.

"Well, it's lunch time!" Her voice quivered with the artificial remark. "I'll fix you a sandwich."

"Rainey, I didn't mean—" Travis began curtly.

In a flash of hurt feelings, she turned on him. "Yes, you did," she accused. "I'm not anybody's stand-in! I never have been and I never will be!"

A muscle flexed in his strong jaw. "I never said you were."

He hadn't needed to say it. Ignoring his reply, she walked to the refrigerator. "I have some cold roast beef. Is that all right?"

There was a long silence before he answered. "That'll be fine."

CHAPTER TEN

The tan and white pickup crested the rise and the familiar, weathered-gray building came into sight. A kind of contentment drifted through LaRaine. Coming home after a long afternoon in Delta was . . . she almost said the word aloud: heartwarming. The groceries were in the back of the truck, perishables stored in an ice chest. Most of the time had been spent waiting with Travis for a pump motor to be repaired.

Her gaze strayed to Travis. The wind blowing through the open window had ruffled the silver strands above his ear and her fingers itched to smooth the hair into place, a liberty she felt entitled to take after more than six weeks of almost living with the man. But her hands didn't leave her lap.

LaRaine hadn't forgotten that mud bath day— nor the crushing discovery that he thought of Natalie when he held her, not the glorious ecstasy she felt in his embrace. The incident hadn't been repeated. Joe had unknowingly acted as a deterrent on many occasions since.

During unguarded moments like these, she would look at him with all the intense longing she kept hidden. In a sense, they lived as intimately as man and wife. She cooked his meals, washed his clothes, cleaned his house, and went shopping in town with Travis at her side. But she wanted the pleasures that went with such a relationship . . . and the commitment.

The truck rolled to a stop in front of the house. "Home at last," Travis announced in a tired voice.

LaRaine looked away before he glanced at her. She didn't want him reading what was in her expression. Opening her door, she stepped down from the cab and her eyes focused on the house. Suddenly she was seeing it as she had for the first time, paint blistered away to expose the boards and a general air of neglect.

Shock waves trembled through her. The sun must have begun to affect her brain. When they drove up, had she really been wishing that she was married to Travis and this was her home? This ramshackle old house? The man she hoped to marry someday would have a mansion and servants. Had she lost her mind?

"What's the matter?" Travis asked. "Did you forget something?"

"Yes." My sanity, LaRaine thought, then realized she'd given him an affirmative answer and took it back. "No, I didn't forget anything."

She walked to the rear of the pickup where the grocery bags were. Travis was lifting a cooler out of the truck bed.

"Why don't you paint this place?" she said. "It looks terrible."

"It does need it badly," he agreed. "I've got as far as buying the paint, but I haven't had time to do it."

"Take time," she retorted.

"When you're running a ranch, it doesn't work that way, Rainey," Travis explained with amused patience, and carried the cooler to the house.

Picking up two bags of groceries, LaRaine followed him. He still used the shortened version of her name, and Joe, who was beginning to lose his shyness with her, had picked it up as well. Travis was in the kitchen unloading the perishables from the cooler. LaRaine carried the bags to the counter.

"There are two more bags in the truck," she told him, and checked the roast in the crockpot. "Is Joe back yet?"

"He might be in the barn doing chores." Travis set the cooler on the back porch. "I'll bring in the rest of the groceries."

The front screen door slammed behind him as LaRaine began unpacking the groceries. When one bag was empty she started on the next.

"Rainey?" Travis called to her from outside.

"What?" she shouted back her answer.

"Come here a minute."

She set the loaf of bread in her hand on the counter and walked into the living room. Through the wire mesh of the door, she could see Travis standing on the porch, looking off to the west. There seemed to be no reason for the urgency in his voice.

"What is it?" She pushed the door open and stepped onto the porch.

He cast her a brief glance backward. "I want you to see the sunset."

"A sunset?" LaRaine frowned. "The sun goes down every day. One's just like all the rest." She turned to walk back in the house.

"Cynic!" he taunted, caught her hand. "You haven't seen one like this sunset." He pulled her to the end of the porch. Placing both hands on her shoulder, he faced her toward the west. "Look at that."

The latent power of his hold tingled through her. He stood behind her, his body warming hers. Her pulse began behaving erratically, reacting to his nearness. She could feel the way his breath faintly stirred the top of her hair and caught the pleasant male fragrance of his shaving lotion.

Out of self-defense, she concentrated on the scene before her. The sun sank behind the far mountains, a blaze of orange-red light fanning upward. A scattering of gray cloud was underlined with the reflected light and the valley floor was tinted with brilliant orange as well.

"It is kind of spectacular, isn't it?" she admitted with awed amazement.

"Watch," Travis ordered quietly. "It will change."

It did. Like a slow-turning color wheel, the orange glow faded into a rosy pink, shading the clouds to a lavender hue. The fanning light of the setting sun began to fold up, leaving pale pink traces across the horizon.

A sigh of regret slipped from LaRaine's lips. Travis's fingers tightened on the soft flesh of her upper arms as the evening star winked from behind a wispy cloud. LaRaine lingered until she felt the provocative caress of his hands slowly moving over her arms.

"Well?" he asked expectantly.

"It was beautiful." Her voice was tight, unnerved by the sensations running through her.

She turned, attempting to subdue the excitement he was arousing, but Travis didn't move out of her way. Instead he smoothed a large hand over her cheek and lifted her head. The lazy smile on his firm mouth sent her heart tripping over itself.

"I'll make a country girl out of you yet," he murmured.

Her breath caught in her throat. At that moment he could have made anything out of her that he wished. LaRaine was suddenly ready to submit to his hands, willing to please as long as he would go on looking at her like that. Then his gaze strayed from her and his hands came away as he released her completely from his touch.

"Hi, Joe," he said.

LaRaine took a shaky breath and glanced over her shoulder to see the young ranch hand walking from the barn. His hazel eyes darted from one to the other and LaRaine wondered how much he had seen. Her cheeks grew warm, and the faint blush made her angry.

Why was she embarrassed? She had done love scenes much more torrid than this in front of a camera with a multitude of people watching. The difference was that this time her partner in the scene was Travis. That knowledge made her want to bolt.

"I'd better see about dinner," she murmured as an excuse, and hurried from the porch before Joe reached it.

* * *

Three mornings later, LaRaine finished the hand washing and carried two of her blouses to the clothesline in back. Travis and Joe had ridden out of the yard only minutes before. She had sent a thermos of soup and some sandwiches and fruit with them, since they weren't coming back for the noon meal.

With the blouses on the line, she started toward the house. She glared her dislike at the bare, weathered siding. Then she remembered Travis saying that he had bought the paint for the house. Pausing, she tried to visualize what it would look like with a coat of paint. It would be a distinct improvement, she decided. There was nothing wrong with the way the house was designed or built. It simply looked shabby and run-down.

If she had to live in the house for another six weeks, it didn't have to look as if it were about to fall on her head. She'd gotten a lot more organized in her housework. Travis might not have the time, but she did. After all, how hard could painting a house be?

Determined to try, she went in search of the paint, finding the five-gallon cans in the storage shed where Travis and Joe slept, as well as a stepladder. She carted the stepladder to the house and had to drag the heavy can of paint. In the house, she rummaged through the junk drawer until she found a brush. Then, armed and ready, she began painting the front of the house, the thirsty boards drinking in the white liquid.

By the end of the day her arms ached from holding the brush. All she had painted was the lower half of the front of the house; the stepladder wasn't high enough to reach the second story. LaRaine stepped back to admire her work.

Pressing a hand against her lower back, she arched her spine to ease the cramping muscles. Then, at the sound of drumming hooves, a smile curved her mouth and she turned expectantly to greet Travis and Joe as they rode into the yard. Her smile deepened at their stunned looks.

"What the hell do you think you're doing?" Travis demanded, the big bay dancing beneath him.

"What does it look like?" LaRaine laughed. "I'm painting the house. You may not have the time, but I do."

"So you propose to do it all by yourself?" he challenged.

She had expected him to be pleased by what she had done, not angry. After all, she wasn't getting paid to do this.

"Yes, I plan to do it myself," she retorted with stinging swiftness. "All I need is a taller ladder to reach the second floor."

"There's one in the barn," Joe volunteered the information.

"Go and get it," Travis ordered. "We have a couple of hours of daylight left. Between the two of us, maybe we can get most of it done before it gets too dark to see." His gaze slashed to LaRaine. "Now you get in the house and start dinner."

"I said I'd paint the house. You and Joe don't have to help me," she protested at the heavy-handed way he was taking over.

"Let's get this straight, Rainey." His dark eyes narrowed dangerously. "I'm not going to have you hanging twenty feet off the ground with a paint-brush in your hand when you don't know one end of a ladder from the other. You'd fall and break your neck . . . and expect met to pick up the pieces. Get in the house like I told you.'' He reined the bay toward the barn, muttering to Joe, ''Like it or not, we've got a house to paint!''

Subdued by his reasoning more than his anger, LaRaine went into the house to finish the last of the preparations for the evening meal. The next day Travis relented and permitted her to help as long as she kept both feet on the ground. In two days, the three of them had completely finished the exterior.

After Travis rode out the third morning, LaRaine tackled the low shed, painting the outside, washing the windows and wiping down the interior walls. It looked amazingly good when she'd finished. That only left the barn—but Travis had threatened her with dire consequences if she attempted it.

''But with the house and shed freshly painted, the barn is an eyesore,'' LaRaine had protested.

''In another month, I'll rent a sprayer and paint it. Until then, leave it alone,'' he had warned.

Instead of being satisfied with the transformation of the exterior, LaRaine was depressed by the ugli-ness of the inside. She glared at the dreary gray tile on the lower half of the kitchen wall. This room was the worst of them all, and the one she spent the most time in.

Absently she picked at a loose gray square with her fingernail. The tile popped off onto the floor. The one beside it came loose just as easily. LaRaine set to work. A few tiles were more stubborn, but they came off eventually with a screwdriver.

Three hours later, small heaps of tile lay on the floor near two walls. LaRaine was halfway through with the third when she heard footsteps on the porch followed by the opening of the screen door. It was Travis. She had learned to recognize his footsteps by now. She glanced around at the destruction she'd caused and braced herself for his reaction when he entered the kitchen.

Two strides into the room Travis came to an abrupt halt. He took a slow, sweeping look at the wall. When he finally met LaRaine's wary look, his mouth was grim.

"You couldn't stand it, right?" The question was dry.

"Could you, if you had to be in here hour after hour?" she challenged.

"Do you think that yellow glue dried on the walls looks any better?" Travis countered.

"No," she admitted. "I thought if I couldn't chip it off, maybe I could sand it smooth so the walls could be painted."

"Not a chance," he said. "If you want to paint the walls, they'll have to be replastered, and I'm not going to that expense."

"I'll try anyway. At least, I won't have to look at that ugly gray tile anymore."

LaRaine returned her attention to a stubborn square of tile and hammered the point of the screwdriver under its edge. Her hand slipped, grazing her fingers against the roughness of the dried glue, snapping a fingernail. With a startled cry of alarm she dropped the screwdriver and clutched the finger of the broken nail.

"What did you do? Cut yourself?" Travis was at

her side in an instant, reaching for her hand. "Let me see."

"I broke a fingernail," she wailed.

"You broke a—" His mouth snapped shut on the astounded exclamation. "Good God, Rainey, I thought you were hurt," he muttered.

"I was always so proud of my nails." Tears misted her eyes as she stared at her hands. "They were so long and now . . . just look at them."

She spread her fingers out for Travis to see. Half the nails were broken or chipped, or filed down short.

"Rainey, I'm sorry." He attempted to be sympathetic, but she heard the underlying amusement in his voice, as if it were a silly thing for her to be so upset about.

"No, you're not. You don't understand." She snatched her hands away and sniffed angrily at her tears. "I need nail clippers."

She found some in the bathroom and proceeded to snip off whatever remained. Travis frowned, "You aren't cutting them all, are you?"

"They might as well match the rest," she announced.

He shook his head, his mouth quirking. "I don't understand you, Rainey. One minute you're crying because you broke a nail—next, you're cutting them all off."

"I never asked you to understand me." LaRaine brushed past him to return to the kitchen and resume her demolition of the gray tiles.

"Yes, but I want to," Travis argued calmly, and took the screwdriver from her hand when she picked it up.

Setting it on the counter, he grasped her shoulders and drew her toward him. Her hands came up automatically against his powerful chest. His heady nearness shook her senses.

"You aren't the same woman who came to work for me. You aren't pampered or spoiled anymore. You're still headstrong and determined to have your own way"—his gaze flickered to the havoc she had raised with the kitchen, to prove his point—"but you've changed."

"Have I?" was all LaRaine could think of to say.

"Two months ago, would you have done this? Or painted a house?" He eyed her mockingly.

"No," she admitted.

"You see?" A dark brow arched complacently.

His gaze shifted to her lips to see her answer. They parted tremulously, but LaRaine had lost her voice somewhere in the turmoil of her senses. The distance between their mouths was slowly shortened by Travis until it didn't exist at all. A warm, rushing tide surged through her as her fingers spread across his chest, feeling the heavy beat of his heart. His drugging kiss demanded a response. LaRaine, who had long been addicted, it seemed, to his brand of kisses, responded willingly.

Before passion could run away with either of them, Travis was lifting his head and enclosing her in his arms. Her head rested against the hard musculature of his chest and she could feel his chin just brushing the top of her hair.

"Instead of replastering the walls, I could panel the lower half of the room," he suggested. "How would that be?"

"That'd be fine. Think you'll get lucky enough to find wood paneling to match the awful color of the cabinets?" LaRaine asked dryly.

"No new cupboards, Rainey," Travis said with a mock growl. "I have to go to town tomorrow. I'll see what I can find." Sliding a finger under her chin, he lifted it up. "Is that all right?"

If he had suggested gray tile, LaRaine felt she would have agreed. "Yes."

His hard kiss was much too brief. Then he handed her back the screwdriver. "I'll let you get back to your work so I can do mine."

It was several minutes after he had left the house before LaRaine got back to prying off the tile. He was such a handsome brute. She knew she was dangerously close to falling in love for the first time in her life—if she wasn't already in love with him.

Late the following afternoon, she dashed out of the house to meet Travis when he returned from town. Sheets of wall paneling were in the rear of the truck.

"You've bought some!" she cried, as delighted as if he had brought her home a new car.

Travis slammed the truck door shut and walked to the bed of the truck. "Yes, I did, but I'm not sure you're going to like it."

"Why?" LaRaine frowned. Then he lifted the top sheet and she knew. "Gray!" She stared at the paneling in disbelief. The birchwood was attractive—but gray?

"Don't say it," he said dryly. "You just got rid of the gray tile. But before you explode, let me show you what I have in mind."

He carried the paneling into the house and propped it against one wall. LaRaine followed, liking the sublety of the light birch but skeptical that it would work.

"What are you going to do about the cabinets?" As attractive as the paneling was, it clashed badly with the cherrywood stain of the kitchen cupboards.

"We'll paint them white and antique them with gray to match the paneling," Travis explained. "It'll lighten the room."

The idea immediately ignited LaRaine's imagination. "And for color, we can paper the walls in a red, gingham-checked fabric with curtains to match. And you could do the table and chairs to match the cupboards. The floor could be recovered in large squares of black and white tile."

"I hadn't thought about the floor, but"—Travis hesitated—"I suppose we might as well go all the way."

"When can we start?" she said excitedly.

"Is tonight soon enough?" he asked with amusement. "I can only work at this in the evenings, Rainey. I can't take any more time away from the ranch work."

"I'll help," LaRaine promised.

When Joe learned of the project, he volunteered his assistance. Except for the painting, the two men did most of the work. LaRaine held paneling sheets and spare nails and pasted the wallpaper for them to hang. It took a week's worth of nights before the kitchen was finished.

When it was done, LaRaine stared in amazement. She had never believed the room could look so stunning. Even the old black and white gas stove fitted in perfectly with the cheery new décor.

"Well?" Travis challenged. "Do you like it?"

"Like it? I love it!" In a burst of spontaneity, she hugged him. Locking her arms behind him, she tipped her head back. "We should toast it with champagne or something. Do you like it?"

"I love it." He huskily repeated her answer.

A painful lump became lodged in her throat and she suddenly wished that Travis was referring to her instead of the kitchen. But his love was already given . . . to that girl named Natalie. Forcing out a breathless laugh, LaRaine glided away from him.

"We don't have champagne, but there is some coffee. Would you like a cup?" She walked to the kitchen counter.

"No," Travis refused. "It's late. I'd better be turning in."

Her first impulse was to object, but she stifled it.

"You're right," she agreed. He walked toward the door. "Good night, Travis."

"Good night, Rainey."

CHAPTER ELEVEN

The packages were almost heavier than LaRaine could carry, and so bulky and cumbersome that she could barely see where she was going. She hurried down the sidewalk. She was supposed to have met Travis twenty minutes ago. She would have been on time, too, if she hadn't happened to glance in that fabric shop.

The truck was parked at the curb. LaRaine almost sighed in relief when she saw it, knowing she would at least be relieved of her burden. The driver's door opened and Travis stepped out.

"It's about time." He lifted the packages out of her arms and set them in the rear bed of the truck.

"Sorry I'm so late," LaRaine apologized, her arms aching from carrying the heavy load. She hurried around to the passenger door, aware that Travis was anxious to get back to the ranch.

"What did you spend your money on this time?"

He slid behind the wheel and started the motor, casting a bemused glance her way.

"Oh, I didn't spend my money," she answered brightly. "I spent yours. You owe me seventy dollars." She took a slip of paper from her purse. "Here's the receipt. Just wait until you see what I bought!"

Travis frowned at the receipt but didn't take it. "What do you mean, you spent my money? Or maybe I should ask what did you buy?" As he turned the truck onto the street, his gaze pierced her for a lightning second.

"You know how tacky the living room looks now that we've fixed up the kitchen," LaRaine began, unable to check the excitement in her voice. "Well, I was walking by this fabric shop, and there was a table of remnants, all upholstery material. There was one large piece of velour material. It's blue and gray with a touch of black. It's just perfect for the sofa. Plus, I found two pieces of fabric, each of them big enough to cover the chairs. One is blue and one is gray. I thought we could reupholster the furniture, strip the wallpaper and paint the walls oyster white, or maybe repaper them. A gray carpet with black flecks would be perfect on the floor."

"We aren't redecorating the living room, Rainey," he said firmly.

"It wouldn't be as much work as the kitchen," she reminded him. "Besides, you already have the fabric for the furniture."

"No, you have it."

LaRaine suddenly realized that Travis meant what he was saying. "But I bought it for you," she argued.

"I never asked you to do it. If you spent seventy

dollars for that material, that's your business. I'm not going to pay for it or reimburse you." The set of his iron jaw was as unyielding as his stand.

"But it's part of the money I've been saving to go back to California," LaRaine protested.

"You should have thought of that before you spent it," Travis answered without a trace of sympathy. "Now you'll have to return the material and ask for your money back."

"It was on sale. They don't make refunds on sale items," she told him in a stiff little voice.

"That's too bad. Guess you're stuck with seventy dollars' worth of material, huh?" There was something arrogant in the mocking look Travis gave her.

"That's cruel, Travis," LaRaine snapped.

"Don't blame me for your own impulsiveness," he said with infuriating calm.

"What is this? Another lesson?" she demanded bitterly.

"I guess it is," he admitted. "I gave in to you twice—painted the house and remodeled the kitchen—but this time you aren't going to get your way. Maybe you'll learn that you can't decide for me what I want or when I want it."

"What am I supposed to do with the material?" She sat close to the door, on the verge of sulking.

"I don't care. You can reupholster the living room furniture if you want, but you won't get any help from me."

And she didn't. Travis didn't lift a finger to help her when she attempted to recover one of the chairs. Fortunately Joe came to her rescue. He didn't know any more about recovering furniture than LaRaine did, but his mother was experienced at it, so Joe asked her for help. Pride made LaRaine insist that she do it herself with only instructions from Mrs. Benteen. She wanted to prove to Travis that she could do it.

The recliner was reupholstered in the blue fabric; the chair to the sofa in dove-gray. And the sofa, LaRaine's maroon monster, was recovered in the blue-and-gray-patterned velour. When the three pieces were finished, she waited for a comment from Travis.

For an entire evening he didn't make a single reference to them. Finally LaRaine challenged him. "Well? Aren't you going to admit that it's an enormous improvement over those maroon monstrosities?"

"Definitely." His dark eyes danced with wicked laughter. "You did an excellent job, too."

"Thanks to Mrs. Benteen." LaRaine gave the credit where it was due. But that wasn't where her interest lay. "Of course, the furniture doesn't look as good as it will once the walls and ceiling are painted and the floor's refinished or carpeted."

"True," he agreed tersely.

LaRaine sighed with exasperation. "If you know that, why won't you let me tear off that yellowed paper and do something about the floor?"

"Why do you care what this place looks like?" Travis tilted his head to one side, studying her curiously. "You'll be leaving in a couple of weeks."

It was true. Two more paychecks and she would have almost the five hundred dollars saved. The discovery jolted through her. There wasn't a thing waiting for her in California. But LaRaine could think of a reason that would keep her here—Travis, if he'd ask her.

"I care because . . . it gives me something creative and challenging to do." She answered his question as best she could under the circumstances.

"In that case, go ahead."

LaRaine blinked. She hadn't expected him to give in without arguing. "Do you mean it?"

"Yes, on the condition that I paint the ceiling," he qualified.

Joe came into the house as Travis spoke. He glanced at LaRaine and smiled, "Did you talk him into painting the living room?"

"Well, I didn't exactly talk him into it," she admitted, still surprised by how easily Travis had given in when he'd been so adamant before. "He just agreed."

"When do we start?" Joe asked.

"You don't have to help," LaRaine protested. "Travis is going to do the ceiling. I can paint the walls."

"I don't mind. In fact, I enjoy helping you two fix this place up," he insisted. "Besides, it isn't going to be easy to get this paper off the walls."

Since Travis didn't object, LaRaine accepted Joe's offer to help. But she wondered if Travis had noticed how Joe had linked them together. She wasn't the only one who was beginning to think she belonged there on a permanent basis. Why couldn't Travis? She reminded herself that this wasn't the kind of life she wanted. . . . Was it? But that was ridiculous. Everything about her seemed to be undergoing a change, her values, her lifestyle and her ambitions.

Removing the old wallpaper was the most difficult part of redecorating the living room. The painting was accomplished over the space of two days. For the time being, the floor would stay as it was until the carpeting could be selected and laid.

Even without the carpet, the room showed the promise of the country elegance that LaRaine had in mind. She wandered about the room, running a hand along the length of the sofa back. She stopped at the desk where Travis worked most evenings, sitting in its straight-backed chair. She glanced curiously through the papers stacked on top of it.

She wasn't consciously snooping. The action was prompted by a curiosity to know more about how the ranch was run than anything else. There was very little to do this afternoon until Travis and Joe returned. She was filling time.

Absently she opened a side drawer. It contained ledger books and canceled checks. Bookkeeping was something that she didn't understand. She closed the drawer and opened a second. In among the papers, a splash of color caught her eye and she took a closer look.

It was a Christmas card. LaRaine wondered why an unsentimental man like Travis would be saving a Christmas card. And why would he keep it in this drawer? She knew she should leave it where it was, but curiosity got the better of her.

Taking it out of the drawer, she opened it. The usual Christmas message was printed inside, and beneath it one name leaped out from the others— Natalie. Her heart seemed to constrict with sharp pain. It hurt to breathe. She read the rest of the names on the card. It was signed, *Merry Christmas! Colter, Natalie, Missy, Ricky, and Stephanie.*

It was obvious that Colter was Natalie's husband. LaRaine supposed the other names were their children. Natalie was married, but that didn't necessarily mean she was married when Travis had known her. She could have chosen this Colter instead of Travis. Although LaRaine couldn't imagine why.

None of that was important anyway. Travis had kept the card—that was what mattered. He'd kept the card because it was signed by Natalie, and despite the fact that it carried her husband's and children's names. It hurt to know he loved Natalie that much.

Strangely, she didn't feel any jealousy of the other woman—an emotion she had experienced in the past. This time she really cared about the man—and she couldn't escape the deep, abiding ache that no tears could assuage, much worse than mere jealousy.

Footsteps clumped on the floorboards of the porch. Startled, LaRaine rose from the chair. She forgot the brightly colored card in her hand. When she remembered, there wasn't time to return it to the drawer before Travis walked in. She barely managed to hide it behind her back. Her guilty conscience made her wonder whether it was her furtive movement that got his immediate attention or if he'd been looking for her.

"Hi, Rainey." His half-smile seemed natural enough. "What are you doing?"

"Nothing," she rushed, enforcing the answer with a quick, negative shake of her head.

A quick brow lifted. "Nothing?" His gaze swept her, alert and inspecting. "Looks to me like you're up to something." He seemed amused rather than suspicious.

The card behind her back was scorching LaRaine's fingers. Her breathing was quick and uneven, panic quivering through her nerve ends. She had to distract him; she didn't want him to think she had been snooping through his papers, however innocently.

"Don't be silly." Her denying laugh was brittle.

"Now I'm convinced. What are you plotting, Rainey?" His attitude remained amused and indulgent. "There aren't that many rooms left in the house. Which one is next?"

"Actually"—his comment reminded LaRaine of what had been only a half-formed idea—"I was thinking about my bedroom."

"Thought so," Travis nodded.

"It isn't what you're thinking," she hurried.

"Oh, no?" he questioned skeptically.

"No." LaRaine couldn't move away from the desk for fear Travis would notice the card she was trying to hide from him. "What I had in mind was turning the downstairs bedroom—my room—into a study."

"A study?" He leaned against the wall, crossing his arms and bending one knee to hook a heel over the arch of a boot.

Her hand moved nervously over the smooth wooden back of the chair. "Every man should have a place to work in private. The bedroom would work perfectly." She improvised as she went along. "We could panel the walls, move your desk in there and build some shelves so there'd a place for your husbandry books."

"It would give me a chance to spread out a bit and keep down the clutter," Travis admitted.

"We could even put in an outside door, make it your ranch office as well as your study. You could conduct business from there. Cattle buyers and grain sellers and the other people you deal with could come there to meet with you," she elaborated.

"You make it sound like there are people coming and going all the time," he said dryly.

"Maybe not now, but in time I'm sure they will. I've listened to you and Joe talk at the table. You've made a lot of improvements on this ranch since you bought it—drilled more wells and acquired more grazing leases," LaRaine reminded him. "I've listened to you and Joe discussing the possibilities of putting more land under irrigation to raise hay and other crops."

"My, my, what big ears you have!" Travis drawled.

"If you didn't want me to know, you shouldn't have talked about it in front of me," she defended herself. "You can't deny that you're ambitious. You intend to eventually make this ranch the biggest and best around."

"Well, it won't happen overnight. It's going to take years and a lot of hard work." His gaze became aloof and thoughtful, measuring her in a way that disturbed her.

"I realize that." She gave him a wide-eyed look of innocence. "What do you think of my idea about changing the bedroom into a study? There are three empty bedrooms upstairs, so it isn't as if there's a shortage of places to sleep."

"It sounds like a practical idea." Travis straightened from the wall. "I'm just curious about whose future you're planning."

"I don't know what you mean." Her fingers trembled around the Christmas card. "I'm not planning anyone's future."

"Aren't you?" Travis moved toward her.

LaRaine wanted to retreat, but the wall was only two feet behind her. She didn't dare turn or he'd see the card.

"If I'm planning any future, it's for the house," she insisted.

"What about yours?" He was towering in front of her, only a corner of the chair separating them.

"Me?" she laughed nervously. "I don't know what you're talking about. I'm going to California in a couple of weeks—or did you forget? Turning the bedroom into a study doesn't have anything to do with me."

Travis took off his Stetson and set it on the desktop. "Are you leaving?"

Not if you don't want me to—but LaRaine couldn't say that. "Do you think you'll miss me?"

"Yes." He replied without elaboration.

"I'll miss you and this place," she admitted, then gave him a wry smile. "Although I won't miss washing dishes—my hands get so chapped."

She instantly wished she hadn't added the last. It drew his gaze to her hand on the chairback, and he instantly noticed that her other hand was behind her back.

"What are you hiding?" He asked the question out of simple curiosity, but when LaRaine stiffened guiltily and the color faded from her face, his eyes became hard with suspicion. "Don't play games with me," he demanded.

"Nothing." Denying it was the worst thing she could have done.

"I want to know what it is, Rainey."

"Travis, no," she protested.

With calm deliberation, he pushed the chair up to the desk, eliminating the one obstacle in his path to her. As he moved forward, LaRaine backed up until the wall stopped her. She was trapped with no escape. Her heart hammered against her ribs.

"Show it to me." Travis stood before her, challenging her in a quietly dangerous way.

"No." Her dark eyes implored him not to force the issue, but he ignored their plea. She pressed herself tightly against the wall, protectively shielding the card with her body.

Firmly, without roughness, Travis grasped her waist and pulled her away from the wall. She struggled frantically, but he simply overpowered her. Reaching behind her, he caught her wrist—and her hand. When he saw the colorful Christmas card she held, LaRaine felt his muscles tense with silent rage. She flinched under his harshly accusing eyes.

"What are you doing with this?" he demanded savagely.

"I . . . I found it," she whispered.

"You've been going through my desk." His words were swift and cold, shivering over her skin in icy chills. He ripped the card from her hand and let her go. "What were you looking for, my bank statements? You picked the wrong drawer. They're here." He snapped open a drawer to show her.

"I wasn't snooping, Travis, I swear." Her voice broke and she tried to steady it. "I was just curious."

"What were you trying to find out? How much I was worth?" he snarled over his shoulder, his mouth thin with contempt.

"No," LaRaine said quickly. "It never even occurred to me. It's the truth. I don't even know why I was looking through the drawers."

"Just idle curiosity, I suppose," he taunted.

"Yes, that's all it was," she insisted. "I didn't touch a thing." Her gaze fell on the Christmas card in his fingers. "Not until I saw that card, anyway. I couldn't imagine why you were saving a Christmas card. Then when I opened it and saw Natalie's name, I . . . I knew."

Travis stared grimly at the card before he tossed it in the wastebasket. The involuntary gasp of surprise from LaRaine drew his pinning gaze.

"There isn't any reason to keep it anymore," he snapped, and raked a hand through his hair, rumpling its thickness.

"Colter is her husband?" LaRaine asked.

"Yes." His one-word answer only raised more questions.

"Did she . . . jilt you to marry him?" she asked hesitantly.

Travis tipped his head back, a mirthless chuckle coming from his throat. "You've been aching to know the whole sordid story for months, haven't you?"

LaRaine swallowed. The crazy thing was she didn't want to know about it, not anymore. There was already too much pain. But Travis took her silence as a yes.

"I worked for Colter." Travis held her gaze, refusing to let her look away. "I was his ranch foreman for more years than I care to remember. I met Natalie for the first time after Colter had married her. She wasn't happy there from the beginning, but then Colter's home was never a happy place. She wasn't there for long before I realized I was falling in love with her." His voice seemed devoid of emotion. "I should have left then, but I couldn't as long as I thought she might need me. When I realized she didn't—well, it was a toss-up as to whether I was fired or quit." His mouth quirked in a cynical smile. "That's the story. Are you satisfied?"

"No," she muttered.

"Sorry I couldn't fill you in on all the details of our affair, but there weren't any," Travis said flatly.

"And the other names on the card are their children?" LaRaine's voice was brittle.

"Missy is Colter's daughter from his first marriage. Ricky is Natalie's nephew. Stephanie . . . is their daughter."

"Travis, I'm sorry." Her heart ached for him.

"Are you, Rainey?" he challenged, a brow lifting in mockery. "I'm not."

There was a lump in her throat as she turned away. "I don't know what to say."

"Neither do I." His voice sounded tight, heavy with impatient anger. "I thought you'd changed, but I was wrong."

"W-what?" LaRaine faltered in confusion.

"One of the few times that I don't bother to lock my desk, I find you going through it." His condemnation was all too clear.

"I told you I wasn't snooping," she protested again. "It was an accidental thing. I wasn't looking for that card."

"Would you like to see my financial statements?" Travis eyed her coldly. "Outside of yourself, I thought money was your sole concern," he jeered.

"Maybe it was once," she admitted, "but—"

"But not anymore." Travis finished the sentence for her. "You're no better at lying than you were at acting. Just plan on packing your things and leaving for California the day after tomorrow."

"But—"

"I'll give you whatever money you need." His offer stung.

"I don't want money!"

"Consider it a going-away present," Travis stated. "You're used to accepting presents from men. What's the big deal?"

Grabbing up his hat, Travis moved toward the door with long strides. When the screen door slammed shut behind him, LaRaine winced. The door was being slammed on her. Travis was ready to pay her to leave. He didn't want her around anymore.

If he had given her money two months ago, she would have kissed him for it and gone happily back to California. Now, the only place she wanted to be was here, on this ranch with him. But Travis didn't want her to stay. He wanted her out of his house and out of his life.

Inside LaRaine was frozen with pain, but there was no one to blame but herself. This was one lesson she hadn't counted on learning—how to hurt, especially her heart. She didn't feel bitter. This was only what she deserved for the thoughtless, selfish life she'd led before Travis.

CHAPTER TWELVE

One suitcase was packed and another was barely half-filled. LaRaine had been attempting to pack her clothes all day, but she kept finding excuses to postpone it. First, she did wash so all her clothes would be clean. In order not to waste water, she did the men's laundry, too—at least that was the reason she used.

Of course, there had been food to cook and dishes to clean afterward. The meals were silent affairs with neither LaRaine nor Travis saying more than a few words. Joe noticed their frozen silence, but he seemed unaware of the cause, and equally unaware that LaRaine was leaving.

Convincing herself that she didn't want to leave the house dirty, LaRaine had thoroughly dusted each room. Now it was evening and she was alone in the house. There were no more excuses not to pack. She stared at the suitcase sitting open on the chair. Sighing in resignation, she changed into the nightgown that she would wear to bed that night and picked out her clothes for the next morning to save time.

With that done, she began taking the folded clothes from her dresser drawer and putting them in the suitcase. As the suitcase slowly overflowed, so did the tears in her eyes until they began spilling down her cheeks. Her sniffling attempt to hold them back became hiccuping sobs.

Finally she gave up trying to check the flood and crumpled on the bed to bawl in earnest. She wasn't crying because she hadn't gotten her way or because her pride had been hurt. She cried because the one person she loved was sending her away. The lumpy bed shook with her sobs.

"Rainey?" Travis's haunting voice came to her, gentle with concern.

A hand touched her shoulder and she realized she hadn't imagined his voice. She rolled away from his touch with a start, her blurred gaze finding him sitting on the edge of the bed. His rugged features drew into a frown at the sight of her face. She could imagine how terrible she looked with her eyes all swollen and red, and straggly black hair clinging to her wet cheeks.

"What's the matter?" he asked.

LaRaine turned her back to him and sat up. She didn't want him to see her like this. "Nothing." She choked out the word between sobs. She scrubbed at the tears with her hands, but more kept racing down to take their place.

"Why are you crying?" Travis wasn't put off by that lie.

"I'm not crying." LaRaine managed a painful smile. "These are crocodile tears. Can't you tell?"

"No, I can't tell."

Iron hands clasped her shoulders to turn her toward him. She made a futile attempt to ward him off, but her efforts were pathetically weak. She kept her face averted, burying her chin against her shoulder and letting her tousled black hair fall forward. Travis seemed determined to see what she hid. When he attempted to push the hair away from her face, she tried to elude him and brushed his hand away.

"Go away. Leave me alone," she pleaded.

Weaving his fingers into her hair, he cupped her head in his large hand and forced her face up to him. She kept her eyes tightly closed, but more tears squeezed through her lashes. Each time she breathed it was a sob.

"Those are real tears," Travis said simply.

"Why are you here? What do you want?" LaRaine sobbed. Her shaking hands attempted to strain against the steel muscles of his arms.

"I knew you were packing, so I came to return your makeup," he explained. "I promised I'd give it back to you when you left."

"My makeup?" Laughter bubbled hysterically through her sobs. "Gee, thanks so much. I'd forgotten all about it!"

The hard shake Travis gave her stopped the laughter, but it also took away what little control LaRaine had over her tears. She no longer tried to fight out of his hold, but simply covered her face with her hands and began crying anew.

She didn't offer even token resistance when Travis folded her in his arms and pressed her head against his chest. It was the one place in the world she wanted to be, whatever the reason. There was comfort and warmth and something strong and solid to lean on.

"Rainey, what's wrong?" Travis asked in a low, soothing voice.

"Hold me, Travis. Please, just hold me," was all she said.

He held her close and LaRaine buried her face in his shirt and cried. Her fingers curled into the material, holding onto him in case he let her go. His shirt absorbed her salty tears; and when her crying softened into sobbing breaths, she felt the gentle pressure of his mouth against her hair.

Travis repeated it near her temple, then brushed to her forehead and down to the damp lashes of her eyes. He kissed them dry and went on to her cheeks; he seemed intent on kissing away her hurt. LaRaine surrendered silently to his tenderness.

Soon her pain-dulled senses began to feel again. There was more than just comfort in the warmth of his mouth against her skin. She felt a slow stimulating of her nerve ends, making them tingle with awareness. His hands were no longer simply holding her, but had begun a sensual exploration of her back and shoulders.

When his mouth moved near her lips, LaRaine moved her head the fraction of an inch necessary to intercept him. Immediately his mouth hardened in possession, claiming the trembling softness he had previously avoided. She could taste her salty tears on his mouth. It only seemed to increase their thirst for each other.

Her hands crept around his neck, fingers sliding into the sensuous thickness of his jet-black hair.

The silk material of her nightgown allowed his hands to glide over her body in searching and exciting caresses. Travis lifted her the rest of the way across his lap, holding her close to him.

The blue silk of her nightgown twisted beneath her and rode up. She could feel the roughness of his blue jeans against the bareness of her thigh. The buttons of his shirt made a row of imprints on her middle.

His mouth worked over her lips, then moved to her ear, his warm breath igniting fiery responses before he shifted his attention to the creamy curve of her neck. His nuzzling melted her last ounce of resistance as waves of exquisite pleasure rushed through her.

The strap of her gown slipped from her shoulder. Tipping her head back, LaRaine enjoyed his skillful foreplay as his mouth explored her throat. The fresh, clean male scent of him, an intoxicating fragrance to senses that were already heightened, surrounded her. She felt as hot as the sun itself— bathed in golden light, afire with amber flames, and glorying in the magic.

Her fingers sought his face, trembling over the strength of his rugged features and drawing his head up so her lips could find the hard male shape of his mouth. Locked in a heated exchange of passion, LaRaine pressed lingering kisses over his face.

"Love me, Travis," she pleaded in a husky murmur. "Even if it's only this once."

"I will." Not letting her go, Travis began to lean back, drawing her with him until they were lying side by side.

She had heard the rawness in his voice and knew

he ached with the same needs she had. His hand slid across her stomach to cup the fullness of her breast. It seemed to swell beneath his touch with all the love she felt for him. To know his possession, she was willing to sacrifice her pride.

"It doesn't matter if you pretend I'm Natalie." She abandoned herself completely. "Just love me, Travis."

His mouth bruised her lips, as in punishment for raising a ghost. Just as roughly, it moved down her neck. The faint bristle of beard on his jaw scraped at her skin. A hand at her hip molded her more fully to his length, letting her feel all the hard muscles and taut desire.

"I can't hold you, Rainey, and pretend you're Natalie," Travis said softly.

Shivering from the rejection, LaRaine felt her hope dwindling. She had wanted him to show feeling when he made love to her, even if it was for someone else. She didn't want it to be just a physical thing, prompted by lust.

"When you're in my arms and I kiss you and touch you, all I feel is you." His voice seemed to vibrate over her skin. "I can't hold you and think of anyone else."

LaRaine breathed in sharply, then couldn't seem to release it. His large hand was sliding the shoulder strap the rest of the way off her arm. The strong fingers running down her skin sent delicious goose bumps over her flesh.

"But Natalie—" She stopped, frightened of misunderstanding what he had meant.

Travis brought his attention back to her lips, his mouth teasing the parted softness. "You aren't standing in for her, Rainey." It sounded like a promise.

The bodice of her gown was pulled down, the opposite strap digging into her arm, and his hand caressed both her bare breasts, stroking her white skin and rosy nipples until her own hand made him stop.

Wanting the same freedom to touch that he granted himself, LaRaine worked at the buttons of his shirt, loosening them until all were undone. His hard flesh burned with life. Curling, dark chest hairs tickled her palms, as sensitive now as every other part of her.

One minute she was on fire in his embrace; but in the next, Travis was levering himself up to sit on the bed. Confused, LaRaine half rose, with an arm braced to hold her. She reached for his arm, wanting him beside her.

"Don't leave me, Travis." She knew she was begging, but she didn't care.

His gaze took in the sensual cloud of her raven hair, and moved to the kissed softness of her face. Her dark eyes held a pleading look.

"I'm not leaving," he told her, and shrugged out of his shirt to toss it on her suitcase.

Then he was leaning back to her, his hand reaching out to slide off the one strap before he gathered her into his arms. The bared softness of her body met his naked torso, flesh to flesh and kindling one consuming desire. His embrace was unhurried as he kissed her eyes closed. Assured by his answer, LaRaine felt no need to rush, wanting only to spend forever in his arms.

"Why were you crying?" He nuzzled her ear. "You never did tell me."

He knew so much about her and soon would know so much more, there seemed no reason to hold back the truth. Vaguely, LaRaine was amazed that he hadn't guessed the reason. Her actions seemed to have made it so obvious.

"I don't want to leave tomorrow," she admitted.

"I thought you could hardly wait to get back to California." His teeth tugged at her lobe, his warm breath sending an indescribable thrill right through her.

She denied that. "I want to stay here."

Then the hard pressure of his mouth covered her lips and a long, stirring kiss made her forget what she was going to say. When it ended, she had no time to recover before Travis moved downward to kiss her breasts and she was lost in a whirl of sexual sensations. An erotic yearning suffused her entire body at the intimate touch of his tongue. When he had her just where he wanted her, he came back to her lips.

"I love you." She spoke without thinking, overwhelmed by the limitless joy that filled her heart.

His mouth became still for an instant. Lifting his head, he framed her face with his hands. There was a frowning look to his rugged features as his wary gaze ran over her expression.

"What did you say?" he demanded.

LaRaine wouldn't take it back, no matter what. "I love you, Travis."

"Do you know what you're saying?" There was an angry tightness to his mouth.

Unable to meet the blackness of his eyes, LaRaine looked down at the tanned column of his throat, then over the breadth of his muscled shoulders to the springing mass of dark hair that wandered down his chest to the flatness of his hard stomach.

"I love you," she repeated. "I don't want to leave tomorrow. I want to stay here."

"A bird in the hand, is that it, Rainey?" The caustic edge in his question lifted her gaze to his. "Have you decided that I might not be bad husband material after all since you don't have prospects in California?"

His doubt that she truly loved him hurt, and that hurt shimmered in her dark eyes. "I do love you, Travis." Her voice was small.

"Enough to give up the glamorous parties, limousines and designer clothes?" He was skeptical. "Nothing out here but hot sun, dust, and hard work. Is that what you want?"

"I've had glamour . . . and a certain amount of fame. It's pretty empty, Travis," LaRaine whispered, fighting the ache in her heart. "Look at my hands. I have stubby nails and some serious calluses. I know what I'm letting myself in for when I say I want to stay here."

"Do you, Rainey? My God, do you?" There was an almost desperate note in his demand. His hands unconsciously tightened around her face. "It might be years before I can give you any of the luxuries you dream about."

"I don't want you to give me anything," she protested. "I only want to love you—and help you and work with you to make this ranch the best in Utah. I know it's hard to believe, coming from me, but deep down inside that's the way I really feel."

His angry tension began to disappear. "You didn't hate it here? All the hard work? The isolation?" he questioned.

"No, I didn't hate it. In a way, I've kind of enjoyed it." Which was something she had been slow to admit to herself. LaRaine ran her hand lightly over his powerful shoulder. "Except at night. It was empty in this house all by myself." She looked at him, loving the vital, male face. "Would you sleep with me tonight, Travis, so it won't be so lonely in this bed?"

She could almost hear his silent amusement before his mouth came down to lightly take her lips and nibble at their softness.

"If you thought it was lonely here"—his warm breath mingled with hers—"you should have tried sleeping in that shed! It was hell sleeping in that cot and imagining you in my bed."

"Did it really bother you?" she whispered.

"Bother me? You've bothered me since the day I saw you in that sultry pose when I rode up." Travis kissed her hard, as if he remembered it all too well. After a passionate minute, the pressure eased to a gentler level. "That's why I moved to the shed. I knew you wouldn't be sleeping in this bed alone if I stayed in the house."

"Really?" LaRaine drew back, wanting to see his face.

"Yes, really." A smile deepened the corners of his mouth.

"But . . . why?" She didn't understand.

"I'd already been burned once by falling in love with the wrong woman. I didn't want it to happen again. Problem was, there wasn't a whole helluva lot I could do to prevent it," he told her.

"You mean . . ." She breathed in. "You said you loved Natalie. That I almost made you forget her."

"In the beginning, it was true. But it didn't take

me long to realize that when I kissed you, I wasn't thinking about Natalie." Travis kissed her again, as if to prove it, and it was a while before he let her up for air.

"Do you still love her?" LaRaine questioned. His hands had begun a series of arousing caresses. Soon she wouldn't care about his answer.

"Not in the same way I once did. I care about her, I admire her. If she needed my help tomorrow, I'd be there," Travis told her. "I felt gentle and protective toward her. With you, the love I feel is strong and fierce, something I can't control."

Rocked by his confession, LaRaine wound her arms around him, too happy to speak. When she attempted to hide her face in the curve of his neck, Travis lifted it to claim her lips in a branding kiss. She abandoned herself to his loving skill and the persuasive ardor of his mouth. Putting herself in the hands of an expert was an ideal way to learn all about what turned him on.

"We can drive to Nevada in the morning and get married in Ely," Travis told her. "Unless you want to go tonight." LaRaine trembled with the passion he had deliberately aroused.

Rubbing the roughness of his cheek against hers, he warned, "We won't have a honeymoon, Rainey. I can't spare the time away from the ranch."

Her fingers lovingly traced the chiseled outline of his face, so powerful and strong. "Do you think I care?" she whispered, then smiled. "Mrs. Travis McCrea isn't going to be able to spare the time, either."

When Travis lifted his head, her hand slid to his mouth to brush his lips with infinite tenderness.

Before they could flutter away he caught them and
kissed them individually. His eyes locked with hers.

"Rainey McCrea. That name will never light up
any theater marquee. Are you sorry?" he asked.

"Not a bit," she assured him. Personally she
thought the name sounded magical. "I have something more wonderful than make-believe. I have
the real thing. Why would I be sorry about that?"

"I just want you to be very sure," said Travis.

"Believe me, I am," LaRaine promised.

Travis rolled onto his back, pulling her on top
of him, cupping her breasts. Her nightgown slid
down a little farther before a muscled thigh got in
the way of its downward progress. Tucking her hair
behind her ears, LaRaine leaned down to kiss him.

Dodging her for a moment, he asked, "You sure
you want to turn this room into a study?"

Deprived of his mouth, LaRaine settled for the
sexy dimple near it. "Why? Don't you?"

"It's a good idea," he agreed, a hand sliding
around to the small of her back. "But I was thinking
it would be nice if our baby could sleep here, until
it's old enough to sleep alone upstairs."

"Baby?" A thread of panic ran through her voice.

"Don't you want to have a family?" Travis kissed
the lips he had been avoiding.

"I don't know," she murmured. "Travis, I don't
know if I can take care of a baby. I've never held
one in my life. What if I dropped it?"

"You won't," he chuckled. "We'll hire some
experienced help with the first one. Then,
depending on how quickly you learn, we can see
about enlarging the family."

He made it sound so simple and uncomplicated.
He actually believed she could cope with anything.

And because he believed it, LaRaine did, too. The idea of holding an infant didn't seem quite as frightening. In fact, she felt a faint thrill of excitement at the thought.

"Do you want a baby right away?" she asked.

"Nature decrees a nine-month waiting period." Travis gently mocked her lack of knowledge about babies and their care. "I don't know about you, but I'm not getting any younger. I'd rather not wait too long before starting a family."

She touched the silver strands of hair at his temples. "You're in your prime, Travis."

"Think so?" A wicked light danced in his eyes as his mouth slanted.

His strong arms held her as he shifted on the bed, turning them together until her shoulders were on the mattress and his crushing weight pressed her down. LaRaine only had a second to marvel at how easily her smaller frame fit the hard contours of his male length—it felt utterly glorious, a discovery that was soon blotted out by the searing fire of his kiss. All her senses turned to him as her desire reached a fever pitch of longing. She cried out when he suddenly rolled away.

"Travis, no!" Her fingers dug into the muscled flesh of his shoulders. "You aren't going to do the gentlemanly thing and sleep in the shed, are you?" she protested.

"I told you once that I'm not a gentleman."

A boot hit the floor with a loud thud . . . and the other one followed three seconds later.

Here's a thrilling preview of
SHIFTING CALDER WIND by Janet Dailey.
A June 2004 paperback
from Kensington Publishing.

———————————————————

A blackness roared around him. He struggled to surface from it, somehow knowing that if he didn't, he would die. Sounds reached him as if coming from a great distance—a shout, the scrape of shoes on pavement, the metallic slam of a car door and the sharp clap of a gunshot.

Someone was trying to kill him.

He had to get out of there. The instant he tried to move, the blackness swept over him with dizzying force. He heard the revving rumble of a car engine starting up. Unable to rise, he rolled away from the sound as spinning tires burned rubber and another shot rang out.

Lights flashed in a bright glare. There was danger in them, he knew. He had to reach the shadows. Fighting the weakness that swam through his limbs, he crawled away from the light.

He felt dirt beneath his hand and dug his fingers into it. His strength sapped, he lay there a moment, trying to orient himself and to determine the location of the man trying to kill him. But the searing pain in his head made it hard to think logically. He reached up and felt the warm wetness on his face. That's when he knew he had been shot.

Briefly his fingers touched the deep crease the bullet had ripped along the side of his head. Pain instantly washed over him in black waves.

Aware that he could lose consciousness at any second, either from the head wound or the blood loss, he summoned the last vestiges of his strength and threw himself deeper into the darkness. With blood blurring his vision, he made out the shadowy outlines of a post and railing. It looked to be a corral of some sort. He pushed himself toward it, wanting any kind of barrier, no matter how flimsy, between himself and his pursuer.

There was a whisper of movement just to his left. Alarm shot through him, but he couldn't seem to make his muscles react. He was too damned weak. He knew it even as he listed sideways and saw the low-crouching man in a cowboy hat with a pistol in his hand.

Instead of shooting, the cowboy grabbed for him with his free arm. "Come on. Let's get outa here, old man," the cowboy whispered with urgency. "He's up on the catwalk working himself into a better position."

He latched onto the cowboy's arm and staggered drunkenly to his feet, his mind still trying to wrap itself around that phrase "old man." Leaning heavily on his rescuer, he stumbled forward, battling the woodenness of his legs.

After an eternity of seconds, the cowboy pushed him into the cab of a pickup and closed the door. He sagged against the seat back and closed his eyes, unable to summon another ounce of strength. Dimly, he was aware of the cowboy slipping behind the wheel and the engine starting up. It was followed by the vibrations of movement.

Through slitted eyes, he glanced in the side mirror but saw nothing to indicate they were being followed. They were out of danger now. Unbidden came the warning that it was only temporary; whoever had tried to kill him would try again.

And here is a preview of
CALDER PROMISE by Janet Dailey
A July 2004 hardcover release
from Kensington Publishing.

"What happened, Laura? Did you forget to look where you were going?" The familiarity of Tara's affectionately chiding voice provided the right touch of normalcy.

Laura seized on it while she struggled to collect her composure. "I'm afraid I did. I was talking to Boone and—" She paused a beat to glance again at the stranger, stunned to discover how rattled she felt. It was a totally alien sensation. She couldn't remember a time when she hadn't felt in control of herself and a situation. "And I walked straight into you. I'm sorry."

"No apologies necessary," the man assured her while his gaze made a curious and vaguely puzzled study of her face. "The fault was equally mine." He cocked his head to one side, the puzzled look deepening in his expression. "I know this sounds awfully trite, but haven't we met before?"

Laura shook her head. "No. I'm certain I would have remembered if we had." She was positive of that.

"Obviously you remind me of someone else then," he said, easily shrugging off the thought. "In any case, I hope you are none the worse for the collision, Ms.—"

The old ploy was almost a relief. "Laura Calder. And this is my aunt, Tara Calder," she said, rather than going into a lengthy explanation of their exact relationship.

"My pleasure, ma'am," he murmured to Tara.

"And perhaps you already know Max Rutledge and his son, Boone." Laura belatedly included the two men.

"I know *of* them." He nodded to Max.

When he turned to the younger man, Boone extended a hand, giving him a look of hard challenge. "And you are?"

"Sebastian Dunshill," the man replied.

"Dunshill," Tara repeated with sudden and heightened interest. "Are you any relation to the earl of Crawford, by chance?"

"I do have a nodding acquaintance with him." His mouth curved in an easy smile as he switched his attention to Tara. "Do you know him?"

"Unfortunately no," Tara admitted, then drew in a breath and sent a glittering look at Laura, barely able to contain her excitement. "Although a century ago the Calder family was well acquainted with a certain Lady Crawford."

"Really. And how's that?" With freshened curiosity, Sebastian Dunshill turned to Laura for an explanation.

An awareness of him continued to tingle through her. Only now Laura was beginning to enjoy it.

"It's a long and rather involved story," Laura warned. "After all this time, it's difficult to know how much is fact, how much is myth, and how much is embellishment of either one."

"Since we have a fairly long walk ahead of us to the dining hall, why don't you start with the facts?"

"I suppose I should begin by explaining that back in the latter part of the 1870s, my great-great-grandfather Benteen Calder established the family ranch in Montana."

"Your family owns a cattle ranch?" He glanced her way, interest and curiosity mixing in his look.

"A very large one. And early ranch records show numerous business transactions that indicate Lady Crawford was a party to them. Many of them involved government contracts for the purchase of beef. It appears that my great-great-grandfather paid her a finder's fee, I suppose you would call it—an arrangement that was clearly lucrative for both of them."

"The earl of Crawford wasn't named as a party in any of this, then," Sebastian surmised.

"No. In fact, the family stories that were passed down always said she was widowed."

"Interesting. As I recall," he began with a faint frown of concentration, "the seventh earl of Crawford was married to an American. They had no children, which meant the title passed to the son of his younger brother." He stopped abruptly and swung toward Laura, running a fast look over her face. "That's it! I know why you looked so familiar. You bear a striking resemblance to the portrait of Lady Elaine that hangs in the manor's upper hall."

"Did you hear that, Tara?" Laura turned in amazement to the older woman.

"I certainly did." With a look of triumph in her midnight dark eyes, Tara momentarily clutched at Laura's arm, an exuberant smile curving her red lips. "I knew it. I knew it all along."